*Totally Bound Publishing books by P. Stormcrow*

**The Playgrounds**
The Words to Bind
The Will to Serve

**Collections**
Rules of Summer: The Knots that Hold
Some Like it Haunted: The Fae Effect

I0681320

# The Playgrounds

# THE WILL TO SERVE

## P. STORMCROW

The Will to Serve
ISBN # 978-1-83943-938-4
©Copyright P. Stormcrow 2021
Cover Art by Louisa Maggio ©Copyright January 2021
Interior text design by Claire Siemaszkiewicz
Totally Bound Publishing

# THE WILL
# TO SERVE

# Dedication

To those who have started me on this journey —
thank you.

# Chapter One

It was inevitable. They had teased each other all day with texts back and forth that whetted each other's appetite—but not enough, never enough. How many times did she zone out at work with blank stares and thoughts of things he would do?

The anticipation throughout the day was excruciating, but in some ways, the drive back to his place was worse. Silence filled the car, so much that at first she feared she had crossed some line and it would be punishment, not pleasure, that awaited But a tiny, barely perceptible steady increase in speed gave her the courage to steal small glances at him. The tightened jaw, the intense focus on the road, the grip on the wheel... Her breathing hitched. The signs were easy to miss, but she had known him for a long time. And now she wondered if she had pushed him too far in other ways.

Well, too far was...one way of putting it.

As soon as they stepped through the threshold of his apartment, he was on her. He pinned her to the door with one large hand holding both of her tiny wrists above her head. A button had flown off somewhere, her shirt half ripped open in haste to expose the bare skin — skin that he proceeded to first bite, hard enough to mark. Then came the lazy licks as his control exerted itself once more. He swept his tongue across to ease the pulsing pain. She squirmed and moaned as he nibbled with his lips and the occasional graze of his teeth down along the edge of her bra. But that was all. It was all teasing, drawing out the anticipation.

Almost against her will, she thrust her hips forward in an attempt to seek some relief as she ground against him and tried to entice him for more. A groan of frustration spilled from her and he smiled against her skin in response. She shifted her weight to try another tactic, sliding her leg up, rubbing her inner thigh along his hip while she mentally cursed the layers of clothing in between that undermined the effectiveness of the move.

"Eager, aren't we?"

She flushed and squirmed again as he glided his free hand down her side and hooked it underneath her thigh.

"Hold on."

His command startled her a little, but her body obeyed before she could register his words. Hazy fog clouded her mind. As he released her hands, she wrapped her arms around his neck and swung her other leg up, marveling still at how easily he could pick her up. She buried her face against the crook of his neck and inhaled, his scent faint with apple and cinnamon. The man had been baking again. Sweets, however, were very far from her mind at the moment.

It didn't take long before she felt the softness of his bed against her rear. She settled and released her legs to let them drape with languid grace over the bed. But she remained reluctant to let go and kept her arms around his neck.

"Sweetheart."

That was all it took. With a soft sigh, she released her grip and leaned back on her elbows while her gaze followed his every move as he straightened. With a boyish, crooked grin, he undid one button, then another until his white shirt parted to reveal the lines of toned muscles beneath it. In her head, she cursed the man's ability to frame himself in the best light, always tempting her. She already knew she could never deny him anything, but when he was in *that* mood, she was helpless against his whims — and they both knew it.

He chuckled as he leaned forward and smoothed the pad of his thumb over her lower lip. "No biting yourself. That's *my* job."

She trembled once more at his touch but released her teeth's hold. *When did I start chewing on my lips?*

Before she could formulate half a reply, he covered her mouth with his, kissing her with the softest touch that began to deepen her groan. He slid the remains of her shirt off her shoulders then splayed his fingers across one breast to stroke the lace. The movement drew louder moans from her.

She reclined and he chased her with more kisses until, at last, she lay on her back. He broke their contact then, and as he hovered over her, he smiled, smug. "So pretty, all spread out for me." His words always made her cheeks flush, even as they heightened the pleasure within. He tugged one bra cup down with his fingertips then ceased his movements to watch as her chest rose with a deeper inhale.

"Love?" she asked, hesitant at his pause. When he looked up in response, her breath caught. The intensity and focus he looked at her with was almost dizzying. They held each other's gaze for moments longer, with only the sounds of their breathing filling the silence — his slow and measured, hers struggling to match.

She was the first to look away, a sudden shyness overcoming her earlier lust-driven bravado. A slight incline of her head and a lowering of her eyes showed her submission. But it seemed that he was in no mood for such gestures, for he slid one figure under her chin and guided her head back up. "Don't. It pleases me to see your eyes."

*It pleases me.* Those words were a trigger. She dared not look away again, lest the gesture end the night before it fully began. She would please him. She *wanted* to please him.

He eased back and rebalanced himself. His grace always awed her, but there was nothing feminine in each movement. Precise. Decisive. They spoke of a well-honed hunter, and unbeknownst to her at the time, she had been his prey since that first fateful night.

He slid his hands down her arms, trailing heat down her skin from his fingertips. When he reached her wrists, he led them up above her head. "We will play a game tonight."

Her breathing grew shallow, although she managed to refocus her thoughts. They had discussed it before, how her brain could not disengage from the daily rat race. It took a man like him to hold her undivided attention in both body and mind, and he did so by challenging her at every turn.

"Tonight" — he tightened his grip around her wrists — "I will not bind you and no rope will constrain you. But you will keep your arms up right there, no matter what I do to your body." With a last squeeze, he let go of her wrists and trailed the backs of his hands all the way down. "You will want to touch." He brushed one finger by one exposed nipple. "You will want to pull me close." He replaced his finger with his tongue and swept it across, drawing a loud gasp from her. But even as she arched upward and begged with her body for more, he withdrew again. "But you will keep those hands where they are, for no reason other than knowing it will please me."

She whimpered, the cold air hardening her nipples further. Heat pooled in her center. Her gaze stayed on him and she watched as he released her other breast while his eyes darkened. She wanted to pull him down so his body covered her own, wanted the touch of his lips on her, wanted him to lose control and thrust deep into her. Instead, she flushed and squirmed under his scrutiny.

"So taut and perky." He tugged her skirt down and a low moan escaped his lips, even as he pressed his fingers against her already-soaked panties. "So hot and wet for me."

"All for you." The words came out as a bare whisper, her voice husky with need. He shifted his hands and tucked them under her rear, stroking her lace-covered cheeks. An unbidden smile tugged at the corner of her lips as he groaned.

"Good girl."

Coming from anyone else, she would have fought back tooth and nail against those words and thrown them back in their face with fire and fury. She had worked too hard in the world of men for anyone to patronize her with such a simple phrase. But here in the safe space, with the man who she knew respected and thought the world of her, she glowed with pride from his approval.

"Lift your hips, little one. I want to unwrap my present."

Without hesitation, she pushed her hips up and felt more than saw him tug her panties down with deft fingers. She strained to keep him in her view, but it was near-impossible without breaking her arms' position.

When he next resurfaced, there was that smirk and hint of mischief in his dark eyes before he tucked the undergarment into his back pocket.

"You owe me new panties." She'd meant for the tone to be flat, even deadpan, but it came out more like a squeal and she cursed herself for how weak she was against him.

He chuckled and leaned forward once more. The heat and hardness of him bumped up against one bare thigh and she shivered. That she had this kind of effect on him always delighted her. Rather than a reply, though, he reclaimed her lips with his, even as he cupped her breast. He took his time to massage it while he circled his thumb over one nipple, rolling it back and forth. It sent a shot of heat to her groin and she bucked upward against him.

"Patience, sweetheart," he murmured as he withdrew, as if to calm her eagerness. She whimpered and almost moved her hands to pull him back, only to remember their game at the last second.

"Please," she whispered and heard his dark chuckle once more, the sound holding wicked promises. A new gush of wetness soaked her thighs. *God*. And he had barely touched her.

"Please?" he teased. She widened her eyes as she watched him sink lower to settle on the floor. She raised herself, licking her dry lips at the sight of him resting between her legs. There was nothing submissive about his posture, however. Every line, every movement, every expression spoke of dominance, of precisely who was in control.

"What would you like, sweetheart?" He ran a hand up her leg and stroked along her inner thigh. Everything in her tensed, held still lest he cease his hand's journey. "Perhaps you want me to bring you to the edge." The breath of his words brushed against her skin and she shivered. "Tease you mercilessly until the only thought consuming you is the need for sweet release." A single kiss as he pressed his warm lips against her… "Or push you over, then keep you on the other side, making you come for me over and over until you cannot take it anymore." He scraped his teeth against her thigh and she felt more than heard him inhale her scent.

The juxtaposition of imagery he placed in her head with the physical teasing that had been building up all this time drew more whimpers from her. When he looked up once more to meet her gaze, she saw the desire mirrored in his expression. But how he liked to draw it out… Sometimes it made her want to tear her hair out in frustration. In this instance she wanted nothing more than to pull his head to her sex so that his tongue and lips would give her the much-needed release. Only sheer willpower and stubborn determination to follow his orders kept her hands above her head.

"Please." She tried again. "Please, I need you." The words were no more than a whisper.

"Soon, little one, soon. Relax." His voice washed over her as he switched to kneading her inner thighs. She tried…and slumped back to stare at the ceiling. Her gaze became unfocused, her eyes half closing. The sharp edge of the heat eased back ever so slightly as she surrendered to his ministrations. Her mind drifted and her hands moved as if they had their own will, lifting before she remembered their game.

Next, he parted the folds of her labia. But before she could react, his tongue was on her, a broad sweep upward that ended with a flick of her clit. Her hips jumped as she snapped her eyes open. He chuckled and shifted his hands on them to position her to his liking, then stayed, applying just enough pressure to keep her there.

Again, he eased back and pressed small butterfly kisses along her thighs instead. She let out a long moan with frustration weaving into the sound. She moved her hands once more then stopped again, as if they tugged against bonds that only her mind could see — bonds made of his words, his command and her own desire to obey.

He moved with tantalizing slowness until the light kisses hovered at her entrance. With the same agonizing pace, he worked his way around her folds with his tongue and drew out glorious shudders from her body. Seemingly on purpose, he left her clit alone, knowing how sensitive she was.

She zeroed in on his attention to her sex, to the warmth and pleasure that coursed through her body. Her nipples hardened in their yearning for more simulation, and she clasped her hands as she fought her own body to stay in position. He built her up with every touch, every sweep of his tongue, layer upon layer of pleasure until she was once more on the edge. Somewhere she heard low, continuous moaning, punctuated by whispers of "please," then realized the sound was coming from her.

Then nothing. Her mind screamed in frustration and railed against her building climax being ripped away with no warning. She whipped her head up as she strained to catch a glimpse of the reason for such cruelty and he smirked, meeting her bewildered look.

"Please what, sweetheart?" He used one finger to stroke her heat, to keep her simmering. Her own slickness coated her thighs and she was fairly sure she was soaking his hand.

She flushed and whimpered. The spoken word had never been her forte, but he had been training her to be more articulate her needs, to communicate more. Now he sat back and waited, clearly with all the patience in the world, as he kept toying with her—but never enough to push her over.

"Please, let me come." The words came out staccato, punctuated by ragged breaths.

"Good answer. Come for me." He gave her clit a hard flick.

That was all it took. She exploded and her body bucked against his hand as the orgasm ripped through her. Her every nerve was on fire, overwhelmed with pleasure as he continued to draw out her climax with expert fingers. Just as she felt herself coming down, she heard his command.

"Again." He replaced his fingers with his tongue and lashed almost cruelly against her oversensitive clit. He slipped two fingers inside her and crooked them to press against her G-spot. She screamed, her entire body arching as she spasmed out of control, the orgasm even harder than the last. The intensity overwhelmed her mind and stripped her world down to nothing but that single moment of ecstasy.

What felt like an eternity later, he withdrew his tongue, then his fingers. But he kept his hand where it was to cup her sex with a gentler touch. As he slid up onto the bed, he smoothed her hair back with his free hand and pressed a kiss on her forehead.

"You're so beautiful." There was a reverence in his voice that shook her and touched something deep inside her soul. Everything felt floaty and surreal, and in a detached part of her brain, she noted that she had likely entered subspace, that special mental state of euphoria that submissives could achieve from an intense session.

"Come back to me, sweetheart. You did good...so good."

She focused on his words, using them as her tether to find her way back.

It took several minutes before her vision cleared, and she gave a weak smile at the sight of his face, hovering close. His expression was like that of a cat that had just eaten a canary. "There you are, little one."

She didn't quite trust her voice yet. Instead, she swallowed. Out of nowhere, he produced a bottle of water and held its straw to her lips, ever observant and sensitive to her needs. She sucked on it and took the water in slowly.

He groaned and muttered to himself. "Maybe a straw was a mistake."

The comment drew a giggle from her, and he chuckled in return. He set the water bottle aside then blinked for a moment. She wasn't sure what had caught him by surprise until he reached up to touch her hands, which were still clinging together above her head. "You can let go now."

She blushed and worked her fingers loose, even as he stroked the back of her hand to encourage the release. As she pulled them apart at last, he took one, held it up to his lips and pressed a kiss on her knuckles. "Good job."

"What do I win?" she asked with a cheeky grin, a sign to both of them that she was on the way to recovery.

He grinned in reply. "We'll see what the score is by the end of the night. We still have a way to go."

# Chapter Two

Luna Weir stared at the sea of emails on her screen and chewed on her lip as the phrase 'victim of your own success' ran across her mind. The quicker and more efficiently she worked, the more they piled on her. She was already juggling three side-of-the-desk projects while managing her own queue of content edits, and on top of that, she had agreed to back up a co-worker while he went on vacation for his honeymoon.

*What was I thinking?*

With a small groan, she pushed back a lock of blonde hair, so light that it was almost silver. In the back of her mind, she could almost hear Jacob's disapproving voice. He never liked it when she overworked herself.

The thought of her Dominant brought a blush to her face and she shifted in her seat, all too aware of the thong riding up her ass crack. She'd never been much of a lingerie person until she'd noticed how much it delighted him. And once she'd dipped her toe into the world of lacy underthings all those years ago, she'd been hooked. They made her feel sexy and much more confident in her body.

Like a chain reaction, the thought of lingerie brought up memories of the previous night, of the games he'd played with her and of the pleasure they'd found in each other's bodies. Her cheeks heated further, and she clenched before she looked around to make sure no one had noticed her burning face. Thank God she had her own office.

She needed to calm down before someone walked in.

Rather than returning her attention to the computer screen, she studied the small space instead. Printouts of all sorts lined the gray office walls, ranging from company paraphernalia and creatives from past projects to charts and diagrams that expounded on theories of good conversion writing. A huge whiteboard hung from one wall, full of scribbles of her ideas for various projects.

A modest bookcase stood flush against one corner, laden with rows of notebooks and reference books on grammar and writing styles. The adjustable sit-stand desk she worked at was pushed up against the opposing wall with two large monitors perched on top, sticky notes lining the bottom of the screens. She had worked hard to make the space her own, a home away from home.

Her cell phone came alive with a buzz. The device's vibration sent it skittering across the desk and startled her out of her reverie. She almost jumped out of her chair but kept her rear in her seat, just barely. Luna took a breath to steady herself, then picked up the phone to see the notification showing two new messages.

The first was from her friend, Lani. A well-known female Dominant in the community, she was the one who had introduced her to Jacob in the first place...sort of.

Luna owed Lani a lot, and she had always been grateful. Lani had taken one look at her during their first munch, a brunch meetup for the local kink community, and had taken her under her wing. Given how naïve Luna had been at the time, she could have gotten into a lot of trouble had Lani not acted as her guide and paired her with the gentle and experienced trainer that was Jacob.

But as much as she loved Lani as a friend, she delayed opening that message in favor of the second — the one from Jacob himself. She skimmed her fingers over the screen and with a light touch, opened the message. Her heart pounded as she straightened, only to slump back in her seat a second later.

*Sorry, sweetheart. Curveball on some stuff that came in today. Got to work some overtime tonight so I can't meet up. I'll text you about Friday night once I get a better handle on the situation here. Miss me a little?*

A small sting of disappointment pricked her heart, but Luna smiled, nonetheless. She did not miss the tone of affection in the words he sent. That man was a charmer, and Luna knew well enough that even after three years, she was still completely under his spell.

*Sorry to hear. Good luck. And I always miss you.*

A message came back almost right away.

*Good girl. GTG. Text you later.*

She grinned like an idiot. Funny how he always provoked such a reaction from her with the smallest of gestures, the simplest of words. With a soft, happy sigh, she flipped to her other message.

*Lunch today? I want to sneak in some shopping.*

It was exactly the distraction she needed, though a small part of her wondered if she would regret the shopping part. Lani had a notorious appetite for shoes and boundless energy when it came to fashion. But they would only have the lunch hour to shop, so how bad could it be?

She glanced at the clock on her computer. *How can it be almost noon already?* She typed a quick response back.

*Sounds good. Meet at the usual in fifteen?*

Another buzz.

*See you there.*

She locked up her computer and pushed her chair back. There was nothing that couldn't wait until she returned from lunch. She grabbed her jacket from the back of the door and left the office, a renewed bounce in her steps.

Luna navigated the maze of cubicles, down the escalator and out into the early spring sun. She squinted as she adjusted to the brilliant light, then turned her face upward to bask in the warmth of it. Being pent up in the office most days gave her little opportunity to enjoy the improving weather. She drew in a breath of fresh air and made her way to the nearby cafe where she and Lani often met for lunch.

It was a cozy place with soups, sandwiches and the usual array of beverages. But it was the pastries they served that kept her and Lani coming back again and again. As she pushed through the door, she inhaled to savor the rich scent of butter that made her salivate and her stomach growl in anticipation.

Rows of croissants, cinnamon buns and other various confections in wicker baskets served as a backdrop to the front counter where staff bustled to serve the growing number of patrons. *Oh God, is that a fresh tray of apple turnovers?*

The place was busier than usual, and Luna scanned for either an empty table or a sign of her friend. Relief released the tension in her face when she caught sight of her. With a mass of curly, fiery-red hair, paired with a perfect complexion and a body that curved in all the right places, Lani was hard to miss, even standing at five-foot-three. Luna was half convinced that Merida from the Disney movie *Brave* was based on her. Next to Lani, Luna almost felt colorless and shapeless with her pale hair and skin and more waif-like body.

Yet, if anything, it was that something about her friend's presence — a mix of charisma and confidence — that attracted most of the submissives and even half the Dominants to her, regardless of gender. When Lani waved to Luna, she could see at least one or two disappointed faces at the surrounding tables.

Somehow, Luna doubted that Lani was oblivious to the attention but she simply ignored it. After all, it was part of her business as a counselor to read and observe people. But she knew her friend had little interest in others for now. Still in mourning for a love lost close to three years before, Lani had never taken on a serious partner since. But one day, she would heal. Luna was certain of it.

With a small chuckle under her breath, Luna waved back, matching her friend's enthusiasm, then lined up to order her own lunch. She retrieved her bowl of broccoli cheddar soup, coupled with a half chicken salad sandwich, threaded her way around and eased into the chair Lani had reserved for her.

"Oh, thank God." Luna relaxed into the chair and dug into her food. Lani had already eaten most of her salad and was sipping her tea.

"Poor thing. Beastly day?" Lani leaned forward, her voice soft in sympathy. But she enunciated each word beautifully, and Luna had no trouble picking them up over the cafe's din.

"Just work." Luna shook her head. "And I didn't really get much sleep last night."

A peal of laughter made Luna redden and regret her last words.

"Of course, of course. As if the dear boy would let his pet do something as simple as sleep in his presence." Mischief sparkled in Lani's eyes.

Luna covered her face with a groan. "We did sleep, eventually…" The words came out as a mumble and Luna jammed more of her sandwich into her mouth so she wouldn't put her other foot in it too.

A silence settled as Luna ate. She could feel Lani's eyes on her and gulped down the last few bites of her lunch. The proverbial elephant in the room grew larger with every conversation they had, and the handful of times Lani had tried to bring up the topic, Luna had managed to avoid it by changing the conversation. Still, it was only a matter of time before she would have to face the music, given how persistent Lani was. *Might as well be now.*

"Before you ask, we're about a month and a half away." Luna pushed her empty plate and bowl aside. She left the apple turnover in its paper bag next to her elbow.

"Have you guys talked about it?" Lani's voice was kind, her warm hazel eyes filled with compassion.

"No. And I'm not sure how to bring it up. I mean, I don't want to make it seem like I want things to end. And since he hasn't brought it up..." She trailed off as she realized just how pathetic she sounded.

"Except, as a trainer, he never keeps a sub for more than three years, and that's the end date of your contract too."

Her tone held all the care and concern Lani had for them both, but the statement still stung. Luna winced. They were words that had been sitting like stones in the pit of her stomach for weeks, but she had tried her best to not give them shape.

Lani reached her hand out to cover Luna's on the table. "Well, has there been any other Dom who has caught your eye? Maybe at The Playgrounds? Jacob never just abandons his pets, you know."

A shudder threatened to pass through Luna at Lani's questions, but she clamped down on the reaction. When Lani looked at her with worry tugging the corner of her lips downward, she shook her head. It was in the past — and it was a past she never wanted to discuss with anyone in her life. The last person — the only person — she'd ever spoken with about her past was now dead.

"Not really, no." Luna was proud that she could keep her voice steady.

Lani sighed in return and squeezed her hand. "Talk to him, sweetie."

Luna looked up and nodded with a weak smile. "Okay." She made no promises and was thankful that Lani didn't try to extract one from her. So, she straightened and strengthened her smile. "Besides that, tell me. Where are we going for shopping?"

# Chapter Three

Luna studied the girl in the full-length mirror with a critical eye. Silver hair piled on top of her head in a loose bun with tendrils escaping framed a pixie face with features a little too sharp for her liking. A red corset covered with black lace wrapped around her upper body and pushed her modest-sized breasts up to appear fuller than they were in reality. Below, layers of black fabric trimmed with red edges flared out at the hip as the skirt she wore ended well above the knees while the back trailed down longer. Sheer black stockings encased exposed legs, and modest black stilettos completed the classic cabaret outfit. It was a new one that Lani had helped her design, and she shifted her weight from foot to foot, trying to find a more flattering angle.

"Confidence," she muttered to herself and straightened.

The sound of a toilet flushing startled her. She blushed as a woman emerged from one stall and went over to wash her hands. Their eyes met for a brief moment in their reflections, and the woman gave her a warm smile. "Hon, you look great."

Luna smiled back. "Thank you." In truth, that was one thing she loved about the community, although it had taken a while for her to discover it. For the most part, they spent more time building each other up rather than tearing each other down, and people were so much more willing to embrace their bodies, no matter their size or shape…or their sexuality.

The woman gave another nod and left. Luna took a breath, shallower than she'd like, given the restrictions of the corset, then stepped out of the washroom.

The Playgrounds was a local fetish club that took up all three stories of the building. Situated in the industrial part of town, the club itself was inconspicuous on the outside, giving little indication of the kind of establishment it truly was.

Luna's gaze traveled across the space. Jacob had said to meet at nine, but she always liked to arrive early, just in case. The lounge was already half full of available subs looking for partners for the night or beyond, while fewer tourists than usual milled around. The dance floor, in contrast, was still empty, but the DJ of the night was just setting up. Later, the lights would dim and strobe lights would flash across the dance floor as house music would pulse in the air. For now, conversations and laughter generated most of the ambient noise.

As no one she knew was in sight, she made her way to the bar. A larger group of men and women sat on one end, but she chose the emptier side. Careful with her skirt, she pushed herself up on the plump red cushions of a bar stool. Everything about The Playgrounds had that kind of understated elegance.

"Hey, Luna." Darryl flashed her a smile and gave a slight nod. But he returned to the task at hand quick enough, busy with concocting fancy drinks.

"Hey-hey," she replied with a slight smile. She liked Darryl. The man took up much of the space behind the bar and the scar above his eye made him appear intimidating to many, but his easygoing-ness always made Luna feel safe rather than scared, even if the man was a sadist. They had first met at Lani's birthday party, and ever since, Darryl seemed to have made it his business to watch over her.

"Can I get you something?"

"Just water, please. I know you're super busy, though, so please, just when you have time."

Darryl flashed her another grin and a brief nod before he moved away to the other side of the bar to serve the cocktails he'd finished making.

"Silver Doll?"

Everything in Luna tensed and her heart pounded in her ears. There were only a few who would call her by that name, and she knew exactly who it was.

She pressed one hand against her chest as if that would help slow her fast-beating heart and swallowed once, then again to find her voice. With deliberate movement to buy herself time to brace herself, Luna turned around. "Mephisto? I mean, Bryan?"

There he was. Blond and blue-eyed, at six foot one he was innocence and bad boy wrapped in one. Dressed in a crisp, tailored white shirt and slim slacks, he looked like a model who had stepped out of a magazine. There was a certain charisma to him, a magnetism that promised fun with a tinge of wickedness.

Bryan's eyes hardened for a moment, so brief that Luna wasn't sure if it was just her imagination. A hint of a smirk, however, lurked in the corners of his mouth and he made a *tsk* sound. "What happened to 'Sir'? I trained you better than that."

Luna swallowed and shrank a little in her seat. A part of her felt ridiculous in the outfit in the presence of someone so smartly dressed. "Sorry, Sir."

When they'd first started their relationship as Dominant/submissive, Luna had asked Jacob what he wanted her to call him. Jacob had replied with that crooked grin of his that when she did scream in pleasure, he wanted it to be his name. Bryan, her first, contrasted against her current Dom in more than one way.

"Good girl." Bryan laid a hand on top of her head and Luna froze, afraid to move as he stroked her hair. Every fiber in her screamed how wrong it was, but her body refused to move. It took all her willpower to keep from hyperventilating.

"Relax, doll. Relax." His words were near-hypnotic, and she blinked for a moment. She remembered that about him. They had only met a handful of times in real life, but she remembered that voice well enough. Unlike those many years back, though, her body refused to obey.

She caught a whiff of his cologne and struggled to hide a cough as he leaned forward. He trailed his hand down her neck to the simple strip of black silk there, the only sign of ownership Jacob ever required her to wear at The Playgrounds. He was quiet, his eyes calculating as he stroked her neck through the silk, and she shivered at the touch, goosebumps rising on her skin. Part of it was familiar, but another part screamed inwardly at the violation. Her skin crawled as Bryan leaned forward to whisper in her ear. "Hmm-m, it seems my pet did not wait as I expected her to."

Fear twisted her gut, but it was the rage that unfroze her body at last. She slid off her seat and took a step back to create the much-needed space. "I. Am. Not. Yours." Luna forced each word out through gritted teeth, bolstered by her anger.

"No, she's mine." Someone wrapped an arm across her chest and pulled her back with gentle pressure. The familiar voice caressed her neck and erased the earlier unwelcoming touch, even as it eased her fear. Luna leaned back and relaxed into the embrace as she reached up to lay a hand on his arm. *Jacob.* Out of the corner of her eye, she saw Darryl move to their side of the bar, observing in silence and clearly ready to help his friend.

Bryan paused for a moment then smiled while he held up both hands. "My apologies." Of course, he was all charm once again. "Luna and I go way back, and it was a surprised to see her. That's all." He held out a hand to Jacob. "Bryan Walsh."

Luna tilted her head back to look up at Jacob. His gaze never left Bryan and he shook against her, his muscles vibrating with rage. She heard Darryl clear his throat and snuck a peek in his direction. The bartender's eyebrow raised in surprise, probably at Jacob's reaction, and she concurred. The last thing her Dom was ever known for was possessiveness. It terrified a part of her. Another part grew wet with arousal.

"Lovelies!" Lani strode over in her impossible heels. Luna was pretty sure that Lani never wore the same pair twice. Dressed in a black pair of dress pants coupled with a golden cincher and a matching top hat, Lani exuded easy command and control.

"Oh, don't you look wonderful, Luna. I told you that you would do the outfit justice. Don't you think so, Jacob?"

Lani's casual attempt at conversation worked to slice through the tension, and Luna felt Jacob loosen his hold on her just a little. Before either Luna or Jacob could reply, however, Lani spun around to turn her attention to Bryan.

"Oh, do we have a newcomer?" Lani turned without waiting for an answer from Jacob.

Bryan bowed toward Lani, his gesture gentlemanly rather than submissive. "Bryan Walsh. I just moved into town and thought I'd see what's around."

Lani patted Bryan on the arm. "Well then, my dear, why don't we leave these lovebirds to their devices and let me show you?"

Luna did not miss the subtle nod her friend gave her. Lani was her hero right now. She watched as Bryan accepted Lani's suggestion and offered her an arm. She wasn't sure who led who away, but she breathed a sigh of relief, nonetheless.

"What the hell was that?" Jacob released his arms and she shivered at the sudden lack of his warmth against her. The anger was back in his voice and caused her to turn around, while caution kept her tongue from running. When she didn't reply right away, he groaned in frustration and pushed his inky hair back. "Fine... You will answer me in private."

Without another word, he turned. She was left staring at his back—his oh-so-sexy back. Clad in a simple black shirt and black slacks, he towered over almost everyone at six foot three. Where Bryan was manicured and refined, an image that he purposefully cultivated, Jacob's casual naturalness made him even more attractive. Luna could just make out the muscle definition beneath his shirt, his every movement speaking of strength. She remembered tracing those muscles with her fingers and tongue, remembered the power radiating from them as he surged above her. Those thoughts were most inappropriate at the moment, considering that the way he held himself right now radiated anger, and she shoved them away.

Luna trailed after him, wondering just how much trouble she was in exactly. She missed him already and ached to reach out for his hand, but she knew instinctively that right now he would not welcome her touch. All she knew was that she'd better brace herself for the conversation to come. Because somehow, she knew it would be one of the hardest they would have since they'd started their relationship.

# Chapter Four

Jacob clenched his fists and held them to his side with all the rigidity he could muster, although what he really wanted was to punch the wall. Well, he wanted to punch Bryan more, but the wall would suffice as a target, and it'd be far less likely to get him thrown out. Maybe.

They made their way upstairs, past the second floor with the dungeon where members of the club could play in public. When they reached the third and top floor, where private rooms lined each side of a long hallway, Jacob paused in his stride to wait for Luna to catch up. The walk upstairs had given him the time to calm the cauldron of emotions churning inside him, and he fought for control over the wicked temper he rarely let loose.

He scanned for an unoccupied room and, without another thought, opened the door to one. At least it was a standard rather than the themed ones. He was in no mood for play.

The room was lit with soft, warm lighting, with walls lined with panels of cherry wood to give it a red tinge and an atmosphere of subdued elegance. To one side, a Saint Andrew's cross was secured to the floor while various whips and floggers hung from hooks on the wall. A glass case leaned against one corner, displaying a variety of gags on one shelf, vibrators and other toys on the others. A sink with a shelf of gentle cleaning agents was installed in the far corner, along with a drinking water station right next to a nest of pillows and blankets available for aftercare. Closer to the opposing wall, a harness hung from sturdy hooks installed in the ceiling, designed for suspension play. *Ideas for another time.*

He held the door open and watched as Luna walked past him, hugging herself, her posture hunched over as if the way she held herself would block out the world. Whatever had just happened had shaken her. It chafed at his instinct, and his grip tightened on the door handle. Part of him wanted to yell at her for scaring him. A bigger part wanted to scoop her up in his lap and tell her everything was going to be okay, to give her the comfort and security she needed to be herself again. Instead, he did neither. As he schooled his face to a more neutral expression, he closed the door behind him with a soft but audible click.

Jacob left her standing by the door as he set up. After stepping toward the nest of pillows, he dragged one away from its peers to the center of the room, knowing Luna had bad knees from her martial arts training injuries. Next, he picked up a hard, wooden chair and set it in front of the pillow, no longer paying heed to the other equipment in the room.

As soon as he'd completed the setup, he turned toward Luna, crossing his arms to regard her. He wished that she'd stop looking so damn defeated.

When she didn't respond, he stalked over, aware of just how much he loomed over her. *Fine.* He would command the truth from her. "Rest position." He pointed a finger to the pillow, his voice cold as his frustration turned from fire to ice.

Luna moved across the room and flowed into compliance. She knelt, toes flat, keeping her shoulders straight as she eased back to sit on her heels. *Seiza.* It was in line with her martial arts training. The posture forced alertness without being too uncomfortable for those trained such as herself. It had been a long time since he had used positions with her. Then again, it had been a long time since her last transgression.

A remote part of his mind admired the grace with which she obeyed him and savored the image of her submission. But the task at hand was too important to indulge. Instead, he walked over to the control panel, cutting off the audio feed to the security camera. He hovered his hand over the video feed. Normally both of them preferred privacy, and their bond had proceeded to a level of trust where security monitoring was no longer needed. But tonight… He left the panel alone, leaving the video feed on. It was what he needed to chain the rage inside.

He sat in front of her and braced his hands against his knees, his back stiff as a board. Silence settled between them, the only sound their breathing, both in slow rhythm. He gave no other order but waited for her to come to her own words.

"I…" Luna swallowed, the movement drawing his gaze, and he studied the way the black silk moved against her throat.

She cast her eyes downward as her words came at a slow, hesitant pace, spilling out, one by one. "Bryan and I met online, in one of those chat room sites, when I first started getting curious about the scene. He…"

Luna paused and snuck a quick peek at him before she bowed her head again, but Jacob only sat, still as a statue, watching as Luna grappled for the right words. People felt a need to fill in silences.

"He laid claim to me quickly enough online. We met up a few times, scened even. But then he just…just ghosted." The words came tumbling out faster from her lips now, but her voice broke with the last two.

*'Are you sure you still want me? I don't go where I'm not wanted, you know.'*

The memory surfaced unbidden in Jacob's mind as he recalled what she'd said to him once. Early on, when they had still been figuring each other out, she had asked while teasing him after their first night together. He remembered flipping her over and spanking her before showing her just how much he wanted her. Now her words, spoken then in jest, took on a whole new meaning.

There was something else, though. He sensed it was not the entire story, not by the fear response the other Dom had invoked in her. She had clung to him earlier, and he had felt the stiffness of her body. Luna met every challenge head on, and it was rare for her to be that afraid. "He hurt you." He had meant for it to be a question, but it came out flat, monotone.

Luna's eyes widened. "No. I mean, I was new to it and I didn't understand my limits. He was just a little rougher than what I would have liked." She looked up and gave him a weak, self-deprecating smile. "You know how eager I am to please."

He clenched his fists and it took all his willpower not to explode. It was a Dominant's responsibility to gauge their submissive's limits, especially if they were brand new to the scene. He knew first-hand how easy it was for Luna to slip into subspace, that special zone where subs could no longer make rational decisions about their own safety. It was what made her trust in him such a precious treasure. And here she was, defending that sorry excuse for a Dominant for abusing such a gift.

With painstaking control, he worked his jaw loose and unclenched his fists, willing his body to relax, even as he stood. "Why was I not informed of this at any time during our relationship?"

Luna lowered her head farther, choosing to fixate on the floor. "I'm sorry." He needed her to stop looking like such a beaten dog, but in his current mood, he had no idea how.

"Answer the question, Luna."

"I— I just wanted to forget." The words came out as a whisper. "I was ashamed...that I was not...good enough..." Her shoulders slumped.

The icy rage threatened to turn molten once more. He gritted his teeth and counted to ten before he spoke again. "Bryan's actions are his own. I do not blame you for that. But this omission—" He paused before his mouth ran away from him. "What is our relationship based on? What is written in our contract?"

"Open communication."

Helplessness was perhaps one emotion Jacob hated the most. And he felt helpless—at Bryan's past treatment of Luna, at Luna's unwillingness to trust him enough to tell him and at her belief that even after all this time, she was not good enough. It was hard to see past any of the anger, to sort out the roiling emotions churning within him. He needed space, needed time before he said something regrettable that would hurt her further. Right now, he didn't trust his control enough to be able to lead them both out of this. "Go home, Luna."

A tear escaped and he leaned forward and cupped her cheek with infinite gentleness, rubbing it away with the pad of his thumb. "I will come back for you, but I need time. Three days. I'll text you then." He kept his voice quiet, low. It was important for her to understand that she was not being abandoned. He would not prey on her insecurities that way. So he would maintain control, just for a little longer. He brushed his lips against her forehead and inhaled the scent of her coconut shampoo. It would be torture to be away from her, but they both needed the space.

"I'm sorry," Luna whispered and nodded in acknowledgment of his words.

"I know, sweetheart." Jacob straightened and crossed the room to let himself out. As soon as he closed the door, he leaned against it and ran his hand through his hair.

With a sigh, he pushed himself off and began to walk. As he did, he pulled out his phone and typed at a furious speed that did not match his slower pace.

*Is Bryan still with you?*

He stalked down the familiar hall and stairs.

A quick notification flashed along with a buzz that followed within seconds.

*No, he found a sub to play with. I think they're in the dungeon.*

A knot in him loosened and he let go of the breath he didn't know he was holding. *Good. Bryan's not waiting for Luna like some crazed stalker.*

His phone buzzed again.

*Is everything okay?*

He paused at the foot of the stairs then headed straight for the exit. It was a cloudless night, but there was a chill in the air that did nothing to cool his temper.

*I need a favor.*

*It'll cost you! What is it?*

"Pest," he muttered under his breath. It almost guaranteed that Lani was going to stick her nose into the matter, and her favors did not come cheap. But he needed to know Luna was going to be okay.

*Make sure Luna gets home okay.*

*You betchya.*

Jacob raised an eyebrow and stared at his phone, waiting for the next message. When no questions came, he muttered something under his breath about women and stared up at the night sky. Out here, the lack of city lights and a new moon meant the stars shone brighter. He resisted the urge to go back in, to collect Luna and whisk her away to a rural road where she could find calm and happiness in gazing at the stars and he could bask in her enjoyment.

Instead, with a sigh of frustration, he got into his car. It was time to figure out how to deal with his wayward sub.

# Chapter Five

Three days. Three long days that dragged on and on without a word from Jacob. Luna knew it was his way, that once angered, it was how much time he needed to cool off, but that didn't make the time pass by any easier.

She made a point of ignoring her silent phone that she had tossed haphazardly on the table. Instead, she alternated between scrolling and typing at a maddening rate. And if her fingers pounded on the keyboard with more force than usual, she chalked it up to the eighth stupid typo she'd had to fix so far in the article she was working on.

Yeah, that was it.

"You know, at some point, you'll have to eat."

Luna blinked and looked up to see her friend and co-worker Ted leaning against the frame of her office's door. As soon as her mind caught up to his presence, she made a face in response, if only to cover her guilt. Her gaze trailed back down to her desk, littered with candy wrappers, a half-eaten chip bag and a now-empty can of Sprite.

"No, Luna, those don't count. I mean proper food."

She groaned and pulled the hood of her sweater up. It was just deep enough that it flopped down over her forehead.

"Luna, come on. At least a walk would do you good. You can't keep up with the pace you're going at. Just because you had a fight with your boyfriend doesn't mean you're suddenly married to work." Ted strolled in, then without warning, tugged her office chair with her still in it away from her desk, yanking her away from the keyboard. She flailed her arms, still trying to reach the keys. Any of their co-workers walking by would find it to be a pure comedic moment, but right now she didn't care.

"Come on. Don't make me call Brandon," he threatened.

"Okay, okay!" Luna held her hands up in surrender. If Ted was like an older brother, his other half was more like her father. Stern, no nonsense. He would not be afraid to give some tough love, both in the form of a tongue lashing and in the dojo, where they practiced.

She sighed and rose from her seat, still sluggish, perhaps from the stiffness of her legs. With reluctant shuffles to the door, she grabbed her jacket and allowed Ted to usher her out of the office. He kept them moving until at last they arrived at their destination.

The food truck with the amazing grilled cheese was out today and they made haste to snag their meals before the rest of the lunch crowd got there. They headed to the nearby park where they sat on the benches and unwrapped their sandwiches. Silence settled as they ate. Luna savored the food and prolonged each bite for as long as she could in an attempt to avoid the interrogation she saw in Ted's eyes.

"So, what is this fight about, anyway? You don't usually have fights with your boyfriend. What's his name again? Jack?"

"Jacob." The name sounded warped in her full mouth and she winced a little. Although not a conventional relationship, Jacob had been happy to stand in as her boyfriend and had no problems with her referring to him as such to her more vanilla friends. But as Luna wasn't comfortable coming out of the closet yet, so to speak, she was reluctant to have her two worlds collide. As a result, very few people had met Jacob. Ironic, considering Ted was the gay one, but in this day and age, his sexual preferences were much more socially acceptable than hers, at least within her more conservative circle of friends outside the scene.

"Right…Jacob." Ted made the name sound more like a question, eliciting another groan from her.

Luna stared at the last bites of her sandwich and sighed. "Well… we ran into an ex of mine the other night while we were out. I hadn't told him about that guy before, so he's pretty pissed." None of it had been a lie, per se, but as she had learned the other day, that omission was just as bad. Still, for Ted, who didn't know, it would have to do.

"Serious? That's what he's pissed about? Talk about insecurity."

Luna winced and stuffed the last of her food in her mouth to keep from babbling something she would later regret. 'Insecure' was the last word she would use to describe Jacob. Confident. Sexy. *Yeah, definitely sexy.* But without the context of their relationship dynamics,

Jacob did sound like an ass. Still, if she explained any more, she would let on too much.

"No, he's not," she mumbled, settling for the lame protest as she still felt a need to defend Jacob. After all, she was the one who had screwed up by not telling him earlier. A D/s relationship depended on communication and openness. She had broken that trust.

"There you go again, blaming yourself for everything." Beside her, Ted huffed and took a long sip of his lemonade. "I've seen you toss around guys twice your size in the dojo." Luna felt Ted's gaze on her and shifted a little under the scrutiny. "Look... Don't let this guy push you around, okay? You're not some slave catering to his every whim."

The words caught her mid-swallow and she spluttered, except then the food went down the wrong way. Luna bent over as her body tried to eject the food in a coughing fit while she pounded her chest with one fist. *Oh, dear God.* That was how it was going to end, choking on a piece of bread from an innocent comment that had hit too close to her dirty little secrets.

"Luna!" Ted set his own sandwich aside and patted her on the back to help. When she waved him off as she recovered, he offered her his lemonade. She grabbed it and took a huge gulp, in part to help but also just to exact revenge.

"Hey, don't finish it! Go get your own."

Luna stuck her tongue out at him when she felt her phone buzz in her pocket. She froze, her eyes widening. Her heart started beating twice as fast. A pause, then another buzz drove her to action. She handed the drink back to Ted and dug into her jacket's pocket for her phone.

As Ted was about to speak, she held out one finger to signal pause. She worked to unlock the phone then scroll to her message app.

*Come over after work tonight.*

There was another quick follow-up.

*What time do you think you'll be done? I'll pick you up. We'll talk.*

Luna sucked in a breath. The pounding didn't slow. The messages held no clue to what the talk entailed, nor did she have any idea what she would step into tonight. Would he end their contract now, a month and a half early? With shaky fingers, she typed back.

*Okay. I'll be done at 5:30.*

"Luna?"

She looked up while she tucked her phone back into her pocket and forced a smile that she was in no mood for. "Yeah, I'm good. Let's head back."

Judging by Ted's expression, she hadn't fooled him one bit, but at least he asked no more questions as they walked back to the office.

For the rest of the afternoon, restless energy fueled by her anxiety filled Luna. She tried to switch to standing, then pacing. She tried loud death metal. She tried chamomile tea. Nothing helped and she found herself checking for messages every thirty seconds. In the end, Luna gave up all pretense of being able to concentrate and instead cleaned her office.

At five-fifteen, she made her way to the washroom to try to salvage some of her appearance. Luna swore beneath her breath as she made an attempt to smooth her hair. There was nothing she could do about the puffiness of her eyes. And she had dressed like crap too, favoring the need for comfort rather than looking good. She didn't have a backup pair of heels to change out of either, having opted for sneakers earlier that morning. Without much thought, she pulled the baggy green hoodie tighter around her. Jacob had let her have it a few weeks back.

Luna returned to her office to grab her jacket and backpack before she navigated her way out, careful to avoid Ted or anyone who might intercept her. By the time she was outside, she was fidgeting once more, rocking back and forth on the balls of her feet while she picked at a loose thread on her bag strap.

At five-thirty exactly, Jacob's black Jeep pulled into the parking lot.

"I'm not going to make a scene. I'm not going to make a scene," she whispered to herself under her breath as she watched him park and exit the car.

*God, he's gorgeous.* She remembered tracing the curvature of the wiry muscles beneath his tall and lanky body a mere few days before. He was clean-shaven today and she could almost imagine the smell of his aftershave. Jet-black hair brushed against his warm chocolate eyes, usually twinkling with humor. Today they were serious, but there was still a warmth to them. Luna allowed herself a glimmer of hope.

"Hello, little one." Soft. Kind.

Luna burst into tears.

# Chapter Six

"Come here."

Luna stepped into Jacob's arms and buried her face against his chest. She had held it together until that very moment, but now that he was there, she was falling. With shaky hands, she clung to his shirt and as he wrapped his arms around her, shielding her from prying eyes, she allowed herself that good cry she needed at last.

They stood there, who knew how long, with Jacob rubbing slow circles on her back. By and by, the sobs turned into gulps for breath. When he pressed a kiss on top of her head, she leaned back and rubbed her face roughly.

"Hey, hey. Gentle. I like that pretty face."

She gave a slight, stuttered laugh as he tugged her hand away from her face to replace it with his own to dry the last of her tears. *It's going to be okay.*

"Better?"

At Luna's nod, Jacob stepped back but kept one hand at the small of her back. "Come on. Let's go home."

It was an odd turn of phrasing, something that made Luna look up at Jacob with a tilt of her head.

"My place." He corrected himself with a shrug as he guided her to the car.

The drive back did not take long, but they held hands the entire way. Jacob traced random patterns across the back of her hand with his thumb from time to time. It was soothing and Luna relaxed, both hollowed out and relieved.

When they arrived, he surprised her with food already on the table, but her gaze wandered across the familiar place all the same. Jacob's apartment was not large, and his dining table dominated much of the living room. Behind it, an old-fashioned three-seater couch perched in front of a wall-mounted TV. An entryway to the galley-style kitchen stood to the left of the table while on their right, a short hallway was lined with doors that led to a small powder room, an office and the master bedroom. The place was sparse but tastefully decorated, and over the last three years, it had almost become a second home to Luna.

The smells caught up a second later, pulling her attention away from surveying the place and eliciting demanding growls from her stomach. She wrapped her arms around her midsection as her cheeks flushed with embarrassment.

A small chuckle made her look up at Jacob. "Lani told me you turned down her lunch invite yesterday, and I'm guessing you've been on the junk food diet the last few days."

"Traitor," Luna muttered beneath her breath as she took off her shoes and hung her jacket up. She turned to help Jacob take off his jacket, but he waved her off and took her by the shoulders to guide her toward the food instead.

"You haven't been taking care of your body. You know that is a punishable offense, right?"

A whimper escaped her lips as she quaked on the inside at his statement. Her list of punishments was going to be a mile long at that rate.

"Eat, then we'll talk." He pulled a chair out and urged her to sit down. Once she settled in, he put a fork in her hand. Only after she took her first bite did he nod in satisfaction and move to the other side of the table to sit down to eat.

They tucked into their dinner, Luna with enough enthusiasm for both of them, despite the threat of punishment hanging over her head. Maybe it was because no matter what it was, the food was a sign that he wasn't mad anymore. She loved Jacob's cooking and every meal by him was a treat.

Only when she ate the last bite did she realize that Jacob had already finished his and was watching her, a small smile playing on his lips. She blushed. "What is it? Oh God, I have something stuck in my teeth, don't I?"

He shook his head, amusement dancing in his eyes. "It's satisfying watching you eat. I have rarely seen anyone in my life relish food the way you do, Luna. No wonder people like to feed you."

Before she could reply, he rose and offered his hand. When she placed hers in his, he led her to the couch and sat her down. He watched her in silence, and she cast her eyes downward. After another moment, she couldn't stand the scrutiny anymore and started.

"I'm sorry. I know I should've —"

"Luna."

She looked up at him, the words she had prepared dying on her lips.

"Do you understand what you've done wrong?"

"Yes." It came out as a bare whisper.

Jacob tilted her chin upward with two fingers. Luna found his eyes boring into hers, his focus on her almost overwhelming. "Tell me."

"I let my fears get in the way of open communication." She was proud that her voice did not crack.

"Good." He let go of her chin. "Then consider that from this point on, your slate has been wiped clean. It's bad enough what you put yourself through in your head these last couple of days."

Luna breathed a sigh of relief.

"However, now we must do the hard work together. I know the written word is easier for you, so I want you to write down what the scenes you and Bryan had entailed and how they made you feel. I expect the writeup on my table by this time next week."

A shiver passed through Luna's body. It was going to be difficult, but she could do it. She would do it for him. She owed him that much. "Yes, Jacob."

He cupped her cheek. "Good girl."

Leaning into the warmth of his palm, Luna smiled and closed her eyes.

"Now, there is still the matter of you not taking care of yourself."

Her eyes flew open and she sat up, her lips forming a small O.

"Up. Strip. Slowly."

Heat blazed on Luna's cheeks once more as she rose from her seat. She shuffled with her bare feet across the hardwood floor until she stood in front of him. *Inhale.*

*Exhale. Inhale. Exhale.* She reached up to unzip her hoodie and tugged the slider down one agonizing inch at a time. The garment slipped off her shoulders and down her body until it lay like a pool of green around her feet. Next, she gripped the edge of her black T-shirt and tugged it over her head with a little more haste to expose the off-white lace bra beneath.

Next came the pants. Warmed up now, she grew more daring, her eyes meeting his as she curved her lips into a teasing smile. She reached down to undo her belt, then the button and zipper to her jeggings. As she tugged them down, she gave a little hip wiggle and grinned wider when she was rewarded with a quiet groan.

Luna bent down to retrieve the clothing on the floor while offering him a full view of her backside, then folded each item before she placed the neat pile on the arm of the couch.

"All the way, sweetheart."

She laughed under her breath, feeling more and more comfortable in her body. His reactions and his focus on her quieted all her self-doubts. With him, she felt empowered, sexy and desired.

With practiced ease, she reached back to undo the clasp to her bra and slipped the straps off her shoulders. And at last she tugged her panties down, placing both on top of the clothing pile before turning to face him in all her naked glory.

He reached out with one hand to wrap around her wrist. If his grip was a little tighter than usual, she didn't mind. Instead, she followed his lead as he tugged her toward him.

"Lie face down on my lap." She grew wet at his command in that husky voice of his, full of need.

She obeyed, positioning herself so that her stomach lay in his lap while her breasts brushed against the side of his jeans. She could feel the sign of his own arousal pushing against her stomach.

Fingertips trailed across her buttocks, sending goosebumps across her skin. "Remember your safewords, Luna?"

"Yellow for slow, red for stop."

"Good. I want you to count out loud. We will go up to ten since this is your first infraction in a while."

"Yes, Jacob." She drew in a deep breath and let it out to prepare herself. When he started kneading one butt cheek, she let out a small sigh.

The first slap from his hand still came as a surprise. She gave a small yelp and her body jumped a little. In response, he pressed on the small of her back with just enough pressure to remind her to hold still, but not enough to pin her down.

"One." She spoke clearly after a moment of recovery.

He kneaded again, just for a brief minute, before he delivered three quick successive blows, the third one ending more as a thud than a sting. Each time, she breathed out with the number.

Again, he paused and rubbed the pain out before he moved to the other cheek. She squirmed a little and began to part her legs, which earned her a quick, light slap. "Five."

*Message received.* She held herself still. For a while, there were only the sounds of their breathing. That and she was pretty sure he could hear the hammering of her heart.

Two more came in rapid succession then nothing. A small moan of anticipation escaped her lips, her rear burning wonderfully, endorphins kicking in.

He chuckled, raking his nails across her skin with light pressure. "So beautiful," he murmured, and she couldn't help but wiggle her rear in response, sure that at that point she was leaving a large stain on his jeans.

"You minx." He dipped one finger downward between her legs. "So wet."

She groaned and tried to part her legs for him more, encouraging him to play. Instead, without another word, he delivered the last blows.

"Eight. Nine." She half-yelled out the words.

He shifted his hand and before she could catch her breath, he delivered the last blow right on her center.

"Ten," she screamed out a split second later, pain mixing with pleasure. At her shout, he plunged two fingers into her, thrusting back and forth hard and fast.

"I need to come. Please." She barely gasped out the words, her body singing with need, her entire world narrowing to just his fingers.

"Come."

Her muscles clenched tight around his fingers and she lifted her head, her back arching as she came apart in his lap, his name on her lips. The world faded. Vaguely, she registered that he had an arm around her midsection to keep her from rolling off.

He slowed his fingers' movement as she came back down. When he withdrew, she gave a small groan but remained on his lap like a limp doll.

"So beautiful," he repeated. Jacob helped her slide off without falling and to steady her when she tried to stand, but her legs were just too wobbly.

He stood and scooped her up, kissing her forehead. "And that last bit was for finishing your dinner and having a proper meal again."

Luna moaned in appreciation and nuzzled his neck.

Jacob chuckled, his lips still half-buried in her hair. "Come on, sweetheart. I'm not done with you yet."

# Chapter Seven

Emotions surged within Jacob as he watched the woman in his arms blink in a hazy fog. Delight. Contentment. Pride. Joy. Arousal. But underneath it all was an undercurrent of something he could not quite name. All he knew was that regret colored the emotion.

After he carried her down the hall to the bedroom, he pushed the door open with his back. A single bedside table lamp cast deep shadows across the furniture. A full-length mirror stood in one corner, an armchair and footstool with a thick throw over the arm in the opposing one. Against the wall, the tall chest of drawers held most of his clothing while a footboard chest spanned the width of a large king-sized bed, containing his more personal possessions. Hidden from the eye were built-in D-rings for various rope attachments. Those were fun things for another night.

He set her down as close to the center of the bed as possible. She was so close to subspace that he was not sure if proceeding further would be wise. So, with a small sigh, he tucked the duvet around her, stripped off his clothes then slipped underneath the covers himself.

Luna curled up against him, pressing her feet against his calf. He hissed at the icy sensation but braced himself as he reached down with one hand to reposition her feet closer to warm them up.

She moved to lay her head on his shoulder and he in return wrapped an arm around her. The movements were so natural that he once more marveled — as he had for more times than he could count in the past three years — at how well they fit together.

Still too keyed up to sleep, Jacob contended himself with stroking her upper arm, tracing random patterns across the smooth skin. His own desires would have to wait. Instead, he allowed his thoughts to wander.

He craved her. Few subs in his life had made him desire them the way she did. When they had first met three years ago, her shyness and her reactions to him had intrigued him. There was a vulnerability and openness to her that tugged at the Dominant in him. He wanted to protect her, to make sure no one could take advantage of her willingness to submit. But over the years, her submissive nature had blossomed with confidence and boldness that brought thoughtfulness to how she served, whether it was in all the ways she anticipated his needs or in the creativity she brought to the bedroom.

She was a treasure and he admitted to himself that he was reluctant to pair her off with another Dom. Perhaps that was why he'd reacted the way he had the other night with Bryan. Normally he was not that possessive.

His arm tightened at the memory of the other Dom's hands on Luna.

He had imposed the three-year limit for a reason. Without moving on, he would stop growing as a Dom, and Luna deserved to have more experiences beyond him. He had been clear with her on the subject since the beginning and that was why their contract term was also only three years. The contract, a common practice among the BDSM community, served as a symbolic gesture to signal consent for both parties to enter a power dynamic relationship and it had given him a suitable opportunity to explain his expectations in the beginning.

Still, he could tell that Luna was not ready to leave. Not that she gave him any grief about it, but he knew by the way she would chatter with excitement about something they could do in the future then trail off, shaking her head with a small, sad smile.

It was his fault.

Jacob tensed at the thought before willing himself to relax when he felt Luna shift next to him, as if reacting to his body. But his mind would not let him off so easily as it continued on that road of guilt. That was where he had gone wrong, wasn't it? He should have kept mentioning it to acclimatize her to the idea, but as the day loomed closer, he also found himself reluctant to discuss it.

The simple way out would be to take on another sub. But he could tell that that would sadden Luna, and that was the last thing he wanted — not that any other sub had even remotely caught his interest ever since she had become his.

Jacob huffed at the dilemma. He needed to figure something out soon. With a heavy heart, he turned his head, buried his nose in her hair and inhaled. He would miss the faint scent of her coconut shampoo.

*Great, now I'm mooning over her like a moody teenager.*

The sudden sensation of fingers trailing down to stroke his cock chased all the thoughts away. It did not take much for it to harden. As Luna looked up at him with utter adoration, he moaned. "Sweetheart…"

"I want…need…" Confusion fluttered across her face before she furrowed her forehead in frustration. So, she was halfway back. He chuckled at what she was asking in her delicate emotional state.

"Ride me, sweetheart," he whispered in his ear. "Show me how beautiful you are."

A slow smile spread across her lips before she slipped the covers off them and shifted until she straddled him. He watched in fascination as her body blushed red with arousal. In the dim light, framed by the long hair cascading down her back, she was his very own ethereal creature.

She ground against him, smearing her wetness along his cock. Every time she hit a certain angle where her clit rubbed against him, she would shiver. Her gaze met his and her smile turned teasing as she reached to cup her breasts, circling her thumbs over the hardened nipples.

"You keep that up and the nipple clamps are coming out." He moved his hands to her hips, using his grip to guide her. "Ride me." His tone had changed, and a hint of impatience crept into it. Now it was an order.

She dropped her hands from her breasts to brace herself against his chest. With sweet, agonizing slowness, she raised herself up, lined his cock up to her entrance then lowered herself, inch by inch. Her eyes never left his, though her lips parted with small moans. Did she realize how sexy her wantonness was?

When she bottomed out at last, taking in all of him, they each let out a long groan in unison. He reached up to cup her face then trailed his hand down to stroke her arms, then back to her hip. "Mine." Only in these moments did he give himself free rein to be possessive of her.

"Yes," she hissed and began rocking against him.

Part of him was not sure if she was answering his claim or stating the pleasure that was taking her over once more. It didn't matter. He gripped her hips a little tighter and thrust back, setting an easy rhythm. Even if he was lying on his back, he was the one in control.

"More, more, please," she whimpered as she closed her eyes, tossing her head back as she rode him.

He smiled, letting go of one side to move his hand forward while he slowed his thrusting almost to a stop. The pause allowed him to move his thumb to find what he sought. Above him, Luna whimpered again, this time in protest.

As soon as he touched her clit, she cried out, her body stiffening.

"That's it, sweetheart. Come for me. Show me all of you." Without mercy, he flicked her hardened nub back and forth in rapid succession and was rewarded by her bucking against him. Her back arched to an almost painful angle and her inner muscles clamped down hard on his cock.

The sight of her orgasm combined with how she milked him was enough to push him over the edge. With a low groan, he grabbed her hips and thrust. In three deep strokes, he came hard inside her, filling her with his seed.

Luna fell on top of him in a heap and they both spent the next few minutes panting for breath. He rubbed her lower back in an automatic gesture of comfort, and when he found his voice at last, he spoke. "Come on. We can't fall asleep like this."

"Can too," she mumbled in protest. "You're warm."

He chuckled and kissed the top of her head once more. "Let me clean you up. Then I can warm your feet."

The bribe was enough. She lifted herself up weakly and both of them moaned as he pulled out of her. While she slid off the bed, Jacob kept an arm out to steady her then rose to lead her to the washroom, where he took a warm cloth and set to work.

The harder part done, he settled them both back in bed, pulled her feet up and tucked them between his legs. At least they hadn't quite had the chance to turn back to ice-coldness again. Luna closed her eyes with a sigh of contentment, a sign of a well-fucked woman, and fell asleep within seconds. In his own weariness, he felt and ignored the absurd urge to strike a superhero pose. He blinked and, in the end, he gave in to the comforting darkness, but not before one last very odd question rose in his mind.

Luna was on birth control. They'd never envisioned a future together. So why was he, for a moment there, wishing that Luna would get pregnant with his child?

# Chapter Eight

Saturday. Oh, glorious Saturday. Luna bustled around in the kitchen, humming along with the folk music playing from Jacob's bluetooth speakers. She had figured out how to connect her phone to them first thing in the morning and was rather proud of herself. Technology rarely worked for her at the first go.

Coffee was brewing and she had thick slices of bread going in the toaster. Bacon was cooling on the side. Onions, mushroom, spinach... She was just flipping the omelet when movement from the corner of her eye made her pause. Caught in the middle of a wiggle dance while she was cooking, Luna flushed.

Clad only in jeans, with his inky hair tousled and his eyes hooded with sleepiness, Jacob still managed to make her knees weak without a single word spoken.

"Mmm-m, so that's where my blue shirt is." The way he looked at her, she might as well be naked. He was hungry for something beyond food.

Conscious that she was dressed only in his shirt with the sleeves keeping her arms covered to prevent oil splatter, she tugged the collar back up as it began to fall over one shoulder.

That crooked grin of his graced his lips and lit up his face. He stalked closer and her heart raced a little faster. Quick as lightning, he snatched a piece of bacon from the plate.

"Hey! That's supposed to go with the omelet!" she protested.

In response, he gave her the puppy-dog eyes and offered the bacon to her. When she tried to grab it, he snatched it away.

"Open up."

Luna shivered and parted her lips, letting him feed her the bacon. She savored the saltiness with a small moan and watched his eyes darken.

A ding from the toaster startled both of them and she looked down. "Gah!" She lifted the pan from the heat and slid the omelet onto a plate, intending to split it in half.

"Leave it. One plate is fine." His words were causal, even as he moved to take the pieces of toast out to butter them.

She nodded and brought the plate to the breakfast nook. He set the toast down then left, returning with two mugs of coffee.

Sunlight filtered through the window, warming the tiles of the kitchen floor. As Jacob settled into a large wooden chair, Luna admired the way the light framed him in a halo effect. *Like an angel.*

He pulled her into his lap and wrapped his arms around her, nuzzling along her jaw. "I missed you in bed this morning." His whispered words tickled her ear.

Luna chuckled and reached over to run her fingers through his hair. "Someone has to make sure you eat too. It's my job to serve you."

Wicked mischief sparkled in his eyes. "Then serve me."

*Okay, a very sinful fallen angel.*

Amusement tugged the corner of her lips upward. She took the fork and offered him a bite of the omelet. Her gaze followed the path of the fork as he took the food in his mouth and he darted his tongue out to capture a stray piece. Luna gulped. *No, I will not get distracted.*

For the next hour, they alternated between little chaste kisses and feeding each other. *Enjoy the now.* That was what she kept telling herself. But another traitorous part of her whispered fears and doubts.

*All this will be gone soon.*

*If he really cared about you, he wouldn't be ending it. You can't just stop intimacy like this, arbitrarily.*

*Ergo, he's just paying lip service to you whenever he tells you he cares. This is just part of training to him.*

No, she was not going to self-sabotage.

*Stop it. Not everyone approaches relationships the same way.*

"So what's the plan today?" he asked, cutting through her inner dialogue. She forced a wide smile onto her face but slid off his lap and turned away, lest he sense the falseness. Jacob had always been too good at reading her. Instead, she focused on collecting the plates and taking them to the kitchen. It gave her the space to recover. She was going to enjoy what time they had left, come hell or high water.

"I have some work to catch up on," she called out instead and nodded to herself. She could do it.

Luna poked her head back out of the kitchen in time to catch the frown on his face. If she didn't know better, she'd say that he was actually pouting. With a soft sigh, she walked out once more to explain.

"We have a new client on Monday that the big-wigs are pretty excited about, but it means I have to clear my plate with the other projects so I can be ready to consult. I have my laptop and notebook and can work here…" She trailed off as she realized she was inviting herself.

"Of course. You can set up in my office." A slight pause. "Wait! So they want you to represent at the meet and greet?"

Luna grinned at that and nodded. For a while now, she had been working to prove herself at the agency and that meant a lot of back-office support work. It was a huge step forward that they wanted her to take on a client-facing role for the new project.

Jacob rose with a grin and pulled her into a hug. "Good girl. I am proud of you."

Those words made her glow. Her work was her pride, and she knew she excelled at what she did. It was icing on top that Jacob recognized and celebrated that with her. She stood a little taller.

He tilted her head upward then leaned down to brush his lips against hers. Luna parted her own with a small sigh, and when he deepened the kiss, her body melted against him.

When Jacob pulled back, he reached up to run the pad of his thumb over her lower lip. "That would be a preview of our celebration later if you are a good girl and get all your work done." He winked. "Got to give you some incentive."

Luna laughed, her cheeks warming once more, and took a step back toward the kitchen before Jacob laid a hand on her shoulder.

"Go work. I'll take care of the rest of the kitchen." When she opened her mouth to protest, he shook his head. "That's an order. Besides, the sooner you're done, the sooner we can play."

"You're insatiable. Fine, fine." Laughter bubbled up inside her as she internally stamped out the idea that he had ruined all other men for her. Thoughts of work and play crowded out her earlier doubts…for now.

"Oh, and you're not?" he asked with a smirk and reached down to spank her with his palm. "Now git."

Luna yelped then shook her head. "Yes, Jacob." She turned and went to set up in his office. Setting aside Jacob's own laptop, she plugged hers in and set it on the oaken desk. The large office chair dwarfed her smaller figure so much that she could sit cross-legged in it. Jacob had made sure to cover the floor with soft rugs, and photos of his trips around the world hung on the walls.

Time ticked by as she immersed herself in her various projects. At some point, Jacob brought in a mug of tea and she murmured her thanks without looking up.

She chuckled when she caught the unmistakable sound of a fight music sequence, then after a few minutes, a shout of utter anguish and despair. Jacob was playing Final Fantasy again.

Luna shook her head in amusement and closed the last of the files. One more project wrapped up. Next she pulled up all the documentation for the new client. If she was going to represent, she better damn well be prepared for the meeting on Monday. She reached for her mug, brought it closer to her face and inhaled the aroma of the ginger and honey before taking a small sip.

As her eyes scanned the details of the project, she continued to scroll downward until she reached the project team list. On the left was the standard team from their side, her name nestled in the middle of the list. On the right, next to the client list, a name jumped right out at her.

*Bryan Walsh.*

Her heart skipped a beat and her hands shook. Luna took deep breaths and struggled to set her mug down without spilling the tea. *Breathe in. Breathe out.*

She stared at the name on the screen again.

*Well, shit.*

Her first instinct was to move on and pretend she hadn't seen the name. After all, Bryan Walsh was a pretty common name. *It's a big city, right? What are the chances?*

*Who am I kidding?*

*Okay.* She could deal with it. He was just an ex, after all, and they were on civil, if not amicable terms. She scrolled down more and scanned for all the pertinent information. In order for Bryan's company to have signed the contract, Bryan would have had to accept her on the project resource list. That had been nearly two weeks ago. That meant...

*The bastard knew.*

Blood roared in her ears as she shot up. The office chair rolled back from the force of her movement. "You...you son of a bitch," she yelled and glared at her laptop as if accusing it of treachery. Bryan was having a laugh at her expense. He was toying with her. He...

"Luna?"

She spun around, still shaking in fury.

"Luna. Calm." Jacob stepped up to her and laid both hands on her shoulders, catching her eyes.

His command, combined with his touch, was enough to drain the tension from her body and she let out a deep breath.

"Better. Now, what's wrong?" Jacob's eyes flickered over her shoulder to her laptop and Luna had to resist the urge to run over and slam the thing shut.

She didn't want to answer the question. She didn't want him to worry or get angry. They'd had such a wonderful evening and morning. She didn't want to ruin things.

*I let my fears get in the way of open communication.*

Her own words from earlier in the week echoed in her mind. With a soft sigh, Luna summoned her courage, squared her shoulders and told Jacob everything.

# Chapter Nine

*That son of a bitch.*

In normal circumstances, Jacob disliked Luna swearing, and it was one of the few punishable offenses, albeit a minor one. However, this time he could forgive her, considering he felt the same way.

He struggled to rein in his temper. With a clenched jaw and hands curled into fists, the lick of his wicked temper sought a target, and he willed deep breaths into his body. That meant Luna or the wall, and even the remote inklings of taking his anger out on her horrified him. Still, the wall... *No, I don't need another dent I'm going to have to fix.*

He was not a very good man when he was angry.

How much of it was coincidence and how much had the bastard manipulated himself into a position of power over his sub?

"Jacob?"

Her gentle touch, a brush across the back of his hand with her fingertips, brought him out of his thoughts.

For her sake, he worked his fists loose then turned a palm up to engulf her small hand in his. His mind still ran along dark thoughts, ranging from confronting the other Dom all the way to insisting Luna step away from the project. Instead, he did none of those things. He sighed and gave her a gentle squeeze. "What do you want to do about it?"

Luna's sigh matched his as she slumped her shoulders. But then, a transformation took over as she straightened her back and looked him in the eye. "Well, I'll have to tell Joanna, regardless. It'll be her call. But I don't want to let him win. I worked hard for this. I deserve it and I will not let him take it away from me. So if they don't take me off the project, I'm staying. I'll do my job and do it so damn well that it will be beyond reproach."

There was iron in her voice and Jacob felt his chest swell with pride, replacing the rage that had threatened to overwhelm him before. Luna was a submissive for him through and through, but to the rest of the world she was not afraid to be her own person and fight when needed. It was always a huge turn-on to see such a strong woman submit.

He nodded in agreement when he realized that she was waiting for his approval. If there was one thing he trusted, it was Luna and her dogged sense of loyalty. What worried him more was the potential for Bryan to cause harm to her career. The conniving asshole had already shown how manipulative he could be.

"Jacob." The small warning in her voice and the accompanying wince made him release her hand quickly. He turned his gaze downward in haste to check for bruises, and his eyes widened when she grabbed his hand again instead. "Jacob, I'll be okay. I can handle myself." She smiled up at him. "I *will* be okay."

He lifted her hand to his lips and pressed a kiss on her knuckles. "I know you will be. Just promise me to be careful. Don't let that bastard hurt you." If Bryan did, Jacob wasn't sure he wouldn't snap. Maybe he needed to talk to Lani about that.

She smiled up at him, but there was no mirth in the curve of those plump lips. "I promise."

It did little to ease his worries, but he wasn't about to add to her stress, so he only gave a small nod and cast a glance at the clock on the wall. "Well...I think Lani said she wanted to meet at The Playgrounds tonight. Do you feel up to it?"

The last time at the club had shaken both of them, and he didn't want to push Luna into going if she wasn't ready. Jacob watched with care, noting the crease on her brow smoothing over as she threw her shoulders back and tilted her chin up as she braced herself. When she flashed him a brilliant smile, he knew they would be okay.

"That sounds wonderful."

It was too late to play, but they managed a light dinner before Jacob drove Luna back home to get ready. As they stepped into her place, he marveled at how everything she owned was in its own place, the surfaces of every piece of furniture cleared of clutter. It only hit him then that she had also been working on his place bit by bit, straightening and organizing it.

*The little minx.* He waited for the surge of anger to rise at being duped. Instead, he was strangely pleased.

Luna gave him a light kiss before bounding off to change. The Playgrounds did not have a strict dress code, but he had found that the women liked dressing

up for their time there. Not that he minded waiting...
Although if Luna had lived with him, it would have
been a hell of a lot more convenient.

*Where did that come from?*

Jacob shook his head to clear it. That was the last
thing he should have been thinking about. So instead,
he yanked his phone out, slumped onto the couch and
busied himself with a random mobile game. But his
mind kept wandering, his imagination running wild —
Luna waking up in his arms every morning, breakfast
together, falling asleep to her body curled up against
him each night.

*What the hell is wrong with me?*

"What do you think?"

Jacob looked up and something caught in his throat.
White was her theme that night. The corset of silver
with its elaborate patterns pushed her breasts up,
exposing their creamy tops, and gave her that
additional boost of an hourglass figure. A bustle skirt
flowed and flared out from her hips. She looked
delicate, almost elfin, a juxtaposition of innocent and
sultry — and he wanted to devour every inch of her.

Her cheeks pinked under his scrutiny, and when he
took a step forward to draw her to him, she gave a small
moan. The sound was almost his undoing, but he
hadn't become the Dom he was by losing control every
time his little sub looked good enough to feast on.

Jacob leaned down to nuzzle the ridge of her ear
before placing a kiss underneath it. When she tilted her
head to one side to give him more access, he nibbled his
way down her neck inch by inch until he reached where
her neck joined her shoulder. There he bit harder,
eliciting a soft whimper. He worked his teeth to ensure
she would be marked properly, then swept his tongue

across her skin to ease the sting. He felt her pulse quicken and he chuckled beneath his breath.

"I think," he whispered, "that if we don't leave soon, I will spend the whole night eating you up instead."

He felt more than heard her sharp intake of breath. When he eased back to study her, her lips were slightly parted and her eyes were glazed over. She was just so delightfully responsive.

"But let's play a game instead." He grinned and took a step back. Then, from his pocket, retrieved a small bottle of lube and a U-shaped toy. "They call this The Lush. Be a good girl and go put this in before we go. One end should fit against your G-spot. Adjust it so that the other rests against your clit."

Luna's eyes widened into saucers, which only made Jacob smile even wider. She stared at the toy in his hand, then without a word, grabbed it and retreated to the washroom.

He loaded the corresponding app on his phone and waited. After a few minutes, he heard the sign he was waiting for. Luna had turned on the tap, which meant that she was likely washing the lube off her hands. Jacob held back the urge to cackle as he turned the vibrator on and was rewarded instantly by a loud squeal. With no mercy in his heart, he increased the intensity as he stepped closer until he was on the other side of the door and knocked. "You all right in there, sweetheart?"

"Yes, I'm o-*kay*." The last syllable ended with a squeak as he turned the intensity up another notch.

"Oh dear God."

He chuckled. "You need something, Luna?"

Another low moan drifted from the washroom, music to his ears. He could almost imagine how close she was. But she was not supposed to come without permission and she had yet to ask. Perhaps…

He cranked it up two more notches and heard a scream in response.

"Yes…oh God. Please, Jacob, please let me come."

He grinned and turned the vibe off.

"No-o…."

The door flew open. Wide-eyed, her cheeks rouged with a deep blush, Luna stared at him. Jacob decided that he rather liked that wild look on her.

He grinned and pocketed his phone instead.

She gaped at him, opening and closing her mouth soundlessly, and he laughed, drawing her to him. The scent of her arousal hardened his cock, but he paid it no heed.

"Later." He pressed a kiss on her temple. "*If* you are a good girl."

"I need to change panties," Luna whispered, her face red with embarrassment.

"Leave it. I want everyone to know how wet my pet is and how much she is enjoying herself."

A lust-filled whimper. The words were having the exact effect on her that he wanted.

Without waiting for a reply, he ushered her back to the car and off to the club. And if she was walking a little more oddly than usual, at least it was practice for when she would have to wear it in the office sometime in the future.

When they arrived, the place was already packed. They smiled at familiar faces, but Jacob kept Luna tucked close to him. He had, with some mercy at last, stopped surprising her with turning on the vibe on the drive over, but it seemed she was still a little on edge.

"Relax," Jacob whispered in her ear and led her toward the bar with a nod toward Darryl.

"What can I get you two this evening?"

There was a beginning of a smile from Luna before it faltered. Jacob grinned with the intimate knowledge of why she'd reacted the way she had. After all, he was the one who had turned the vibrator back on at a low setting.

"Well, Luna?" He managed his most innocent smile, which turned into a smirk as she cast a murderous glare in his direction.

"A Coke, please," she choked out the words.

"The usual for me, no alcohol."

Darryl was a mask of professionalism as he inclined his head toward Luna, but when she wasn't looking, he raised his eyebrow at Jacob and gave him a knowing wink. They had been friends for too long for Darryl to not know what he was up to.

When Darryl stepped away to pour the drinks, Jacob turned off the vibe.

"I'll get you back for this…somehow."

Jacob almost cackled in delight, but instead, he smirked and gave a disbelieving nod. "Uh-huh."

"Luna, lovely!" Lani emerged from the crowd.

"Hello to you too, pest." Jacob greeted, amused at being ignored.

Lani stuck her tongue out at him just as Darryl came back with their drinks.

"Be nice, Jacob," Luna admonished with a small frown.

He chuckled and held his hands up in surrender as Darryl returned. "Give me a hand here. The girls are ganging up on me."

The Will to Serve

Darryl raised a brow, handed them their glasses and shook his head. "You're on your own. I'm not touching this one with a ten-foot pole."

"Ah-ha! Well, just for that, I'm borrowing Luna to dance with." Lani stated matter-of-factly, already tugging his sub away.

Luna paused and looked up at Jacob with the silent question. Over time, they had developed to the point where sometimes words were no longer necessary, and he liked that about them. Jacob smiled in return and nodded. "Go have fun." He wasn't much of a dancer but knew Luna enjoyed it. And Lani would keep her safe.

"Okay, be back soon!" She turned to take a long draw of her drink then leaned up to kiss him.

The taste of Coke on her lips was better than anything he could imagine, so much that he was almost reluctant to take a sip, replacing it with the flavor of his own Sprite.

"I'm always surprised at how much you let her get away with." Darryl watched the girls join the crowd on the dance floor before turning back toward him, his tone curious.

"Who? Lani?" Jacob knew who Darryl was referring to but mustered his most innocent smile.

"I meant Luna, of course, you little shit."

Jacob chuckled. "She has a saucy streak to her. It keeps me entertained and I know it is not out of disrespect." He chose his words with care. "She is a strong woman and I enjoy her will. It makes her submission"—he paused to search for the right word—"sweeter."

"You just like a brat you can bend to your will," Darryl countered with a raised eyebrow.

"Ah, no. Luna is not a brat." From anyone else, Jacob may have been offended, but he enjoyed these conversations with Darryl. Over the years, they had challenged each other and pushed each other to be better Doms, even if their styles were different. "She's not doing it to push me into certain behaviors. She just speaks her mind. And she is very pleasing as a sub."

His eyes softened as he watched her laugh at something Lani whispered in her ear. "I probably do give her more leeway, but it's because we both know I wield considerable control over her."

"You're completely smitten. You know that, right?"

Now it was his turn to raise an eyebrow at Darryl, who gave him a shrug. "I've just never heard you talk or act this way with any of your past subs."

Jacob held his glass up and took a sip to buy himself time to formulate an answer. He never had a chance, though.

"Ah, Jacob, correct?"

He turned at the sound of his name.

There was Bryan with a smug grin on his face.

# Chapter Ten

"Yes?" Jacob's face was devoid of emotion, even if what he really wanted was to reply with a punch to the man's face. Maybe then the cocky grin would go away.

"Bryan Walsh. I think we got off on the wrong foot last time."

Jacob took the proffered hand, giving it a perfunctory shake. He had no interest in talking to the man and inwardly groaned when Bryan settled into a spot next to him and ordered a drink from Darryl.

Out of the corner of his eye, Jacob studied Bryan more closely. The other Dom was almost his complete opposite. Sandy-blond-haired, well-dressed and at about the same height as Jacob, the man exuded a kind of wicked-boy charm that Jacob could see subs being drawn to.

"So how long have you and Luna been visiting The Playgrounds?"

*Slick. Very slick.* No reason to not give him the information...for now. Perhaps he could use the opportunity. Jacob quelled the undercurrent of anger within him. "We met here three years ago, actually. I believe Luna was new here at the time, but I've been around for a while."

"About ten years now," Darryl added, returning with what looked like a gin and tonic. He set it in front of Bryan.

Jacob gave a nod of appreciation before turning back to Bryan. "And yourself? How did you hear about this place?"

Bryan took a swig of his cocktail and sighed in satisfaction while he scanned the room. Jacob caught the subtle hint of a smirk and followed his gaze to see him staring at Luna. The anger threatened to rise. Instead, Jacob lifted the glass to his lips and downed the entirety of its contents, letting the sugary taste distract him from his anger. Barely.

Bryan mirrored him and downed his liquor, as if trying to match him drink for drink. *Idiot.* Little did Bryan know that his was a Sprite.

"Ah." Bryan grinned. "Luna told me about this place years ago. She mentioned that she'd always wanted to visit, so I thought I'd pop by when I moved into town."

The words unsaid were as loud as the ones spoken.

"I see. And how are you finding The Playgrounds?"

Bryan turned back toward Jacob. "This place is impressive. Where I was from, there wasn't much of a community, unfortunately." He paused and leaned a little closer, his voice lowering as if they were sharing a confidence that Jacob did not feel. "Not nearly as many...delectable opportunities, if you know what I mean."

"I see." Jacob did not miss the predatory glint in the other Dom's eyes. He had a sudden urge to warn away some other subs he knew, but as yet, Bryan had given him no tangible reason to do so. Just a nasty feeling in his gut.

Jacob turned his attention back to the dance floor, his body shifting to turn away, hoping it would signal the end of the conversation. When Lani cast a look at his direction, he saw her eyes widened.

Jacob took out his phone to send a quick text.

*Keep Luna away from the bar for a bit longer.*

He watched as Lani took out her phone then pocketed it again. When she next looked up, she gave him a nod then maneuvered Luna so that her back was entirely toward the bar. Jacob saw Lani giggle at something, then lead Luna farther away to introduce her to another woman.

*Good.* It put him more at ease.

"So, how are you enjoying Luna?"

*The bastard.* Jacob clenched his jaw, every fiber in his body loathing the poor excuse for a Dominant. Luna was many things. An object was not one of them.

"I found her to be quite the fun toy when she was bottoming for me. Fantastic response with the cane. The tears came almost right away."

Now it took every ounce of control not to haul the man by the collar and throw him out. The image of Luna came unbidden, holding still while strokes from a cane rained down on her, welts blossoming across her skin and tears streaming down her face as she bit her lip hard to grit through the pain.

Because that would be how she would have gotten through it. He had seen it before in the aftermath of an accidental injury from her martial arts training.

Brandon, her sensei, had to pop a dislocated shoulder back into place. Had Bryan known what he was doing enough to not break skin and draw blood back then? Had he cared?

*Damn it.* The manipulative bastard was doing it on purpose to get under his skin. He was posturing to show who was the bigger Dom. Jacob heard the bravado beneath the words.

"I think you are mistaken." Jacob's voice had turned to ice and steel, although a haze of red was threatening to fog his mind. "Luna's not a pain sub."

A second glass, this time a Coke like Luna's, appeared at his side. Jacob looked up to see Darryl incline his head. It was enough of a reason to return and he gave his friend a nod of appreciation. Darryl understood.

"Oh, really? Interesting…" The three words held layers of meaning that Jacob did not care for. Disappointment, smugness, superiority. When the man next looked at him, he could see judgement in his eyes.

Jacob had met his share of pain Dominants during his time in the scene. Some, like Bryan, thought it was the only way to lead the lifestyle and anything else was less. Obviously, they lacked any imagination. But this was personal.

"Well, you must know the community pretty well. From what I've heard, you train subs on three-year contracts, right?"

The man had done his research and must have talked to people about him. But it would be hard to narrow down who Bryan had been talking to, considering these were all well-known facts. What Jacob did know was that Bryan had designed every statement here to rattle him. He would have to pay closer attention to who the wannabe-Dom talked to and played with.

Jacob took the second glass in hand and swirled the liquid, observing the bubbles before knocking back some of its contents. He let the silence stretch out. There were different styles of dominance…and intimidation.

"Well, you must point me in the direction of a good one!" Bryan clapped him on the shoulder.

Jacob smiled, seemingly absentminded. "Perhaps," he replied.

Bryan flashed him a grin and leaned in once more, lowering his voice to a whisper. "Or I can always just wait for Luna. I'm a patient man, and I understand that she'll be available soon." He leaned back then gave Jacob another pat on the back. "Nice talking to you." Without waiting for a reply, Bryan walked off. *Power move.*

Jacob's blood ran cold as his eyes narrowed. *Over my dead body.*

"You all right?" Darryl leaned across the bar.

Jacob downed the second drink, although the sugar did little to elevate his mood when Lani and Luna returned. The sight of Luna, her face flushed, eyes sparkling, was enough to soothe his temper. Without waiting for a greeting, Jacob reached and pulled Luna to him, resting his cheek against the top of her head.

"Jacob?"

"Just let me hold you for a minute, sweetheart," he muttered against her hair. The fragrance of her shampoo mixed with the softness of her body drained the last of his tension. She was there. She was safe. She was still his to protect.

Lani cleared her throat while Darryl grinned. He ignored them both until he felt a poke on his arm. As he pulled away, Lani cleared her throat again.

*Lani and her theatrics. Pests. All of them.*

"I believe you owe me a few drinks, Jacob, my dear."

Jacob groaned and pushed his hair back as Luna giggled at his expense. "Would it clear my debts?" *One could hope.*

Lani tossed her head back with a hearty laugh. "Not even close, my boy."

Darryl was already bringing over Lani's favorite drink for her, a bottle of water for Luna and the tab for him.

"What favors does he owe you for?" Luna asked, tilting her head to one side.

"Well, there was the matter of him asking me to make sure you got home okay last week."

Jacob reached over to pinch Lani while still keeping one arm around Luna.

"Ouch. Hey, watch the skin. I have a gig tomorrow!"

Meanwhile, Jacob looked down just in time to meet Luna's gaze. Something passed over her face and for a moment she almost looked like she wanted to cry. Jacob tightened his arm around her and her breathing hitched.

It took only a second or two for Luna to get her emotions under control. "Can I do anything to pay off the debt?"

A growl from the back of his throat emerged. "Stop trying to pay my debts, Luna."

Lani's eyes sparkled in mischief. "Tell you what, lovely. I am missing a model for tomorrow's shoot to promote the club. Come let me dress you up and model with my group, and I'll consider it even."

"Me? A model?" Luna squeaked and Jacob chuckled. But he saw the subtle signs of excitement—the way she leaned forward, her eyes widening and her breathing growing shallower. He knew her, knew all the hundreds of micro-gestures that helped him read her emotional state. Jacob had been paying attention for three years, after all.

"It's your choice, but only if you think you'll have fun doing it." Jacob had to admit he was curious as to how Lani would dress her. *Now only if I can get a copy of those pictures.*

"Okay, I'll do it," Luna murmured and blushed.

She was still so damn adorable.

Lani clapped her hands in glee. "Excellent! Now if you'll excuse me, I see a lost boy needing a firm hand." Their eyes all followed toward Lani's gaze to a tanned, shorter boy who was hovering by the entrance, his gaze darting this way and that. Jacob chuckled, remembering three years ago how that had been Luna. Oh yes, he had known. He had been watching the moment she'd stepped into that public dungeon on the second floor.

As everyone left, Luna turned toward Jacob, tilting her head to one side with an unspoken question in her eyes.

In response, Jacob grinned. With exaggerated, deliberate movements, he took his phone out.

"No, you wouldn't," Luna whispered, panic rising in her face.

After a moment, the toy in Luna came buzzing to life and a loud moan escaped from her lips. She covered her mouth in a rush to stifle the sound.

Yeah, he would take a page from his sub's strength. He refused to let Bryan ruin another night of them together.

Jacob pushed aside the memory of what had happened earlier and checked himself instead. As he refocused on Luna, that crooked grin of his returned to tug his lips back upward. The sight of her inner conflict, desire warring against her sense of propriety and coupled with the way she struggled to hold back her body's reaction was intoxicating.

Jacob let his hand drift down to the small of her back to both gently guide and steady her. "Come on. Let's go take our game to the next level."

They rarely ever played in public. Not that Jacob hadn't before, but there had been something about Luna from day one that made him reluctant to share her with the world. Every whimper of desire, every moan of pleasure, every scream from a climax was all his.

But tonight, something chafed at him and that something led him and Luna to the dungeon instead of the private room, the duffel bag he had prepared earlier in one hand, Luna's hand in the other. They had discussed the scene before but never about it being in public, so he turned to Luna.

He watched as she swallowed, darting her gaze from one scene to another unfolding already in the dungeon. There were at least two other couples, one on the bench getting the flogging of her life, another actively servicing his Mistress. A few others were hanging about, observing. Some were grouped together chatting in low voices, including at least one couple, and another trio lingered around watching. He noted it all as Luna's cheeks flushed and her breathing grew shallower.

He shut off the vibe, drew her aside and shifted his body to obscure the view to ensure he had her full attention. A small tremor shot through her body before her eyes refocused on him.

"We've already discussed the scene I have in mind for tonight." This time his words were not designed to arouse. He was not out to persuade her into doing something she didn't want. "But we never talked about doing the scene in public. How do you feel about it, Luna?"

A cry of pleasure punctuated the air and Luna's gaze flickered over his shoulder unconsciously as she shifted her weight back and forth. She was trying to hide the fact that she was squeezing her legs together beneath the skirt.

Ah, so his little one did have an exhibitionist streak, even if she was as skittish as a mouse right now.

"Luna, I need to hear it out loud. Red, green or yellow?"

"Sorry," Luna mumbled in return. Jacob waited for her to process the emotions and thoughts going through her mind. Minutes ticked by as only the sounds of the strenuous activities behind him filled the silence between them until at last, Luna gave a slight nod. "Yellow."

Proceed with caution. Yes, he could do that. With a nod of an acknowledgement, he took her hand and led her to one of the St. Andrew's Crosses. "Strip, sweetheart."

She did, one item at a time, without the teasing. Corset, bustle skirt. He groaned and his cock stirred as he realized the stockings she wore were thigh high and held up by garters. What was more, as she reached down to pick up her clothes and fold them neatly, her perky ass came into view, framed only by the white lace thong she was still wearing. The heels had already had him hard all night, but this... She had dressed for him. *God help me.*

"Leave the rest." The words came husky with need. "Go stand by the cross, facing me."

For a moment, he froze as he watched her pick her way up the side platform where the St. Andrew's Cross was situated. Without another word from him, she raised her arms and parted her legs to fit herself to the cross.

*I am a lucky man.*

Jacob followed her and secured her limbs with the attached cuffs. When he studied her once more, she smiled. She was nervous, but he could also make out the excitement that danced in her eyes. *Good.* He had found a new edge to push her with.

"I can feel all my fingers. I'm comfortable."

"Good girl."

Once secured, Jacob reached for the supplies in the bag, taking out each item. When he finished, he cupped Luna's cheek with one hand. "Do you trust me?"

There was no hesitation in her answer as she gave him a smile that lit her entire face with adoration that he wasn't sure he deserved. "Completely."

# Chapter Eleven

The last thing Luna saw was Jacob's teasing smile before he slipped the black sleeping mask over her eyes. The cold silk lay soothingly against her face and it shut out the sight of anyone staring at her nude body.

She quelled her imagination as best she could as she tilted her head this way and that to map out the various sounds. Her heart thumped in her chest and she could hear the rhythm of her own breathing. Questing further with her remaining senses, she could sort out motion close by, and beyond, an inaudible murmur of conversation that ebbed and flowed. She jumped at a sudden loud moan a bit away to her right, which crescendoed to a scream of repeated yeses. Blood rushed to her face.

Jacob's aftershave wafted to her nose, as the heat radiating from his body warmed hers. He must be close. A few seconds later, his chuckle in her ear confirmed her suspicion and sent delicious shivers down her spine.

Then he took away her hearing.

Large headphones engulfed her ears and sealed off all sounds. The addition of another sense being cut off made her heart race, and her breathing grew shallower until Jacob's warm hand — or so she presumed — touched her shoulder, trailing downward and leaving fire in its wake.

"What color, Luna?"

Jacob's voice came from the headphones, but it still made Luna look up in surprise, as if seeking his true direction. He flattened his hand against her abdomen, the gesture more reassuring than sexual.

She checked herself. Physically, she was comfortable. Mentally, she knew Jacob would never actually leave her alone. Restrained as she was, the relinquishing of control soothed her. There was no need to think of what to do, what to say. She only had to follow his lead. As she adjusted to her situation, a calm settled over her and she gave a nod. "Green."

"Good." His hand left her body and her skin cooled. "I'm here. Listen to my voice. In this very moment, there is only me. You are safe. Vulnerable to me…but safe. I've got you."

She shivered and swept her tongue over her dry lips. Her every nerve was alive to each subtle change and sensation. Her imagination took off. What would it be like when he truly touched her? Kissed her?

As his voice faded away, she began counting in her head, waiting for his next words, his next touch. The padding on the cross, cool at first, began to equalize in temperature from the way her body pressed against it. In the darkness, devoid of the two senses she relied on the most, time became a distorted concept. For a moment, everything remained the same and caught within it, she searched for a sign of change. Was that his breath brushing against her shoulder or just a movement of the air circulating in the room?

The first sure sign arrived when the toy still nestled inside her came alive without warning. It would have been barely perceptible, buzzing away on the lowest setting. It had been on for a good part of the night. But her body, in the absence of stimulation, had become extremely sensitive. Heat pooled between her legs and she gave a long, soft moan, rocking her hips slowly.

Jacob's hand shifted to cup her left breast, as if testing its weight. She pushed forward, eager for the warmth of his touch.

"So wonderfully responsive." His voice was distorted through the headphones, but it was easy to detect those notes of approval.

He kissed her, his scent enveloping her. She wanted more. She parted her lips and flicked her tongue over his in an attempt to taste him, entreating him to come closer. In response, he pressed harder against her, devouring her moans before he eased back to nibble along her jaw. A purr rumbled from the back of her throat, ending in a squeak when he began circling her nipple with his thumb.

The toy began vibrating faster and she rocked her hips back and forth more in response, trying to set a rhythm. She whimpered, her body tense against the restraints, as she throbbed with need while he built up her pleasure. Nothing else existed as she barreled headlong toward her climax.

Then it was all gone. The toy lay in silence within her, and his lips and hands no longer touched her. She whimpered again, this time in protest, her hips still rolling in the same rhythm as if it could coax the toy back to life.

"My beautiful Luna." His voice was no more than a whisper and held a sort of admiration she did not understand. "You have no idea what a sight you are, sweetheart."

Luna trembled, biting her lip with a low moan, the words arousing her further.

"They see you. They see your tight body flush with need. They see you tremble at every touch." She felt a finger tracing her collarbone then moving lower, inch by agonizing inch.

"They want you." His finger continued its path downward, slipping under her thong to part her folds. He reached down and brushed against the still toy then withdrew, leaving the toy there only to offer his finger to her lips. Her own scent tickled her nose, and when he pushed against her mouth, she opened to take it in, licking and sucking.

"They wish they were me — to touch you, to taste you, to feast on your screams as you climax, over and over again."

She moaned as he withdrew his finger and heard an unmistakable groan.

"So sexy."

That was all the warning she got as the toy started again, this time on what must have been the maximum intensity. His hands made quick work, pulling her panties down, one staying to hold the vibrator in place. Two fingers entered her, stretching her, even as they held the toy tight against her G-spot. His lips returned, sucking one hardened nipple, then the other, alternating between the two.

A scream tore through her throat as she tossed her head back. "Come. Now. Can't hold." She choked her words out. Every part of her body was burning up. The intensity threatened to overwhelm her.

"Come, sweetheart. Show them how sexy you are."

Every nerve was overloaded with ecstasy as the orgasm ripped through her. Her hips buckled against him erratically and an arm moved to pin her lower body down against the apparatus. Every time she thought the climax was ebbing, a subtle shift of the toy would push her to greater heights until she felt lightheaded and the world turned upside down in the darkness.

After what seemed an eternity, he eased off at last. With tender care, he pulled the toy out of her and she gave one last great shudder.

The headphones came off first and a roar of sound greeted her before it equalized. She barely registered the smattering of applause.

"Close your eyes, little one. I'm going to take off your blindfold."

She hastened to obey, and when he tugged it off her, she could still sense the dim light of the room, even behind her eyelids. She struggled to open her eyes, then thought better of it and kept them shut.

One by one, the restraints came off—ankles first, then arms. Jacob rained light, comforting kisses along her shoulders as he massaged her arms and she sighed with contentment. At his urging, she leaned on him as she attempted a step away from the cross, but when her knees buckled, he caught her with a large fuzzy blanket and scooped her up in his arms.

He carried her to an area dedicated to aftercare. There, he fed her water and stroked her hair. "My beautiful Luna," he murmured into her ear, "I am so proud of you. You served me so well tonight. I'm right here. I've got you." Over and over again, he soothed her with his words and his touch.

"Well, that was quite the show."

A semi-familiar voice cut through Jacob's. Luna buried herself closer against her Dom and willed the other one to go away.

"Please leave. I am busy taking care of mine at the moment."

*Angry.* Jacob sounded so angry. *Why? Did I do something wrong?* She cracked her eyes open to look up at Jacob and whimpered.

Jacob pressed a long kiss on her forehead in swift response. "It's all right, sweetheart. It's okay."

Luna relaxed and closed her eyes again.

There was a minor commotion, but Luna kept her head down, half buried against Jacob's chest. At some point, Jacob tensed again, but he never stopped cradling and petting her. That was enough.

At last, as her brain reset, she looked up to see him smile down at her. She worked her throat, still raw from screaming, and only when she managed to find her voice again did she speak. "Home?"

"Yes, sweetheart. Let's get you home."

His tone was gentle, but there was something else, a catch in his voice. For the first time, Luna wondered if perhaps, just maybe, the tinges of regret she'd picked up were not just her own hopeful imagination.

# Chapter Twelve

The weekend had come and passed in the blink of an eye. Jacob had stayed with her on Saturday night and driven her to the photoshoot as promised on Sunday. Luna grinned as she recalled Jacob's face when he had strategically arrived early to pick her up. Heat in his eyes had chased away the surprise quick enough at seeing her in the outfit she wore, until Lani had shooed him out. Jacob had driven home like a demon afterward and spent the afternoon showing her just what he thought of her outfit.

It had been delicious.

Today, however, was back to reality and right now, reality equated to being in the best meeting room of the entire office building. Sandy, the account rep for this client, had booked the kick-off for first thing in the morning and there had been no chance to talk to Joanna, her boss, beforehand. She would have to roll with it for now.

Luna swiveled back and forth in a Herman Miller office chair and glanced at the clock for the fifth time. The client contingent was late by fifteen minutes, and they had a packed agenda.

Sandy was outside waiting for them, but the rest of her colleagues in the room were also fidgeting. Some stared at the presentation deck projected up front. Others were busy responding to emails on their own laptops. She herself had opted to not bring hers in, falling back to the notebook and pen. Luna liked the tactile feeling of ink on paper, but now she regretted not having anything to distract her from her nerves.

At last, unable to sit still any longer, Luna stood to pour herself a glass of water, only to hear voices approaching. With a small inhale, she set the pitcher back and smoothed a hand over her shirt. *Show time.*

Bryan was, of course, at the head of the pack, leading three others into the room. Dressed in a pair of designer jeans and a sports jacket, he was all professional and charm as Sandy introduced him to the others. Luna stiffened as she met Bryan's eyes. His crinkled in humor and she nodded in return as they shook hands, her business smile plastered on her lips. He turned his hand ever so slightly palm down in an attempt to exert dominance while maintaining a firm grip.

She had expected an attempt at a power move, had run scenarios in her mind and planned her response. It was not The Playgrounds and she had never made a habit of letting anyone — a client, no less — walk all over her in her professional career. So, she tightened her grip and held her hand steady.

He lifted a brow, narrowing his eyes with scrutiny, then inclined his head and released her hand. A modicum of respect.

They made no further gesture to acknowledge each other. Bryan sat at the end of the table to her right. But by then, Luna was well in her element. When her turn came to present, she straightened and dove in to explain her expertise, the approach and the plan for her part of the project, detailing the why and the how. Out of the corner of her eye, she could see Joanna smiling in encouragement. She swept her gaze across the room, paying special attention to each member of the client team before turning to look directly at Bryan, since he was the project lead on their end. When he considered her words then nodded in agreement, she knew she was killing it. *Ha. Take that.*

The rest of the meeting passed in a blur. Luna took rigorous notes, both about things said and things she observed. Then it was time for the office tour, also known as 'the dog-and-pony show'.

Fortunately, she did not have to take part. Luna murmured some excuses, parted with the other meeting participants and made a beeline straight for her office. Ideas for the project were already popping up and she needed to capture them before they faded. It wasn't until she heard Bryan's voice that she turned around to take a peek back outside.

"Ted! So, this is where you sit. Swanky."

"Yeah yeah, Cuz. Still on for dinner tonight?"

"Of course! What can I bring?"

Luna tuned out the rest of the conversation as she shut her office door and turned to brace her back against it. *Cuz? Ted's cousin?* Her stomach sank. *No...it can't be...can it?*

She was not too proud to admit that she hid in her office until the client team left. It helped that she also had genuine work to do. She stared hard at the screen, her forehead furrowed, before she sent a meeting request to Joanne for the afternoon at last and titled it simply as *Project Resource Convo*.

Only when her stomach growled in warning did she open the door and stick her head out once more. Few people were left at the office, most having already left for lunch, but luckily, Ted was still there. Now was her chance.

"Hey, Ted, food?" Luna called out as she approached his office, cupping one hand like a bowl, two fingers from the other, imitating chopsticks.

"Sure."

It took most of Luna's willpower to not usher Ted out of there. She bit her tongue and bided her time until they'd settled into window seats at their favorite ramen restaurant, hot bowls of soup and noodles in front.

"All right, Luna. spit it out. What did you want to ask me?"

She startled, looked up at Ted and her jaw dropped. At his chuckling, she snapped her mouth shut and grumbled at him. Ted only laughed harder.

"Stop it!" Luna growled in frustration then sighed. As she peered up at her friend an co-worker, she found his eyes twinkling in amusement. Great, now she was seeing a resemblance. *No, my brain is playing tricks on me.* She was all over the place. *Focus!* "Fine. I'll come right out and ask. I saw you and Bryan talking. How do you know him?"

"Ah, digging dirt on the client. Very smart." Ted nodded his approval. "We're cousins. His company transferred him here for this project."

Luna turned away and dug into her noodles, lest her face gave hints to the sea of emotions sweeping through her. Could coincidence build upon coincidence like that? She swallowed her bite. "So, what's his deal?" Her tone was casual, but she trained her eyes on her bowl to keep him from studying her face too closely. Usually, Ted was all for gossip, and she hoped it was one of those times.

"Poor guy had it rough. He always worked too damn hard, never had time for much of a life. Then the partner he owned the agency with ran off with the money, and the girl he was dating online ghosted him. He was lucky that he got picked up by Telcorus. Worked his way back up." Ted leaned in and waggled his eyebrows. "Why, Luna? Interested? If you want to ditch that cardboard boyfriend of yours, I can always talk you up after the project..."

Luna almost did a spit take and instead tried to swallow too fast, which resulted in hot soup going down the wrong way. A coughing fit ensued and tears trickled down her cheek.

"Whoa...easy there. I was just teasing." Ted patted her on her back while she pounded her fist to her chest. She reached for her glass of water and took a slow sip. Ted really needed to stop making comments like that. Eating lunch with him was becoming a health hazard.

Bit by bit, she recovered her breath, but her mind was muddled over Ted's words and the moral dilemma in front of her. Should she tell? How much? With a start, she realized. *Oh God, I'm the Internet girl who ghosted him.*

In the end, she said nothing. Luna rationalized that if Bryan had wanted it known, he would have said something to Ted by now, since he'd known she would be in the project much earlier than she had.

A hand waved in front of her face. "Hello, Earth to Luna."

Luna looked up and shook her head with a smile before glancing at her watch. "Gah, I'm meeting Joanna in fifteen. Let's finish up." She shoved the rest of her now-cooling ramen in her mouth with haste. Such a picture of elegance... She would never let Jacob see.

Ted nodded as he did the same. They settled the bill, then proceeded back to the office, walking side by side in silence. It lasted for about two minutes before Ted placed a hand on her shoulder. "Hey, look. I'm sorry if I made it awkward for you. I know Bryan is a client. But seriously, I was just teasing..."

Luna flashed him a smile. "Don't worry about it. I'm not bothered."

"Promise?"

"Yeah, promise."

Thirty minutes later, Luna gave her boss the bare minimum of details. She had dated Bryan. Yes, it was several years ago. Yes, they were on amicable terms. Yes, she could keep it professional. Yes, she'd prefer to keep it quiet. They agreed that Luna could continue on the project as long as she checked in regularly with Joanna.

An hour after the meeting, Luna admitted defeat in trying to keep her promise to Ted. His words haunted her and she turned the story of Bryan over and over in her mind. Bryan had told people in his life about her when they had been together. Had they truly been together all those years ago? Had he considered her a girlfriend at the time? Why had she never asked?

She made her way home after work but the doubts continued to swirl in her traitorous mind. The familiar scenery whipped by as Luna leaned her head against the cool window of the bus, trying to relieve her oncoming migraine.

Luna tried to recall the last days of their so-called relationship. She had waited online at the same time they usually met, day after day, but he had always been a no-show. He'd never returned her calls. Eventually, heartbroken, she had stopped trying. But what if it *was* her fault? She'd had no idea he was going through such a rough time. What if it was a case of her not trying hard enough?

*'It seems my pet did not wait as I expected her to.'*

*Oh God, what if I read everything wrong? What if it was really* me *who ghosted* him?

Her head pulsed with pain and she reached to pinch the ridge of her nose. Nausea hit her and she closed her eyes and tried to breathe through it. When the bus arrived at her stop, she staggered off and walked the rest of the way home. The fresh air helped ease back the urge to vomit, but the light worsened the pounding behind her eyes.

When Luna arrived home at last, she sighed in relief, gladdened by the fact that tonight was a quiet night alone. After popping an ibuprofen and forcing some small bits of dinner down her throat, she tried to lie down on the bed. The pain receded, but her mind would not let her rest.

It wasn't long before she gave up on sleeping and sat at her desk instead. She had homework anyway and it might help sort out her thoughts. With almost deliberate, ritualistic moves, she laid out fresh pages of blank paper in front of her and picked up her favorite pen, rolling it in her hand, finding comfort in the familiar weight. She needed to sort out her thoughts. She needed to remember what had happened. Everything to do with Bryan was blurry and uncertain, like her mind had erased all the details.

Where to start?
A title.
*The First Time I Played with Bryan*

# Chapter Thirteen

Jacob tapped his foot as the elevator took him up to Luna's floor. An unease had settled in the pit of his stomach, and combined with his natural impatience, it made staying still even more difficult.

Their usual check-in time for days they were not meeting had come and gone. At first it had annoyed rather than worried him, until he'd received a call from Brandon. Luna had not shown up for practice either, and Ted had mentioned to Brandon later that Luna had looked ill before she'd left the office. It was enough to make her instructor look up and call her emergency contact...him.

He tried his best to not break into a run down the long corridor when the elevator door opened at last, too slow for his liking. But he kept a brisk pace and that carried him to her apartment unit in record time. He knocked. Once. Twice.

The sound of feet dragging along the floor behind the door then the latch being undone interrupted his movements just as he raised his hand for the third, more insistent knock. Unease turned into irritation. It was late into the night already and he had an early meeting the next day. He readied himself and drew in a deep breath. He would not yell but he would be stern.

The sight that greeted him killed the scolding he had in mind.

Puffy red eyes blinked blearily up at him while her hair was a disarrayed mess. Luna was paler than usual, though her skin was blotchy with red patches. Dressed in a ratty oversized T-shirt, her slight body seemed to lack the strength to hold herself upright.

She looked like a ragged doll, hollow and lifeless.

"Luna?" He feared to touch her lest she crumble.

"Jacob?" The first signs of life flickered in her eyes as she looked up at him then winced.

That was when he noticed how dim her apartment was, the brightness from the hall reaching into the darkness with fingerlings of light. Realization dawned on him. "Let me in, little one." He kept his voice low and soothing as he placed one hand on her shoulder.

It worked. Her body responded in a zombie shuffle as she stepped aside. Luna used to get migraines often when they'd first met, but over the years, they had stopped as the two of them had worked on helping her better managing her stress. Something bad must have triggered one today. The unease came back in full force. Her meeting with Bryan had been today.

"What are you...?" Luna trailed off as Jacob stepped into the apartment, kicked off his shoes then guided her to the couch. With subtle pressure this way and that, he guided her until she sat. He settled to her right, pulled her into his arms and took her left hand, massaging the pressure point between her thumb and forefinger. A soft sigh escaped her lips.

"Have you been drinking enough water?"

Luna nodded then shifted to lean her head against his shoulder. When he noticed her trying to rub her temple harder against him, he chuckled and pushed her up.

"Sit on the floor and lean back against the couch."

"I'm okay. Really," she whispered. He was sure the weak smile she gave him was meant to be reassuring, but it had rather the opposite effect.

"No, Luna. Don't make me repeat myself."

She groaned but dragged herself to comply, not so much getting up and reseating as sliding down the couch like a limp dishrag. Normally, she moved with grace. Right now, he was lucky he could get her to move at all.

He took some time to reposition her between his legs, then tilted her head back. As he leaned forward, he dug his fingers around her scalp, testing until he drew the right moans from her lips. She needed it. Why hadn't she called him earlier? With the pain points found, he proceeded with the head massage.

*Oh right, because she never asks.* Some days, she felt so damn low maintenance that he wasn't sure if he was much of a Dominant for her.

"I'm sorry." The words were almost inaudible, but in the silence, they rang like warning bells.

"For what, sweetheart?" Jacob frowned and paused his fingers to allow her to speak.

"I should…be the one doing this. But lately, all I've been is a burden." Her voice grew smaller.

He leaned down to kiss the top of her head. "No, you're not. You serve by being you."

When she turned to look up at him, puzzlement in her eyes, he sighed. "You've had a hard time the last few days. It's okay to lean on your Dominant. You are mine and I take care of what is mine."

Luna blinked at him once, twice. He could see her trying to wrap her mind around the concept. At last, she gave voice to her question.

"What do you get out of it?"

The smile he gave her was wistful. It was both an easy and a hard answer. "It's in my nature to nurture," he began, then paused.

Very few subs had asked him the question before and it took him a while to find the right words. "I take pride in the happiness and wellbeing of my subs. They place great trust in me, in giving me control over them. In return, I do my best to make the decisions that help all of us grow and be better every day. That is my reward." Jacob shrugged a little. "I suppose that's just how I'm built as a Dominant."

He stared into the distance but came back to himself quick enough. "Now stop distracting me and get back into position," he chided.

When Luna complied, Jacob resumed his work. Luna's question had triggered something in him, had made him recall his past subs. But all of them paled in comparison to Luna. He had never met someone so selfless and loving in their service.

They stayed that way, him working up her neck then back again, until she drooped forward.

"Luna?"

"Mm-hmm-m?" The barely conscious reply came back slurred. He chuckled under his breath and maneuvered himself around while keeping one arm out to prevent his pet from falling on the floor. Once he found his balance, he scooped her up and carried her to bed.

The tension on her face had eased, and her color was returning. In repose, she looked angelic, even in that damn ratty T-shirt.

He tucked her in, smoothed her hair back with one hand and kissed the top of her forehead. The small but genuine smile that tugged at her lips for the first time that night went a long way to easing the knot inside him.

Jacob stayed for a little longer, making sure she was asleep before he tiptoed out of the room. As much as he wanted to stay, he couldn't quite afford to with his schedule for the next morning.

With another glance toward the closed bedroom door, he set out to hunt for pen and paper to leave a note. That was when he saw the stack of paper, line after line of cursive scribbles that he recognized as Luna's handwriting. Dried spots where drops of liquid had touched before blurred the ink into splotches. Tears. He stared at the title. *The First Time I Played With Bryan*.

He knew then that he would find the answers to his unease in those papers, papers that he had asked her to write. He thought it would give her space to think. Instead, he had left her to re-live her pain by herself. *What have I done? How could I have been so stupid?*

It was not in him to invade her privacy, but she had written it at his request in the first place. Work became a distant memory as he settled into the chair and began reading. The pages unfolded the relationship they had, hinted at the way Bryan had treated her.

*He was here for a project for a few weeks. It was going to be wonderful spending time with him in real life.*

*We met a few times. Coffee dates grew into dinners. Dinners grew into full days of activities on the weekend. He was gentle at first, saying we needed time to get to know each other. It was nice. The flirting was nice.*

*We talked about scening, about what would happen. He always kept it light so it wouldn't scare me. That was good. By the time it was happening, I felt ready.*

*He told me once that when we would finally do it, he was going to punish me for making him wait for so long. I had laughed it off, chalking it up to more flirting. I didn't mind. He* had *waited for so long.*

*When I got to his place, a service apartment, he kissed me and swatted at my ass before he told me to go into the office. I went in and he bent me face down over the desk, cuffing my hands above my head and my ankles to the desk legs so that I was bent over spread out for him. It was a little scary but a little exciting too.*

*He made sure I repeated the safeword then brought out the paddle. I was told to kiss it and that it would be my new best friend since I was a naughty girl. I didn't really like the label, but he seemed to be excited, like a boy on Christmas Day. That made me happy, so I said nothing.*

*The rest was a bit of a blur. The desk dug into me a bit. The paddle stung a lot. It wasn't really good pain, like when muscles burn from exercise. But maybe that just takes time to develop. Not sure.*

*The next part is harder to write. I remember his disappointment when he found I wasn't getting wet. I remember him going harder, and there was some yelling. When I still wasn't wet, he told me he was upset but he would train me to be better. I was going to be better for him.*

*He left me there for a while. Left the room, though I'm not sure how long. Then he came back, uncuffed me and told me to go home.*

*I was determined afterward that I would be better the next time he came into town.*

The tone, despite being written in first person, was clipped and remote, nothing like Luna's usual elegant writing. It was how victims of abuse talked about their experiences.

Jacob's hands shook, but he forced himself to read on. He would honor Luna's efforts, no matter how sick he felt.

It was subtle, so subtle that a less-experienced Dominant would never question the approach, but there was that pattern. Bryan would talk about his enthusiasm for a particular kink. Luna would express doubts. He would convince her that her doubts were just weaknesses, impeding her focus to serve him. The aftercare was almost always dependent on her performance. Conversations afterward would inevitably end with Luna agreeing she liked it, even when he could read between the lines how she was uncomfortable, ashamed and in pain. Wash. Rinse. Repeat.

With infinite care, Jacob placed the papers back down on the table. He pushed the chair back and rose, every moment deliberate.

*How dare that asshole.*

He clenched and unclenched his fists repeatedly. It explained all the little behaviors he'd had to train Luna out of early on and some they were still working on — her reluctance to communicate, to express what she wanted, the fear of saying she didn't enjoy something, the moments of self-doubt.

Seething with rage, Jacob stalked the tiny living room like a caged predator. He wanted to yell. He wanted to punch something. He wanted…

Luna.

Jacob pulled out his phone and typed a careful email—one to his boss about a sick day and another about rescheduling the meeting. That done, he turned off his phone and tossed it on to the kitchen counter. The phone landed with a thud and he winced. He had used a little more force than he'd intended.

With business taken care of, he let himself quietly back into Luna's room, and without taking off any of his clothing, he slipped under the covers. He shifted to cuddle against her and let her scent soothe the rawness in him.

Luna turned to curl up against him, her sleepy eyes opening. "Jacob?"

"It's all right, sweetheart. Go back to sleep."

She smiled and pressed a kiss against his shoulder, her eyes already closed once more.

He kissed the top of her head in return and comforted himself with running his fingers through her hair. At the sight of her so vulnerable, he swallowed the emotions that threatened to overwhelm him but could not hold back the tears that fell as he grieved for the girl who'd had to go through so much, who had hurt so much.

For the rest of the night, he held her to him, reminding himself that she was still his to protect and he could still keep her safe. Tomorrow… He would decide on what to do tomorrow.

# Chapter Fourteen

Her bed was wonderfully warm. Luna murmured something as she tried to bury herself closer in her half sleep to the heat source. Vague memories of a migraine and a surprise visit from Jacob trailed across her mind. She remembered his gentleness, his kindness...

*Jacob!*

Luna's eyes flew open and she tried to sit up, only to find herself trapped by Jacob's arms. At her stirring, he groaned and tightened his hold. The sound combined with, well — honestly — being held down, sent a shot of lust straight to between her legs. *No. Bad.* She bit her lower lip, hard.

As she reared her thoughts back to the situation at hand, she craned her neck to search for her phone, only to glimpse the time. Eight-thirty. It was way too early for a —

"Crap!" It was nowhere close to the weekend.

"What?" Jacob mumbled as Luna attempted to shove his arm off her.

"Work! We're going to be late for work!" Panic edged in her voice as she tapped his arm with her palm over and over.

He groaned and rolled over, freeing Luna. She shot up and rubbed the last of sleep from her eyes.

"Not for me." He was barely understandable, his words half muffled as he pulled the covers over his head. "Called in sick."

She paused in her franticness to stare at Jacob, wide-eyed. Alarmed and concerned, she crawled back onto the bed on all fours and teased the covers down until she had access to his forehead. When Jacob turned enough to expose his face, she placed a hand on his forehead to check his temperature.

In the blink of an eye, she was on her back, pinned to the bed. Jacob hovered above, staring at her with an intensity that made her squirm. It wasn't sexual. Rather, it was as if he were studying her, searching for something — though what, she had no idea.

"Jacob?" When he didn't budge, she tugged against his grip.

He rose and eased off the bed. There was a quiet about him, as if he were closing off a part and distancing himself.

What had happened the previous night? Luna tried to recall every moment but found nothing that would cause such behavior.

"Are you okay?"

"Yeah." Jacob gave her a smile, but it didn't quite reach his eyes. "Some things came up today that I need some time to deal with." He placed a hand on top of her head and ruffled her hair. "Go shower and get ready. I'll drive you to work."

They lapsed back into routine as they both got ready to head out of the door, and before long, they were on their way. During the drive, Luna alternated between looking out of the window and sneaking glances at Jacob. The silence in the car was oppressive, and she fidgeted, debating whether to take her phone out just so she had an excuse to be doing something. At last, she couldn't stand it anymore.

"Um…thank you for…."

"Do you have another meeting with Bryan today?" His question cut her off, startling her into temporary silence as all other thoughts fled.

"Luna?"

"Y…yes," she stuttered in reply.

"Did he give you trouble at the meeting yesterday? Or after?" There was an unfamiliar edge to Jacob's voice that made Luna nervous. Was he jealous? No, Jacob never got jealous. That's just wasn't him. *Worried? Yeah, I'll go with that.*

"No, he was fine. He was very professional." She paused. "I talked to Joanna and I'll be staying on the project. It looked like from the meeting yesterday that it should be okay."

In response, Jacob made a noncommittal sound as he driven into the parking lot, but instead of dropping her off, he parked the car in a stall, pulled the handbrake then turned to her, catching her eye.

"If he gives you any trouble at all, you tell your boss. There is no shame in walking away."

Part of her wanted to laugh it off, to crack a joke to lighten the mood. But the other part, the career woman part of her, was pissed. And that was the part that won out when she next spoke. "You don't think I can handle it." There was a hint of a growl at the back of her throat.

"No, it's not that." Jacob pushed his hair back, frustration written on his face. "You and this guy have a history...a bad history. You don't need that stress in your life."

Jacob could dictate a lot of things about her life, but telling her what to do with her career had never been part of the deal. Why was he starting now? "Is that an order, Sir?"

As soon as the words were out of her mouth, Luna knew she had crossed a line. Yet her temper, now roaring in her ears, kept her rooted to the seat as she refused to back down, even if she thought Jacob's next words would be to throw her out of his car.

"No." Jacob's voice grew quieter in return. "But it is a request." It was a reply that surprised both of them.

She should have yielded then and apologized for the comment. But it was as if some dam had broken within her. All the pent-up emotions came pouring out to shape into words that have been unsaid for too long.

"You have no right." Luna's voice was equally quiet, but her shoulders trembled. "Our contract is ending soon and you have no right to request something that would impact my future — a future that wouldn't even have you in it." She refused to cry. She would be the ice queen. She would feel nothing. Without waiting for a reply, she opened the car door. "Have a good day off, Jacob. Good luck with whatever you're planning to do." She let herself out and closed the door with a quiet thud. And when she turned to walk away, Luna denied every instinct in her to look back.

In the office, Luna threw herself into her work. This time, there was no nervous energy, no checking her phone every five minutes — just a single-minded dedication that saw her through most of the morning until it was time to meet with the client team.

She had scheduled an hour-long workshop to get at their content requirements. As they filed into the room she had booked, she slapped on her game face. Once more they shook hands before everyone sat around the table. Luna remained standing next to a screen where her presentation was projected. In the back, masking tape held up scrolls of white paper with diagrams and swim lanes. She waited with silence until all eyes were on her, a trick she had learned from Lani.

"Thank you for coming today. The purpose of this meeting is for me to get a good grounding of what your content needs are for this project. I already have some basic ideas from the brief, but now I want to dig a little deeper. We'll work through a series of exercises that'll help me understand both your audience and stakeholders. Questions before we start?"

Luna had expected the crickets to be chirping. Clients usually were until they'd warmed up. But her eyes kept straying to Bryan to watch his reactions, to ensure that she had his attention. After all, he was the lead and his buy-in was essential. It had nothing to do with old instincts kicking in, wanting to be sure he was pleased with her.

As if to emphasize that thought, Luna barged on ahead without waiting for affirmation and gestured for the woman sitting closest to her. "Carly, why don't you start?"

For the rest of the hour, she ran the workshop, walking them through the exercises and asking questions to dig beyond their surface-level thoughts, while reminding herself to stop searching for signs of approval from Bryan. He was just another client, nothing beyond that. Luna remained ruthless at clamping down all her emotions. By the time she was on to the third exercise, Luna had convinced herself that he only needed to be pleased with her results, not her. Her eyes no longer strayed to meet his every five seconds.

As the hour drew to a close, Ted poked his head into the room then backed off again until Luna wrapped up the meeting.

"Hey, you guys head on back to the office. I'll meet you back there." Bryan waved to the others on the team as they filed out of the room. Luna kept an ear out as they said their goodbyes and left, but a moment later, she heard Bryan's voice again. "Lunch?"

"That's what I'm here for!" Ted responded.

Luna envied Ted's joviality but paid them no heed as she took photos of the exercises' results then started taking down the Post-it notes on the walls.

"Hey, Luna, join us. Eating with the client means we can get the bosses to foot the bill!" Ted called out to her and winked as he peered back into the room.

Luna paused, uncertainty battling with hunger. "You guys go on ahead. I still have to pack up here." It was an excellent excuse.

"We can wait," Bryan cut in. "Besides, you deserve it. Running a workshop for me and my team must be like herding cats."

Luna smiled a little in response. They had gotten unruly and had a tendency to go off topic, but it was nothing she hadn't experienced before. Any more protest would sound like an excuse, though, and she was done with conceding to men today. "All right. Let me finish up, then we'll go."

By the time they were out of the door, it was as if Luna and Bryan had an unspoken agreement that they would pretend they'd never met before the project. That was more than fine with her and she was content to remain silent as the two men nattered on.

They arrived at a hipster soup and sandwich place. Luna could almost imagine Jacob's comments, pointing out and making fun of each element, from the Mason jars for water to the uniforms of plaid shirts and skinny jeans. Almost. She stamped out that thought in her mind. Ted and Bryan continued to make small talk until they each got their lunch and found a table.

"Hey, so how are things at Telcorus?" Ted asked as they all started on their food.

"Oh man, I am remembering why I hate working for the big guys." Bryan groaned. "No one wants the accountability, but everyone wants a say in the product. The approval processes are ridiculous." He turned to give her a sheepish grin. "Don't worry. I'm here to deal with all that so you don't have to."

Luna flashed him a small, grateful smile but said little as she focused on eating.

"Nah, it can't be that bad."

"You don't think so? Well, last time…"

She listened as she ate, amused by Bryan's anecdotes. It was a side of him that she hadn't seen before, and as time passed, she grew more at ease as she began to see him more as a person than just a Dominant.

When they finished their food, Ted excused himself to the bathroom, leaving Bryan and Luna alone.

"You know…" Bryan leaned closer and gave her a warm smile. "I have to admit that you're nothing like what I'd imagined when I first realized I'd be working with you. You take charge well and you know your shit. It's very sexy."

Heat bloomed across Luna's cheeks at the unexpected comment. Fortunately, Ted's return right at the moment saved her from having to formulate a reply. She pointedly ignored the look he threw her way and rose instead to put her jacket back on. Once outside the restaurant, they waved their goodbyes to Bryan and went back to their respective offices.

Ted opened his mouth.

"No Ted, I'm not going to talk about it."

"Fine."

Luna laughed under her breath at Ted's pout. Maybe, just maybe, she was going to be okay.

# Chapter Fifteen

Jacob stared at the seat Luna had just vacated as if flowers would grow from it.

*What the hell just happened?*

Never had he allowed a sub to get away with speaking to him that way, but what was more, never had he felt such an urge to run after a pet of his, to beg for forgiveness until she came back into his arms.

*This is getting ridiculous.*

No, what he'd read last night was throwing him off balance and he couldn't trust his judgement right now. There was one person he could turn to. He pulled out his phone.

*Got time today? I'd like your thoughts on something.*

He didn't expect an answer right away so tossed his phone on to the passenger seat and started the car. It was why he started with surprise when his phone buzzed just as he was getting ready to pull out of the parking spot.

*As a friend, Dom or counselor?*

He sighed and stared at the message. Lani was too astute.

*Dom and counselor.*

*Sure. You're lucky I have blocked the morning off for paperwork. Come to the office.*

*On my way.*

First, he made a pit stop at Luna's favorite bakery to pick up coffee and tea, breakfast for him and bribery for Lani. He knew better than to show up on such short notice without an offering. As he stood in line, his eyes fell on the apple turnover that was Luna's favorite, the crust still flaky and sparkling with tiny coarse grains of sugar. On a whim, he picked up one of those too. Then he was off again.

It took longer than he expected to hunt for parking near Lani's office, but when he found a spot at last and pulled into it, he heaved a heavy sigh to brace himself. It took only a five-minute walk before he was staring at the state-of-the-art building Lani worked out of. As one of the best pro-kink counselors in the industry, Lani had a surprising number of high-profile clients. It turned counseling into a very lucrative career that gave her a gorgeous office with a view and supplied steady funding for her vast and ever-growing collection of heels.

When he arrived at the office with hot beverages and most of the baked goods in hand, he gave a friendly nod to Lani's receptionist, who beamed at him. "Good morning, Mr. Dakota."

Jacob gave a brief smile in response. "Morning, Ophelia. Coffee and a croissant." He left it at her desk. It paid to be nice to the receptionist, but he wasn't certain if the woman was taking it the wrong way. Dressed in a low-cut top, he swore she was trying to push her breasts up to him as she leaned over.

"Oh, you're always so thoughtful, Mr. Dakota."

What was it with women and trying to look through their lashes? *Yeah, time to get out of here.* "I better get these to Lani before they get cold." He held up the rest of the food.

"Let me get the door for you!" She rose and walked over, brushing by him. He was sure some people found the short skirt and tall heels on the blonde alluring, but only irritation filled him. Without another glance, he entered Lani's office and sighed in relief.

The office, to put it simply, was massive. Two bookcases leaned against one wall. A large couch and two armchairs surrounded a mahogany coffee table. Toward the back, Lani sat behind a large matching writing desk.

"Hi-hi!"

How the woman could be so perky first thing in the morning would never be something Jacob understood. He muttered a hello in return as he walked up to her and pushed the offering of tea and a croissant across her desk, then crossed the larger office more to plop himself on the couch.

For a moment there was silence as they dug into their food. As he began to feel a little more human, he leaned into the back of the couch and watched as Lani grabbed her notebook then came to sit on the other side of the coffee table.

"It's been a while since you came to my office. Talk to me."

The Dominant in him strained against the command. Jacob felt a gut reaction to clam up and had to remind himself that he'd come here to ask for help.

It was hard to figure out where to start and he struggled as Lani waited. At last, he gave up and just said the first thing in his mind. "Something's not right with that Bryan."

Lani nodded and made a slight noise of encouragement.

"There was just something about her response to him that seemed off. When she found out that they would be working together, she lost it." He was stalling from talking about the main reason he'd come to see Lani in the first place and he knew it.

"They're working together?"

Judging from Lani's surprise, Luna must not have told her. That in itself worried him, considering the two of them talked all the time.

"I told her this morning that if she wanted to back out of the project, she should, and she flipped out on me." Still stalling.

"Luna? Flipped out on you? Wait! Define that."

He could hear the disbelief in her voice and winced a little. It was true. Luna, in all their years together, had almost never been so mad and definitely not so angry as to walk away. Lani used to tease them that he could do no wrong.

"She said I had no right to ask her for something that impacts her future."

"Wow."

"Yeah." Jacob looked to one side and grumbled. "I understand she's been under a lot of stress lately, but I didn't expect her to take it that way."

Lani sighed and shook her head. "You do realize that she's been upset and worried about the three-year mark coming up."

Jacob groaned. That was not what he'd come to discuss. "Yes, but I figured we still have some time to figure it out."

"What is there to figure out?" Lani leaned back a little.

About to reply with the standard 'matching her with the right Dominant', Jacob paused instead then snapped his mouth shut. He hadn't come there to lie either. When he spoke next, it was with a new gravitas in his carefully chosen words.

"Whether I should let her go. Whether she wants to be let go."

At that, Lani leaned forward once more, her eyes now sparkling with interest. He wasn't sure he liked that speculative glint, but they had been friends for a long time and Jacob trusted her more than he did most.

"Let's talk about that for a moment. You used the word 'should', not 'want' for yourself."

Hadn't he been circling the precise issue for weeks? But to give it voice was another matter. *Fine.* If they were going there, he'd go there. "Lani, you know I am a trainer. After a certain period, subs move on to a more permanent relationship. I can only take their growth so far."

"Do you see your identity as a Dominant tied solely to being a trainer?"

The question gave him pause. He had always been a Dominant and he had almost always trained subs. Did he see being one the same as being the other? Could he be a Dominant without being a trainer?

"I'm not sure," he replied after another heavy pause.

"Well, I suggest you think on that," Lani replied with a small, almost enigmatic, smile.

Lani was right. It was an interesting aspect he'd never given much thought to before. But he couldn't leave yet, not until he addressed what he came here for.

"There's something else." Why was that part even harder? Jacob closed his eyes for a moment, and when he reopened them, he was once more the Dom acting in his sub's best interest. "I asked Luna to write up what her scenes were like with Bryan."

Anger returned as he recalled the pages and pages of her handwriting. "He was a shit Dom and I think he hurt her." He spat out the last few words.

Lani straightened, eyes widening. Her tone was neutral as she spoke again. "What makes you think that?"

It was hard not to explode. He gripped the arm of the couch, digging into the fabric with his fingers. "She wrote that she didn't like what he did with her but was convinced she would like it eventually if she kept trying."

He didn't go into more details. He knew he didn't need to, not for an experienced Dominant like Lani.

"I see." If she felt any anger, Lani was much better at not showing it. It was what made her such a good counselor. "I can't help unless she comes to me, Jacob. So what do you want to do about it?"

At that, Jacob rose from his seat and paced along one wall. "That's the problem. I think she's in denial about what happened. She was crying last night, but this morning, she acted perfectly fine and insisted on working on the project still. I'm just not sure what's going on in her head."

He stopped at the window, staring out at the sea of buildings that faded into the horizon. "Part of me wants me to forbid Luna from any contact with Bryan. Part of me wants to beat the daylights out of the little shit and tell him to stay away. But both would cross lines." He could not keep the growl out of his voice and did not trust his own expression right now.

"Well, both urges are coming from a place of wanting to protect her rather than revenge. But you are well aware that what happened between them was in the past. And what damage he has done, you have addressed by showing her a much different relationship as her Dom. So the question is, what do you want to protect her from?"

"From making the same mistake again!" Jacob turned and snarled, then stopped himself, his eyes widening. Everything snapped into focus.

Bryan wanted her. And he feared that with their contract ending, Luna might run back to him.

"Jacob, take a step back. If any other submissive came to you asking how to proceed, what would you do?"

"Educate." The answer came immediately and easily. "Arm the submissive with enough knowledge to make good judgements and keep safe."

Lani sighed and nodded, setting her notebook and pen down. "I think perhaps both of our mistakes came from assuming that Luna had that education in the first place, since she said she had some experience already.

Neither of us dug deeper, respecting her privacy. I think, my dear boy, *that* is where you must start."

Jacob nodded, thoughts and plans churning in his head. They continued to plague him as he left the building and drove home, but at the back of his mind was the niggling of a horrifying doubt.

Did he want to keep Luna because he wanted her — or was it only because he worried that she would get hurt again?

# Chapter Sixteen

Jacob spent the rest of the afternoon making preparations now that he had a plan. Every time his mind strayed to his own feelings about Luna and their impending separation, Jacob savagely shoved the doubts aside. *One problem at a time.* No matter the outcome, he needed to equip Luna with the right tools to keep her safe.

An obnoxious alarm pierced the silence of his apartment. Reaching for his phone, Jacob shut it off then rose from the seat, his muscles stiff from sitting for hours. With a sigh, he pushed his hair back then moved around to tidy the pile of notes and shut off his own laptop.

He was stalling again. As he chastised himself, he picked up his keys and was off once more.

"Hi, can I help you?" A young man in skinny jeans and a black hoodie in his twenties stopped to look at Jacob as he stepped into Luna's office. From the looks of it, he was on his way to the kitchen with his coffee-stained mug.

"I'm good. I'm just here to pick up Luna when she's ready to go."

"Sure. What's your name?"

"Jacob."

"Cool. I think I saw her packing up. I'll let her know you're here."

Before Jacob could protest, Luna's co-worker jetted off. He looked around until he glimpsed one chair by the wall and settled into it to wait. To kill the time, he pulled out his phone, scanning his Reddit app. In truth, however, it was random scrolling as he was too distracted to linger and read any particular posts.

When he heard footsteps once more, he rose from his seat. Luna approached with a messenger bag slung to one side, her expression neutral. As Jacob took a step toward her, she looked to one side and made a subtle hand gesture in front, close to her body so only he would be able to see. It was a signal they had developed a long time ago. *Vanilla friend or family present.*

"You must be Jacob." Ted's voice projected with enthusiasm from behind Luna.

Jacob smoothed his face into a friendly smile and extended his hand out. "And you must be Ted."

They shook hands as Luna smiled up at him. If it was forced, Ted didn't seem to notice. Once they released each other from the handshake, Jacob wrapped an arm loosely around Luna. "Can I take that bag for you, Luna?" he asked. He didn't dare use any terms of endearment right now.

Wordlessly, Luna handed him the messenger bag and he slung it over his shoulder. She grew rigid against him and he knew that his sudden appearance wasn't doing much to help them resolve their earlier fight. *Well, too damn bad.* He wasn't there to appease her.

"Glad to finally put a face to the name."

Jacob nodded in reply. Luna had mentioned a few times that Ted had wanted to double-date, but Luna herself was too nervous about it, as if she wanted to keep her worlds separate. Fair enough – he had always respected that, but now that he was there... "I believe I met your partner once...Brandon?"

"Oh yeah, that time Luna popped her shoulder?"

Jacob smiled in response. "Yes, I was glad that Brandon had called me to take Luna home."

"Okay, okay," Luna interrupted, glaring at both of them. Her expression became a little more genuine and that made Jacob grin. He could picture a future where he got to tease her in front of her friends more often. *Damn it, no, not what I should think about right now.*

"Come on. Let's go. See you tomorrow, Ted." Luna grabbed his hand and pulled him toward the door with a last wave back at Ted.

Still amused, Jacob allowed Luna to lead him outside. "Nice to meet you!" he called out, just before the door closed behind them. Luna continued to drag him away from the building until they were far from prying eyes before she dropped his hand.

"What are you doing here?" With that, she dropped all pretense of them being a happy couple.

*Fine, two can play at that game.* Jacob straightened. "You're staying over for a few days. I'm driving you to your place to pack a bag, then we're going back to mine." He turned to see that Luna's jaw had dropped as she stopped cold right by the passenger side of the car. He stepped around her to open the door and waited, then sighed when she still did not move. His voice softened with his next words.

"I'm still your Dominant right now and I have assessed that it is what you need." He paused. "I'll take the couch if that puts you more at ease, but there's some reading and research you need to do, and it'll be easier for me to answer questions in person."

There was still skepticism on Luna's face, but now Jacob saw hesitation as well, as if she were trying to wrap her head around what he'd outlined. He waited and hid the fact that his heart was in his throat. It was a make-or-break moment. Luna could just walk away. She could turn her back on him, could disregard his command. Submission had always been her choice. Every day.

He could, of course, take advantage of her confusion and natural submissiveness and order her to get into the car. He could point out that if she walked away, it would be the end of their relationship. He could guilt her, remind her that she'd trusted him all that time.

He did none of those things. He would not stoop to Bryan's level. Just like any other decisions in their three years together, it would be her choice.

When Luna stepped into the car with a sigh of exasperation, Jacob let out the breath he hadn't realized he was holding. It wasn't time for celebration yet and the hard work was still ahead of them, but at least it meant that she was willing to stay and put in the effort. It went a long way toward soothing all the anxiety that he had been building up since the night before.

Once in the car, Jacob grabbed the apple turnover from the dashboard and handed it to Luna. "Here… I got it this morning, so it may be cold, but you should have a snack." Bribery or a reward for coming with him—he wasn't sure which one it really was.

Even as he drove, he saw out of the corner of his eye that she was smiling as she peeled back the top of the paper bag. Sugar had always been the way to his pet's heart, and he hoped that the peace offering would be enough for her to hear him out later.

At her place, Jacob waited for her to pack her bag and willed himself to not pace. His gaze, however, kept straying toward the pile of paper that seemed to lie forgotten on her desk. On a whim, he took the stack and folded it in half before tucking it into the large inside pocket of his jacket. He wasn't sure why. Perhaps all he wanted to do was to hide the papers so they wouldn't dredge up those painful memories again for Luna.

"I'm ready." Luna stepped out with a duffel bag in one hand and her messenger slung over her shoulder.

Jacob nodded, reached to take her bag for her and turned to lead the way back out. It wouldn't be the first time they'd spent a few days together, but it had never been under such strained circumstances.

The drive back to his place was still pregnant with silence, but Jacob did not speak. More than once, he caught Luna staring out of the window, her expression pensive. But rather than saying anything, he gave her the space to ponder. When they arrived back at his place, he took both of Luna's bags. He knew she would protest, so he shot her a look before she had a chance. When he opened the door, he let her in first, knowing the sight that would greet her. One end of the dining table held his own laptop. The other end, a brand-new notebook and pen.

"I'll take your bag to the room. Set your laptop up on the table and we'll begin soon. I've ordered delivery for dinner, so we need not worry about cooking." Jacob kept his tone neutral still but could not keep the command out of his voice. It was too much in his nature.

Without hesitation, Luna moved to obey. He watched as she settled in then turned to his own tasks, dropping her stuff off and preparing the couch for a couple of nights of sleeping.

He came back to find her running her fingers across the cover of her new notebook, a wistful expression on her face. Jacob had picked out a small leather-bound book with handmade paper, remembering her love for those things.

"Do you like it?" The words were soft, its tenderness surprising even himself.

"Yes. Thank you." A genuine smile, at last, graced her lips. It hadn't been that long, but he had already been missing it.

"Don't thank me yet." Jacob moved to his side of the table and hit 'Send' on an email he had drafted earlier on. "I've sent you a reading list. I want you to work your way through each article and take what notes you need. I want you to focus on the rights of a submissive, what is and isn't acceptable behavior from a Dominant and what a sub needs to look out for in order to assess if they're in a dangerous situation. Dinner will be here soon, but you can get a head start."

Luna's mouth opened then closed. Something in Jacob begged her silently to not fight him on it. He barged on ahead when no words came out.

"When you are ready to call it quits for the night — or when I deem it's time to stop — we will take some time to discuss each reading. You're also free to ask me questions at any time. Is that clear?"

"Clear," Luna muttered beneath her breath. He knew she was not convinced of why she needed it, but he was relieved when she didn't ask for an explanation.

"Good. You may begin."

# Chapter Seventeen

The first two days were a brutal slog.

Luna didn't understand why he was putting her through it all. Well, no, she did, and if she were being honest with herself, she just didn't want to admit it. Jacob was preparing her for finding a new Dominant.

It would have been endearing if it weren't breaking her heart.

Luna pinched the bridge of her nose as she looked away from the article. How Jacob had managed to put together such a long and detailed reading list, she had no idea, but she had to admit that she had learned a lot in the past three nights. She was even beginning to see where she may have made some mistakes in the past, allowing her submissive nature to overpower her self-respect for her own boundaries. It was an uncomfortable thought.

Her gaze flickered toward Jacob, who was staring at his own laptop with intense concentration, causing furrows on his forehead. She knew he had spent his time off preparing for these next few days and it had cost him. Every night that she had been there, he had been working overtime.

By and by, however, through the quiet hours spent together, her temper had receded into a deep appreciation for the kind of Dominant he was. He had never taken advantage of her desire to please. He always listened and checked in with her comfort level.

A small sigh escaped her lips. She wanted to thank him, to show how grateful she was, but it was as if a new gulf had appeared between them and she didn't know how to cross it. The Jacob now was still dominant, but gone were the little terms of endearment, the small gestures of affection. They had so little time left and she didn't want to waste it waging a cold war anymore.

Jacob looked up as she sighed. *Damn that man and his sensitive hearing.*

"Let's call it a night."

She watched as he shut off his laptop and rose from his seat. "Let me make some tea, then we'll talk."

Luna nodded and eased out of the chair to stretch, and her gaze swept across the mountains of papers, notebooks and binders across the table. She rubbed the back of her neck in an attempt to relieve the tension and reminded herself that she had to stop craning her neck every time she read on her laptop.

Mid-stretch, a stack of creased papers beneath a binder caught her eye. It tugged at her curiosity, and with a glance toward the kitchen to make sure Jacob was still busy, she walked around the table to take a peek.

It was her homework assignment, her descriptions of her times with Bryan. She had forgotten about them, but memories came flooding back, memories that now she could see with a new light. Her hands shook and her breathing grew shallower.

Jacob wasn't doing it to prepare for the end. He was doing it because she had proven she would let a Dom walk all over her. She swallowed the lump in her throat.

"I made some chamomile to help with sleep," Jacob called out as he shuffled out of the kitchen.

Luna hastily tucked the papers back where she'd found them and wiped the corner of her eyes, plastering a smile on her face. "Thanks."

They didn't talk long. Jacob kept nodding off. Burning the candle at both ends was clearly draining him. So when Jacob's blinks grew longer and longer, Luna excused herself to bed. He barely mumbled a goodnight.

She lay there in Jacob's bed, still surrounded by his scent. Tossing and turning, she listened to the gentle snoring outside the room, guilt crawling across her skin. Her eyes remained wide open and she kept staring to the door that separated them. There was no reason for it.

*'A sub holds as much responsibility in the dance of dominance as the Dom themselves.'*

The line, one she had read long ago in August's journal, echoed in her mind. She had never been a meek sub, not since she'd become Jacob's. So why was she waiting for him to come to her?

Before she could even finish that thought, she moved on instinct alone. As she slipped out of the bed, Luna stripped herself completely nude then grabbed one of the large throws to wrap around herself. With lithe grace, she slipped out of the bedroom and approached the couch where Jacob lay.

The city lights sneaking through the blinds cast strange shadows across his face and bare chest. For a moment, she held her breath, wondering at how he seemed like a stranger all over again. It wasn't until he turned and muttered in his slumber that she smiled a little. The couch was too small for a man of his size. She should never have made her Dom suffer.

She leaned down, brushing her lips against his, working her way down to leave a trail of tiny kisses along his jawline. In response, he moaned.

She missed that sexy sound.

Luna continued downward, trailing her lips along his neck while she took her time to trace the contours of his muscles with her tongue. She closed her eyes, savoring the taste of his skin.

"Luna?"

She looked up, baby blues meeting darkened brown, and gave him a small, sad smile. She straightened as he sat up, still groggy.

"What's going on?"

She had been clutching the throw to her body, but at his words, she let go. The blanket fell from her, pooling at her feet, and she heard his audible groan in response.

It gave her courage to keep going. She knelt down with the grace her martial arts training had instilled in her, using the throw as a cushion. As soon as she settled, she gazed up at him and reached up to the edge of his pajama bottoms. He might be sleepy, but something of his was definitely awake.

Jacob grasped her wrists, stopping her from completing her intended task. "Explain."

Luna faltered for a moment. She had hoped he would just go with it, but she wasn't sure why she'd thought that would happen. She held her body still and, summoning her courage, she held his gaze. "I understand why you are doing this, why you wanted me to step away from the project. I know you read what I wrote." Tears welled up and she swallowed again. "I'm sorry." The apology came out more wobbly than she'd intended.

"Luna." He breathed out her name with a sigh and he released her wrists to cup her cheeks and brush away the tears that had started to fall. "We're both at fault here."

Luna smiled through her tears, leaning against his hand until she felt him tug her up. She shook her head. "Please, let me do this." At Jacob's hesitation, she turned to press a kiss against his warm palm. "Please."

Hesitation turned into amusement as he nodded his consent. He allowed her to position him then raised his hips helpfully as she drew his bottoms down, freeing his hard cock. He hadn't bothered with his boxers and she spared a moment to appreciate that.

At her touch on his thighs, he tensed, and his gaze roved across her nakedness in clear admiration. Luna made sure her gaze held his before she leaned forward and flicked her tongue along the tip.

Jacob held himself still while his cock jumped a little, but she did not wait for further invitation. Luna leaned farther forward, dragging her tongue around the head. He rewarded her with a sharp intake of breath, his cock twitching in response.

"Damn it, Luna, you tease."

She laughed softly, enjoying the role reversal for once. They both knew that if he wanted, he could order her to do as he pleased, but it became a new game, how long she could play seductress before he lost his legendary control. She parted her lips, wrapped them around the head and held it in her mouth as she continued to swirl her tongue around it.

"Sweetheart." The word held a hint of warning as he reached around to run his hands through her hair.

Something about the edge of desire in his voice made her feel powerful and proud in her service to him. Her own arousal was building between her legs but she ignored it. The night was about giving him pleasure, to show him she was still his.

Luna wrapped her hand around the base of his cock as she sank her mouth lower to take in more of him. When he groaned again, she dragged the nails of her free hand up along his inner thigh until she reached his groin. She shifted her hand to cup his balls, then began to massage them. He shuddered in response, his grip tightening in her hair, just enough to remind her that she had control only as long as he permitted it.

She took him in as far as she could until his cock hit the back of her throat, then extended her tongue to run along the base. He thrust up and she withdrew until once more only the tip remained in her mouth, leaving him almost chasing after her.

Jacob tugged at her hair, just enough to show his desire. She obeyed, bobbing her head and setting a rhythm until she felt his cock swell. She moaned in anticipation, the sound vibrating along his shaft, and as the ultimate sign of submission, she withdrew her hands to hold behind her back, relinquishing control to him.

"Luna, sweetheart." The words uttered behind gritted teeth were accompanied by a low, animalistic growl that rumbled in his chest. He jerked, his rear lifting off the couch as he abandoned all semblance of control. He fisted her hair at last and pulled her head in to take all of him, holding her in position.

A soft "fuck" was all the warning she had as his body tightened then shuddered in climax, spilling his seed into her mouth. Luna kept her lips sealed tight around him, sucking hard. She struggled to keep up with swallowing his cum until her throat was coated in his taste. A small trail of cum dribbled down the corners of her mouth.

Jacob loosened his grip on her hair as he slumped back into the couch. She kept her lips on him still, following his movements until she milked the last of him. With her hands still resting on the small of her back, she eased back and cleaned him with her tongue.

"Luna." He reached down to caress her shoulders then pulled her up. She rose, her legs stiff from kneeling such that she half fell into his lap.

"Good girl," he murmured and stroked her hair once more before he trailed his hand down along her cheek then to her lips to wipe his own cum away. "I didn't hurt you, did I?"

Luna shook her head and smiled as she steadied herself in his lap. Now it was his turn to position her until he had free access, tracing along her inner thigh with his fingertips, leaving a trail of goosebumps in their wake.

"Jacob…"

She couldn't keep the whimper of need out of her voice and he smiled that crooked grin of his.

"Come on, sweetheart. I'm tired of the couch." With that, he hooked one arm under her legs and one around her back. With one swift motion, he rose and carried her to bed.

# Chapter Eighteen

"I'm off!" Luna struggled to keep the strap of her duffel bag on her shoulder while trying to get her sneakers on at the same time.

Jacob popped his head out from the kitchen, a dishrag slung over his shoulder. "Hey, hey, hey."

Clad in jeans and a simple black T-shirt, he walked over to her, and suddenly she found it hard to leave, even if it would mean an extreme ass-kicking for missing a makeup class at the dojo.

Any thoughts of getting out of that door flew from her mind as he placed his hands on either side of her hips and tugged her toward him. He leaned forward and crushed her lips with his into an almost-bruising kiss. With a soft moan, Luna pressed herself against him and slid her hands from his shoulders and down his arms. In return, he reached up with one hand to tangle his fingers in her hair as they tasted each other until they had to come up for air.

"Be careful at practice. I'll see you later tonight."

*Practice? What practice?* She blinked at him.

Jacob chuckled and placed a light kiss on her forehead. "Off you go, little one, before Brandon makes you do squats for being late."

Luna shook her head clear and smiled before rising on the balls of her feet to give him a kiss on the cheek. "Okay, see you soon."

"Have fun, sweetheart."

With a last wave, she was off.

Ironically, the dojo was closer to Jacob's home than hers. She too a brisk walk and in no more than fifteen minutes, she arrived at front door of the gym and, half on autopilot, Luna entered.

With five minutes before class started, she rushed to change, exchanging her T-shirt and ripped jeans for the crisp white judogi, the uniform of her practice. With a nod to herself, she stepped into the dojo then gave a bow in front.

"Luna, what a surprise! What are you doing here?"

Her jaws dropped as Bryan waved from the side, sitting in one of the plastic chairs reserved for spectators. "Bryan? What...what do you mean... what am I doing there? W-what are *you* doing here?" she stammered in confusion.

A hard slap on her back almost made her jump out of her skin in her bewilderment. "Bryan, I see you already know Luna, one of our senior students."

Luna's head swiveled up toward her sensei, then back to Bryan, then back to Sensei again, still gaping like an idiot. With conscious effort, she snapped her mouth shut. "We...work together..."

"I had mentioned an interest in restarting my training when I was having dinner with Brandon and Ted the other night, and Brandon invited me to his dojo to observe a class." Bryan grinned and winked. "Had I known you were practicing here, I would have come to check out the class earlier."

"All right, no flirting in the dojo," Brandon's voice cut in, iron behind the words, and Bryan ducked his head like a chastised schoolboy.

Luna chuckled, though her cheeks were still pink from Bryan's comment. She had forgotten about that certain charm Bryan always had—a charm that had once made her too eager to please. A shadow of a memory flitted through her mind.

*But I'm stronger now.*

She carried that strength with her to the mats. The first part of the class was stretches and drills to warm them up and train their muscle memory in executing technical moves. Luna was already familiar with most of them, but she could always improve her technique. Her focus narrowed to the hyperawareness of her body, of the angle of her limbs—of which parts would tense and which parts she had to keep relaxed, of the burn of her muscles, the spacing of her feet and the bend of her knees to keep her center of gravity low.

Then Brandon declared it was time for sparring—three-minute matches with five minutes breaks in between. She started with two rounds that were both with beginners. Her first opponent was respectful, so she allowed the fight to draw out, to stay in defense a little so he could learn, understand how to feel his opponent's balance and try a few moves. She didn't need to trounce a newbie for the sake of showing off.

The second, however, came at her with a cocky smirk. "Come on, little girl." It wasn't the first time he'd made such a comment to her. Brandon had pulled him aside before and launched into a full lecture, then had asked Luna to throw him twenty times as punishment. Now he only made the comments when they were outside Brandon's earshot.

The fight lasted thirty seconds. Most untrained people kept their center of gravity high, which made them very easy to throw. When the cocky newbie came at her, it was a simple matter of faking resistance then let him tug her back. His eyes widened as he realized just how off balance he was as the momentum carried him backward, but it was already too late.

Rather than allowing him to step back with one leg to catch himself, Luna stepped in to trip him by blocking his back-left leg with her right. She pushed at his right shoulder and pulled the left, allowing that same momentum to do the rest of the work. They both winced as he landed flat on his back. He had not quite learned the art of break-falling to minimize pain yet. Luna stepped back and waited until he got up before she gave him a perfunctory bow, then walked off the mats without a glance back.

Two more matches with more senior students left Luna a little breathless but sparkling with vitality. She was in her element.

"Excellent job, Luna. You seem in top form today." Brandon rarely handed out compliments and Luna beamed with pride. An infinitesimal part of her wondered if it was because she had an audience and she had something to prove. She beamed at him and bobbed her head but didn't reply.

*I am stronger now!*

Before she knew it, it was the end of class. They bowed to each other then performed the class closing rituals, and that was when she caught Bryan watching her. Their eyes met and he gave her a quick wink. She looked away.

As she came out of the changing room, she saw Bryan talking to Brandon. She paused, torn between a need to be friendly and the desire to avoid further interaction. Although she felt more at ease with Bryan now that they talked almost every day at work, she could not help eyeing him in a different light once outside the office, especially remembering what she had written for Jacob.

It was for that reason that she turned to leave.

"Hey, Luna, wait up."

*Well, so much for the quiet exit.* She pushed aside the memories and managed a smile.

"You were spectacular." There was something in Bryan's admiration that made her straighten with pride. Perhaps it was a remnant left over from old conditioning.

Bryan gave her a wide smile and, for a split second, Luna wondered if he'd noticed.

"Hey, I know you're probably pretty busy, but want to grab a quick coffee? My treat."

She had been thinking about grabbing a drink and a light snack on the way back to Jacob's. And she had to confront her own past at some point. That was at least how she justified it in her head as she nodded in assent. "Sure, sounds good."

They found their way to a coffee shop only a few doors down from the dojo. The baked goods were nowhere near as good as her favorite place, but practice had made her hungry. As they brought their coffees and food — Danish for her, a muffin for Bryan — over to the table, Luna glanced at her phone. Fifteen minutes, then she'd make up some excuse to leave.

"Like I said earlier, you were incredible on the floor. How long have you been practicing?"

"Oh, about five years." She couldn't quite bring herself to tell him that she had started it to get over her heartbreak from him.

"I see." Bryan's voice had softened, and when he looked up at her once more, there was a mix of emotions Luna couldn't quite understand.

"Look... There's no easy way to say this." He stopped, then started again. "You know, over the years, I kept thinking about what I would say to you if I ever ran into you again. I even wrote it out at one point, but now that we're here, the words are not coming."

Luna stared at Bryan, tried not to squirm in her seat and opened her mouth to reply but stopped when Bryan shook his head.

"Please, hear me out." He didn't wait for her to agree but dove ahead. "I always felt bad about how things ended. I was in a rough spot in my life, but that's not an excuse for...." He waved his hand in the air and trailed off with a heavy sigh, his gaze downcast. "Over the years, as I got more experienced as a Dom, I realized how shitty I was with you. I was inexperienced and I mistreated you." Now he looked up at her with the most woeful expression on his face. "I'm sorry, and if I ever got the chance to make it up to you, I would jump at it, be the Master you deserve."

Of all the scenarios that had run through her head when she'd agreed to coffee, that was the last one Luna had expected. Her cheeks reddened and she stayed silent, unsure what she should or could say. She clutched at her coffee mug. Not trusting her voice, she lifted the mug to her lips and took a sip.

"Luna, say something, please? Say you forgive me?"
*Is that a plea in his voice?*

What was she going to do? Throw coffee in his face and run out after such a heartfelt apology? Still in shock, Luna nodded, the coffee mug hiding half her face.

"Thank you, Luna." Bryan leaned back in his chair, relief written all over his face. At last, he took a long draw of his coffee then grinned. "I heard you may be looking for a new Dominant soon. Maybe after the project's over, we can talk? No pressure or anything. We can go at your pace."

How was she supposed to respond to that? And who the hell had told him in the first place?

"Oh crap, I have to get going!" Bryan rose from his seat, the rest of the muffin and coffee forgotten. "I'll be at the club tonight. See you there?"

Luna had no plans of going tonight, but she nodded anyway. He was going so fast that she was getting whiplash just following the sequence of events.

"Great! I'll keep an eye out for you. See you later." Then he was out of there, leaving Luna glued to her seat, still stunned.

*What just happened?*

# Chapter Nineteen

"Luna?"

The sight of his dazed sub took Jacob by surprise. He ushered her inside, closed the door and watched as she flopped on the couch and curled up into a ball. She was functioning on autopilot and Jacob could only wait for her to come to herself. He followed, sat next to her and waited while he summoned his patience. That was what his sub needed at the moment.

"He apologized to me." There was a mix of emotions in those four paltry words.

Jacob's heart sank, but he swallowed the dread that welled up within. "Start from the beginning, little one."

Luna looked up and refocused on him at last. "Jacob." She breathed his name as if it were an anchor back to reality. When he nodded to show he was listening, she swallowed hard.

"Bryan was at the dojo observing a class."

Jacob could imagine that being a shock on its own and reached out to hold her hand. *Why did Bryan even show up there in the first place? Did Luna mention her dojo at work? Did Bryan take that as an invitation?*

"After class, we went out to grab a quick coffee. He apologized for ghosting me and for the way he treated me as a Dom. He said it was because he was inexperienced." Her words, which started slow, came faster as she talked.

*Why did Luna agree to go out for coffee?* Another question. An unfamiliar feeling twisted his gut and, with a start, he realized that it was jealousy. He knew the other Dom wanted Luna. Was that his play? Or was he genuine with his regrets and their conversation earlier at The Playgrounds had just been posturing? *Like a damn peacock.* He found his fists clenched and worked to relax his fingers.

When he realized that Luna was staring at him, waiting for an answer, he nodded again, making a pretense of considering her words. "How do you feel about it?" He was careful to keep his tone neutral.

Luna shrugged before she breathed out slowly. "Surprised. Confused." She chewed her lower lip and he resisted the urge to kiss her to get her to stop. It was an absurdly inappropriate thought. He had better control than that.

So instead, he opened his arms for her. When she crawled over to resettle against him and tucked her head under his chin, he wrapped his arms around her, giving them the comfort they both needed.

"I guess I need time. To process, you know?"

Jacob nodded in acknowledgment. He wanted to tell her to be careful, to not be fooled, that it was an act. But he had learned his lesson and, to be fair, he couldn't be sure himself either. He was too biased.

They remained on the couch that way until Jacob leaned back with reluctance, weighing his limbs down. "Dominique and Erica called."

He saw the questions in Luna's eyes. Although he had been in the lifestyle long enough to know most of the people in the community, including The Playground's owners, they still rarely contacted him. And now he was regretting picking up their call earlier. "There's been a flu going around and they're short dungeon monitors for tonight. They asked if I would be able to fill in."

He saw Luna's hesitation and disappointment. They both knew what his answer was and that he was a man of his word. Luna sighed and unfurled her legs to push herself up from the couch. "Should I go get ready?"

Normally, neither of them had any problems with her hanging out at The Playgrounds without him. They knew enough people that Luna could always go to someone for help if another club guest bothered her. However, this time, there was a reluctance in her voice.

Jacob wrapped a hand around her wrist, keeping his touch light enough to not bruise but still with enough firmness to still her movements. "What's wrong?"

She cast her gaze downward. Her words came out as a mumble under her breath. "Bryan said he would be there tonight and would keep an eye out for me. I would rather not run into him, especially alone. I'm not ready yet to face him." Hesitation snuck into her voice. "I'm being a coward, aren't I?"

Part of him wanted to leap up and holler in celebration, to praise and reward her for her good sense. Instead, he settled for drawing her into his lap then placed a tender kiss on her temple. "No, sweetheart, you're not. This is not a straightforward thing and you should take all the time you need." He brushed her hair back, tucking a stray strand back behind her ear. "Sometimes strength means admitting you need time. I'm proud of you."

The corner of her lips tugged upward in a tired smile, but he noticed her sitting a little straighter. *Good.*

"You don't have to go." He leaned back to catch her gaze. "Tell you what. You can stay here and relax, spend the night in. I'll text and keep you posted, And I'll come home as soon as I can, okay?"

"Okay. Maybe I'll work on the rest of those readings?"

Jacob beamed with pride. "That's my girl."

He knew this time he had approached it from the right way when Luna relaxed against him and nuzzled his neck. It made him regret agreeing to help Erica. It wasn't until after several minutes had ticked by that Luna slid off his lap and gave him a slight smile. "You better get going."

Two hours later, when he was on the floor of the dungeon, Jacob was still regretting his decision, if not more so. He kept his eyes on the few scenes being played out, but there was little of concern, as most were regulars with their usual partners. Across the room, Darryl, also filling in as a dungeon monitor rather than bartending tonight, gave him a nod to confirm that all was well.

Behind him, a giggle and two sets of footsteps signaled new arrivals. With a sigh under his breath, he turned, only to stiffen as he realized who it was.

*Him again.*

He narrowed his eyes as Bryan made his way to the other side of the dungeon with his partner, neither of them paying him any heed. He watched as the Dom helped the blonde onto one bench. He also recognized her as a familiar face, though not one he had spoken with before. Everything in him tensed as if ready to spring into action while Bryan strapped her down with the various cuffs and belts, then placed an O-ring in her mouth to keep it open while still preventing her from speaking.

Perhaps part of him was hoping to see Bryan fail, to prove his instincts were correct and that it was not just jealousy talking. Jacob changed position, moving to a better vantage point in time to see Bryan produce a Taser from his pocket. From where he stood, he saw the sub squirming and tugging against her restraints. *Anticipation or fear?*

The gag muffled her first screams. There was no warm-up. Bryan had gone straight for applying the Taser to one butt cheek. The girl now struggled for real, her distorted squeals holding notes of terror. One hand tried to signal but another shock, this time to the arm, caused her to lose muscle control.

It wasn't play. It had gone way past safe territory. Before Bryan could inflict another shock with the Taser, Jacob interceded, Darryl already moving to back him up.

"We're going to ask you to stop." Jacob managed to keep his tone even as he imposed himself between Bryan and the occupied bench. Meanwhile, he saw from the corner of his eye that Darryl was undoing the buckles and straps, a blanket already close by. The girl whimpered as the other Dom released her from her restraints.

"What's this? I've barely done anything. You have no right, Jacob." Red-faced, Bryan pulled himself to full height, but if he was trying to intimidate, it sorely missed the mark. The attempt only made him look like a petulant child.

"Actually, tonight, I'm one of the dungeon monitors and that gives me full right," Jacob said in an almost soothing tone, his voice only growing calmer.

"This is an abuse of power then. You're biased in your judgement." Bryan smirked and turned toward the sub whose O-ring Darryl had just undone. "Tell them, darling. You were enjoying it, weren't you?"

"That's enough."

Erica's voice cut across the dungeon, ringing with command, a scowl on her face. Where she walked in her five-inch stilettos, reverent silence fell. She was one of the two Goddesses of The Playgrounds, after all. As she approached the trio, she turned toward the rest of the crowd. "Please, carry on." The din returned, albeit subdued.

"Mr. Walsh, may I remind you that the dungeon monitors here act with my full authority. Any questions henceforth should be directed to me, not to one of my monitors and certainly not to the submissive involved in the incident."

Erica was the only one Jacob knew who spoke like she wrote. He stood in silence but at attention, his face a mask of professionalism.

"Understood, Mistress Erica." Bryan inclined his head. His eyes flickered over to Jacob then. "May I then file a complaint—at your convenience, of course?"

*The little shit.*

"You may." She nodded toward the exit. "Return tomorrow at two in the afternoon and we will discuss the incident. In the meantime, I will have to ask you to leave the premises pending a full review."

Jacob watched in fascination as Bryan trembled with anger before he finally managed to rein in his temper. Any other reaction would have risked him being banned for life. "Very well. Till tomorrow."

All eyes were on Bryan as he walked past Jacob. In a low voice, almost inaudible, he uttered words meant for Jacob's ears alone, like a classic villain. "This ain't over." With that, he disappeared down the stairs.

"Darryl, take care of the girl, call for backup then come to my office. Jacob, with me." Erica turned and walked away without another glance at either of them. The implication was clear. There was no doubt that both Doms would obey. Still, Jacob had to remind himself that she had a full right as his employer for the night.

With a heavy sigh, he followed. For the nth time, he regretted agreeing to help and wished once more that he were home with Luna instead.

# Chapter Twenty

*Maybe staying at home wasn't such a great idea.*

She had managed to read through two of the last three articles on the list before her overthinking took over, whispered doubts chasing each other like noisy little mice scurrying in her head. With a groan, Luna pushed the chair back and went to refill her mug with tea and honey. It was her third cup already — *or was that fourth?*

What she seemed stuck on was trying to reconcile what Ted had told her with Bryan's apology. Her ex-Dominant had told others she had ghosted him but admitted to her in private that what he'd done had been wrong too. So which was the authentic version to him? Without thought, she took a sip of the tea then quickly put the mug down, wincing and sticking her tongue out. *Ow, hot.*

The turn of the lock drew her attention. The door creaked open and Jacob lumbered in like something out of a horror flick.

Luna rushed to his side and helped him out of his jacket. While he kicked off his shoes, she hung up his jacket and poured him a cup of tea, adding a large dollop of honey. She walked over to the couch, handing him the mug just as he flopped on it, slouching until his head was resting on the back.

"Rough night at The Playgrounds?" She watched as he inhaled the aroma of the tea then took a careful sip, sighing with a mix of pleasure and relief.

"That's one way of putting it." He pushed himself up enough to set the tea down on the coffee table, then patted the empty spot beside him. When Luna sat, he turned to lay his head in her lap.

Well versed in what he needed, Luna began stroking his black locks, running her fingers through them. "Poor Jacob. Want to talk about it?"

There was a pause. Luna wasn't sure if it was hesitation, but she felt Jacob subtly shake his head "Nah. Tell me about your evening."

Jacob didn't need more stress. So, rather than unloading her thoughts and confusion about Bryan's apology, she opted for a safer topic. "Well, I managed two more articles," she started. Questions on those were for another night. Right now she wanted to keep it light for him. "One of them reminded me of a story Lani told me the other day."

"Oh?"

"Yeah. So Lani's been keeping in touch with a few of August's online friends through FetScene." Even after three years, the mention of August always filled her with a myriad of emotions, but talking about him kept his memory alive. It was the least she could do. Luna cleared her throat. "One of them asked Lani a question on the forums and it snowballed from there." Luna peered down at Jacob to see his eyes closed.

"Mmmhmm, I'm listening." His eyes remained closed and she felt the tension slowly draining from his body.

"So, turns out, this friend was unsure about the Dominant who was interested in him, something about the Dom being too pushy. But their kinks seemed to match so well, so..."

Luna trailed off as Jacob's gentle snoring cut in and she watched in silence as his chest rose and fell, his breathing evening out. Whatever had happened must have exhausted him after the stressful week they'd both had. Her lips tugged upward in a fond smile as she continued to stroke his hair, waiting until he fell into a deeper slumber. Minutes ticked by before she was certain he was sleeping deep enough for her to ease herself out from underneath him. With a deft maneuver, she replaced her lap with a nearby pillow and tucked one of the throw blankets over him before she took their mugs to the kitchen to clean up.

Her phone buzzed on the kitchen counter. Wondering who it was, she peered at the screen as she dried her hands.

*Hey, it's Bryan. I didn't see you tonight. Are you okay?*

Luna nearly dropped the dishrag. For a second, she wondered how the hell Bryan even had her number. Had he kept it after all those years?

She continued to stare at her phone as if it had grown arms and legs. Actually, given the Transformers movies, that was more believable than what was happening.

*What to say?* Luna picked up her phone, still wary, and typed back a quick message.

*Yeah, I'm good. Just tired from practice.*

Little white lies.

*Okay, good. I hit you with some heavy stuff today, but I needed to say it.*

*What the hell do you say to that?* Luckily it seemed like she didn't need to reply.

*Oh, by the way, can you let Jacob know no hard feelings? It's probably all just a misunderstanding.*

What? Luna's gaze traveled over to Jacob, watching as he turned slightly on his side and mumbled.

*Yeah sure.*

*Cool. See you Monday.*

Luna ran a hand over her face. How was she supposed to face Bryan on Monday?

It was not her place to push to find out what had happened. On some level, she didn't want to find out, but she had to deliver the message or it would upset Jacob if he found out another way. Tomorrow, she decided. Let him sleep in peace.

Still, her mind would not cease spinning in a gazillion directions, the mice returning with their chittering at full force. Filled with sudden restless energy, she knew that there was no way she could sleep.

*Well, only one thing to do.*

She rolled up her sleeves, retrieved her cleaning supplies and started scrubbing the counter.

\* \* \* \*

"Luna."

A gentle shaking of her shoulders brought her back to semi-consciousness. With a Herculean effort, she peeled her eyes open and lifted her head from her arms. She groaned, bright light piercing her eyes, and grew aware of every ache and muscle cramp permeating her body.

"Come on, little one." There was a hint of command in the voice. It was enough to push her to full consciousness. She sat up and looked around her.

At some point, after all the cleaning and scrubbing, she must have sat to just rest her eyes for a moment, then fallen fast asleep. Luna attempted to move her arms and winced at the sensation of ants crawling up and down them. *Great.*

"Um-m… good morning?" She could hear her own hesitation in her voice.

As he gazed upon her, Jacob sighed. "What am I going to do with you, Luna?" When she ducked her head a little, he leaned down then kissed her forehead. "Good morning."

Luna closed her eyes to enjoy the simple yet intimate gesture of his lips against her skin.

"Why don't you go soak in the bathtub. Considering the look of this place and how you slept, you must be sore."

She brightened and, when Jacob smiled, she jumped up and threw her arms around him, all the aches forgotten.

He hugged her back and chuckled. "Go on. You deserve it."

Luna ignored her body's protests as she tilted her head back only to close the distance and press her lips against his in a light kiss.

"Mmm-m, you taste like honey." He rubbed his thumb against her lower lip. "I'm a lucky man."

Her cheeks heated at the compliment before one of their phones on the dining table suddenly buzzed. The memory of messages from last night came rushing back. Inside she wailed, clinging to the last shreds of their morning contentment. A voice inside her was screaming to not do it. She told it to shut up.

"Jacob." She inhaled once more deeply before plowing ahead. "I got a message last night from Bryan. He said to tell you that it's just a misunderstanding and no hard feelings." The words rushed out, one tumbling after another, barely coherent.

She watched as Jacob tensed, every muscle of his stiffening. The voice inside her was now whining a loud "why".

"I see."

Luna reached up, brushing his arms with her fingertips. "Jacob, I…" She wasn't sure what she was going to say, just that she needed to comfort him, to let him know that she was still here and that she still served him. And that she was worried.

"It's okay. Thank you for the message." His body remained tense, but he mustered a smile for her. "Don't worry about it, 'kay? Go enjoy your bath." Jacob shifted and gave her a little swat on the bum.

She squealed in surprise. Although she knew it was a distraction, she let it go nonetheless. "Okay okay!" Spinning around, she did as she had been told, but as she left for the bathroom, she cast one last glance over her shoulder. Jacob was frowning again, his face drawn as he grabbed his phone.

As if realizing she was still there, he looked up and raised an eyebrow at her. She held her hands up in surrender and resumed her walk to the master bedroom that would lead to the bathroom with the tub. But she knew that no amount of soaking would wash away the anxiety that had notched up since seeing Jacob's reaction. And, above all, a single question hovered in the forefront of her thoughts.

*Why won't he tell me what is going on?*

# Chapter Twenty-One

"Good morning, Erica." Jacob held his phone to his ear, each word slow while his tone remained carefully neutral. He stood still, both feet planted to the hardwood floors.

"Good morning. I thought we'd best discuss things over the phone rather than leaving such matters to text." He could almost see her in his mind, her legs crossed, head held high and displaying a slightly detached air. Those that didn't know her would think her haughty.

"Of course, I appreciate the call."

"I have reviewed your and Darryl's reports and questioned the submissive myself. By the way, she is grateful for you stepping in and sends you her thanks."

He exhaled, letting out a breath he hadn't realized he'd been holding.

"Are you still there, Jacob?"

"Yeah, I'm here."

"Good. Unfortunately, the submissive is unwilling to file an official complaint, stating that it was also her fault for not being clear with her limits."

*What is with Bryan that make subs want to protect him with shitty excuses?* "With all due respect, Erica, Bryan had rendered the sub unable to speak her safe word or even make the hand signal. She's hardly the one to be blamed." Jacob couldn't quite keep the growl out of his voice.

"Yes, so you reported last night. However, my one unbiased monitor did not witness it...which brings us to the second reason I called."

Jacob winced, switching the phone to the other hand and shifting his weight from one foot to another. *Here it comes.*

"Darryl informed me of your earlier...interactions with Bryan. As your sometimes boss, I don't give a rat's ass about what's going on in your personal life. But when it affects The Playgrounds, it becomes my business." Her voice took on a lower, almost growly pitch and Jacob's eyes widened in shock. Erica rarely swore.

"What were you thinking, Jacob? You know better than this."

*Tread carefully*, his gut told him. "I know, Erica." He paused and gulped as if he could physically swallow his pride. "I'm sorry."

"Because of your actions, I am losing a source of reliable help for at least a month." He knew she was referring to him and was about to reply when he heard Erica's voice uncharacteristically soften with her next words. "Look... I don't know what's going on between Luna, you and Bryan, but from what little Darryl and I can figure out, if you don't do something soon, you will lose her. And you would regret that more than you can even imagine."

Jacob glanced at the door that led to Luna in the bathroom, and his hand tightened around the phone. First Lani, now Erica. Were all the female Dominants trying to gang up on him? "Thanks, Erica. I'll figure out something." A sudden absurd hope welled in his chest. "So, what'll happen to Bryan?"

Erica sighed. "He'll get a talking to and I'll be putting him on probation, which will take away access to any private rooms. Now go mind your own and let me deal with mine...or I may just steal Luna from you myself."

He raised his eyebrow, lips tugging upward as he relaxed. "Dominique may not like that."

A titter of laughter followed. "She may if it's Luna." He heard a slight shuffle in the background, probably Erica moving stacks of paperwork around. "Have a good day, Jacob."

"You too, Erica."

He hung up and sighed in relief. Erica was right about one thing. It was time to mind his own. And right now, that meant a deliciously naked pet in his bathtub.

When he cracked the bathroom door open and poked his head in as silently as he could, he found her submerged. Only her shoulders, knees and the tops of her breasts broke through the surface of the water while she had her head tilted back, her eyes closed, her body relaxed His cock stirred in his jeans and he adjusted himself as subtly as possible.

Luna must have been almost asleep, since she made no move as he slipped into the bathroom. No surprise there, considering how clean his place was and how awkwardly she had slept.

"Luna," he murmured her name under his breath even as he skimmed his fingers over one exposed knee. Rather than waking, she moaned and parted her legs.

*So wonderfully responsive.*

He lowered to his knees and moved his hand up along her leg, sinking deeper into the tub and closer to her sex. A heat radiated from there that had nothing to do with the temperature of the water.

Luna raised a hand idly to brush against her nipple, just barely under the surface of the water. "Mmm-m, Jacob." His name was a breath of desire on her lips as her eyes half-opened, glazed with dreams still. Dreams of him, he hoped.

"Hello, sweetheart." He grinned in anticipation as he cupped her sex, finding it slick with arousal, the feel of her wetness distinctively different from the surrounding water.

A wide, lazy smile spread across her lips as she thrust her hips against his hand. Bathtub sex could be dangerous, but play? Play was always welcomed, and he knew her to be most receptive while in a bath. She was already open for him, so he had no trouble parting her folds to slip his middle finger in to tap lightly against the emerging nub that was her clit.

She whimpered, a shudder passing through her body such that the water rippled around her. At that rate, she would not last long. He eased off, shifting his hand back up to her stomach, then farther up to one breast.

"No-o," Luna protested as he left her lower body now unattended. He watched in fascination as her stomach tightened and she clenched her legs together in an attempt to find relief.

"Legs open. Keep your hands on the sides of the tub. Do not move them." His commands came accompanied by his crooked grin. Pure delight crashed against a deeper unnamed emotion as he watched her obey, despite her clear desire to touch herself.

"Good girl." He resumed his course, drawing wide circles with his middle finger around but never touching her areola. She whimpered again, this time full of want as she tried to maneuver so that his finger would brush her nipple. Chuckling, he gave her breast a light slap—not enough to hurt, just enough to warn her. "Stay still." He leaned forward, his voice dropping to a whisper. "Treats come to pets who wait."

Out of the corner of his eye, he noticed her fingers curling to grip the sides of the tub tighter. That control, that will to obey, to please despite her every instinct to seek her own pleasure, was what made her such a precious submissive and was what called to every dominant instinct in him. Jacob moved his hand across, teasing the other breast, watching as her nipples hardened. He wanted nothing more than to wrap his lips around each one, to tease them with his tongue. *Maybe later. Round two.*

He shifted his hand to cup one breast, kneading with gentle pressure. She closed her eyes with a groan as she relaxed at the different type of pleasure. Just as she let her guard down, he rubbed the pad of his thumb over her nipple in quick circular motions.

Her eyes flew open and her entire body tensed. Unable to help herself, she rocked her hips as if seeking something to fill her.

*God, she's so sensitive I can hold her on the edge just by playing with her nipples.*

Jacob took her hand in his and brought it to her breast. "Play with yourself," he instructed and watched as she wasted no time in teasing and pinching her nipple.

A more primal part of him wanted to lift her out of the bathtub and fuck her hard right then and there but he had more control than that.

He left her to tend to her own nipples and focused instead on her lower body. This time, he sank both of his hands into the water between her parted legs. Like a man on a mission, he dipped one finger into her core, then another, crooking to press against her G-spot. He parted her farther with deft fingers then began a relentless assault on her clit, flicking it back and forth.

He watched as her stomach clenched immediately and, unbidden, a torrent of words spilled forth. "Please, Jacob, please, I can't hold it. Please let me come. Oh God, I'm going to come. I can't hold on."

He had a moment of temptation to not allow her to come, of watching her struggle to hold back, but he never made a habit of setting her up for failure.

"Come."

It took less than ten seconds before a scream of ecstasy tore through her throat. Her body bucked and he had to struggle to keep his position. Water sloshed everywhere, soaking his clothes, but he paid it no heed as he worked through her orgasm, allowing her to ride his fingers. He slowed his movements as she came down from the climax, but instead of stopping and withdrawing, just as she started relaxing, he sped up again, shifting to pinch her over-sensitive clit between two fingers.

She flew to grip the sides of the tub as her second orgasm, even harder than the first, crashed into her, her body thrashing and writhing in its glory. She was always beautiful, but in that moment, she was the epitome of desire.

He brought her down slowly until she lay limply in the cooling water. As he withdrew his fingers, she let out a low groan and squeezed her legs together. He chuckled. "My insatiable little pet."

When they had first started playing, it had pleased him to discover both her sensitivity and her capacity for multiple orgasms. Over the years, he had perfected taking advantage of such qualities to keep both of them more than satisfied in bed.

Luna pouted at him, more playful than shy now. "You're wet. Take your clothes off," she cooed.

Jacob raised a brow as he stood. "Yes, I'm sure that's the only reason you want me to strip."

She rose from of the tub, rivulets of water cascading down her body. "Of course, I wouldn't want you catching a cold," she replied, sniffing delicately as she stepped out and over, then took a towel to wrap around herself.

He almost took his turn pouting, mourning the loss of the view. But instead, he laughed, a wonderful belly laugh that drained away the tension of the morning. Coming to stand behind her, he wrapped his arms around her from behind and kissed the top of her head. "Come on. Let's head out to the bedroom and I'll see what I can do about these clothes and that appetite of yours."

# Chapter Twenty-Two

Luna held the door of the hotel room open with her butt, dragged her suitcase through, then let the door fall shut behind her. If she were to be honest with herself, she had been dreading the three-day trip for weeks now, but there was no helping it. There wasn't long before their contract expired, and while Jacob had assured her before that he wouldn't just abandon her on the day of, Luna still wanted to spend the remaining time with him. But her career was important to her too.

At least the conference was being held in a decent hotel and it was a pleasant change of pace from the daily humdrum of the office. She surveyed her room then hauled her baggage up onto the luggage rack before plopping down on the bed.

Normally, they wouldn't schedule going to conferences in the middle of a project, but this was the biggest one in their field and it was only held once every two years. So, Joanna had negotiated and built in contingency time within the project timeline so that they could all go. She really was a wonderful manager.

Luna reached into her jacket pocket and fished out her phone to type a quick message to Jacob.

*Just checked into the hotel. Miss you already.*

It only took half a minute before the reply came. Her lips curved upward as her heart swelled.

*Good. Miss you too. Now go enjoy yourself.*

A knock on the door startled her. "Hey, Luna, you ready? Let's go grab a bite." Luna recognized Joanna's voice from the other side.

"Coming!" *Wallet, check. Phone, check.* Unpacking could wait until she got back. She crossed the room, grabbed her keycard and opened the door. "Where to?"

Joanna checked her phone then flashed her a smile. As a much older woman, Joanna sometimes liked to 'mom' her, and making sure she ate on these trips was a regular gesture for her. "Well, I think the guys are already downstairs. Let's go see if we can find them."

And that was how they found themselves in the hotel's lounge, huddled over a small table with Scott, Prakash and Jung, the three other guys who made up their contingent. By the time they were halfway through the food, the place had filled up with other conference-goers arriving, and despite the din, Luna found herself enjoying the easy camaraderie among her co-workers. Jacob was right. She should just relax and enjoy herself.

"Well, if it isn't my favorite content strategist."

Luna looked up, her mouth full of food, and almost choked as she tried to swallow too fast. There stood Bryan. Everyone else looked frazzled from travel to the conference, but him? He looked picture-perfect, not a single strand of hair out of place. *Of course.*

She had expected that he was going to be there, so why was she so surprised?

*Breathe.* She grabbed her water and pounded her chest, even as Joanna rose from her seat and extended a hand toward Bryan.

"I'm Joanna. I believe we met at the project kick off?"

At that moment, she couldn't have loved her boss more.

While Joanna did her play-nice-with-the-client song and dance, introducing Bryan to the other guys, Luna focused on recovering. The guys were also putting on their best behavior and made small talk until she could stand up to give Bryan a proper greeting. She had never been more grateful for their presence.

When she did stand at last and extended a hand to him for shaking, he reached out to pull her into a hug instead. Luna forced herself to relax. *It's a hug, right? God damn it. No big deal.* But the physical proximity only reminded her of his offer at the coffee shop—an offer she still hadn't figured out how to tell Jacob about.

"Join us," Scott offered, still looking up at Bryan. Luna wished she was sitting down next to Scott for the sole purpose of kicking him under the table. The last thing she wanted right now was for Bryan to join them.

"Thanks for the offer, but I still have to find my own guys. Let's meet up some time later?"

"Yeah, sounds good."

Luna gave Bryan a brief smile and a slight wave, all the while trying to not look too relieved. He nodded to her with a last grin then turned and left.

"What was that about?" Prakash leaned in, his eyes lighting up with anticipation. The other guys bowed their heads closer and all of a sudden, Luna found herself the target of some very unwanted attention.

"We've just been working well together," she stammered and inwardly cringed. That sounded feeble, even to her own ears.

"All right, all right, guys, leave Luna alone. Yeesh, you guys gossip like a couple of old ladies." Joanna waved them back, exerting her authority as the most senior member there.

Luna really did love her boss, and she mouthed a silent 'thank you' in her direction.

Chastised, they shifted to discussing what sessions they were each planning to attend, coordinating, so that there was as little overlap as possible. Little by little, caught up in the excitement of planning, thoughts of Bryan faded from her mind.

By the time she was dragging herself back upstairs, she was dead on her feet, even though it was just early evening. As she eased back on to the queen-sized bed, she stared at the evil that was her suitcase. There was at least one dress that needed to be hung up for the gala dinner the next night, but right now, all she wanted to do was veg in front of the TV. With her mind emptied of thoughts, she picked up the remote and began channel surfing.

The rest didn't last long, as it wasn't in her nature to sit still when there were things to do. After a sufficient amount of sitting, she began to putter, opening up her suitcase to exchange what she was wearing with a tank top and yoga pants that acted as PJs. The dress came out next, a sleek black thing that emphasized what subtle curves she had then flared out at the hips. She eyed the dress with a wistful smile, wishing Jacob were here to see her in it—or help her into it...or strip it off her.

And Jacob had forbidden her to play with herself for the next three days. *Damn that evil man.*

On a whim, she grabbed her phone.

*What're you up to?*

God, she sounded clingy. She felt clingy. But he always said that if she were being too clingy, he would tell her up front and so far, he had said nothing.

*TV. Syfy is doing a rerun of the first Avengers movie.*

Luna perked up and grabbed the remote. Most hotels didn't carry specialty channels, but sometimes, if she were lucky... *Yes!* She grabbed her phone and leaned back to type a message back.

*Sweet! Watching it now.*

*Yeah? Hey, think they'll ever do an Avengers crossover with Deadpool?*

Luna shifted for a moment to pull the cover off the bed before snuggling into the nest of pillows. If she pretended hard enough, she could almost picture Jacob there with her. In the past, on quiet nights, they would snuggle in with a movie and make each other laugh with funny commentary. She smiled at the fond memory of the first time they'd cuddled. It had been over a rerun of *Hellboy* when Jacob had insisted on sharing blankets. The smile, however, soon faded as she realized that it'd been a while. But at least it was one way to make up for lost time.

*Nah. They'd have to make it rated R.*

*They did it with Logan.*

*Yeah, but that was the swan song.*

*They can always make Deadpool more PG.*

*Can you imagine him agreeing to that?*

*If it means beating his rival in the box office, maybe? You've seen their rivalry on Twitter.*

Okay, so they were both huge Marvel nerds. Luna grinned as she imagined Jacob only half paying attention to the TV screen now. That was certainly the case on her end. It was a fortunate thing that they had both seen the movie at least a dozen times.

Their conversation went on, text messages flying back and forth. It helped her feel a little less lonely.

What was she going to do at the end of their contract when it all disappeared?

Luna paused, her fingers hovering over the on-screen keyboard of her phone, midway through a reply. She had no doubt that they would remain friends, but she could never text him with such casual ease again, especially if he took on another sub to train.

That thought pricked her heart, enough that she had to hold back sudden tears. Picturing someone else exchanging texts with Jacob the same way was going to tear her apart. Her hands trembled of their own accord and she wiped one eye with the heel of her palm, only to drop the phone on to the bed.

A traitorous whisper reminded her of Bryan's offer. Would it still hurt as much if there was someone else she would go to? It might not have been the best experience before, but perhaps he'd changed. She certainly had. She was stronger now. She knew how to draw boundaries.

No. Regardless, she would not use him as some rebound replacement. It wouldn't be fair to him, even if he had offered.

*But he* did *offer.*

"Stop it!" she yelled out and waved a hand in front of her face as if it would brush all the thoughts away — thoughts she hated herself for thinking.

*I'm fine. I will be fine.*

She picked up the phone to text back.

*Act normal. I can do that over text at least.*

She sank deeper into the pillows, determined all the more to live in the moment. And for now, that meant pretending that there would be a future for her and Jacob.

# Chapter Twenty-Three

Luna cursed herself for waking up so late. Jacob had been the first one last night to realize it was already early morning when he'd virtually herded her to bed. But that had only been a few hours before, so she'd ended up sleeping in despite the alarms and missed the free breakfast altogether.

*Breakfast. Coffee.* Luna mourned.

She scanned the room that was rapidly filling up. Rows upon rows of hotel chairs huddled close together to fill the room to capacity. Up front, the speaker of the morning, the warmup before the keynote, was taking a sip of water, waiting for everyone to get settled. Silence, punctuated with indistinct short murmurs, filled the room. No one was up for conversation as most of them were still strangers to each other for now. That was always the case for the first morning of the conference.

*Oh, empty seat!* Luna dove into the crowd and, using her more diminutive form to her advantage, threaded her way until she claimed the last perfect seat in the middle. It was not so far that she couldn't see the projected slides but not too close that if she had to check her phone, it would be that obvious.

As she took off her messenger bag, she slid into her seat with a sigh of relief and went through her mental checklist—notebook and pen out, phone on silent. Once she was settled, she turned to study her surroundings. To her left, more men and women were hovering along the sides, some smiling and waving as they spotted their colleagues. The woman next to her was typing furiously on her phone. On her right... *No, I did not... Oh God, no...What should I do?* If she got up now, it would be too obvious. But if she didn't say something, it would be even more awkward later.

*Act cool.*

"Oh hey, good morning." *Friendly smile, friendly smile.*

"Oh wow. Hi, Luna. How are you this morning?" Bryan turned to face her, giving her his full attention as he smiled.

Luna barely noticed but instead, stared at the plate of muffin and fruit Bryan held in one hand and his cup of coffee in the other. She bit her lips hard to keep a whimper from escaping.

"Let me guess. You missed breakfast." It wasn't a question.

Luna flushed when she realized he had caught her staring, but she managed a small nod. Greeting him had taken all her courage and now she was left rather tongue-tied.

"Here, take this." Bryan offered the plate to her.

"Oh no," Luna found her voice and shook her head. "I can't take your food. What about you?"

He chuckled and shook his head. "This is technically my second helping, and trust me, I don't need it."

Luna narrowed her eyes in skepticism. There wasn't an ounce of fat on him, so she had no idea what he was talking about. As if catching her staring once more, Bryan straightened and winked at her.

"Let's get started!" The speaker clapped his hands together and beamed at the room. He was way too enthusiastic for so early in the morning. Right on cue, the lights dimmed.

"Go on. Take it," Bryan's voice dropped to a whisper.

Her hunger won out. She tucked the notebook away, took the plate and mouthed a 'thank you'. For the rest of the pre-opening session, she managed to stay awake and keep her stomach from growling as she nibbled on the food.

When the panel ended at last and the lights came back on, Luna turned to give Bryan a genuine smile. "Thank you, you're a lifesaver."

"Hmm-m, if I saved your life, does that mean I'm responsible for you now?"

Luna froze. In any normal circumstances, it would be a natural flirty comment. Maybe a little cheesy, but combined with his almost puppy-like expression, it would be kind of cute. But in their world, responsibility for someone took on a whole new meaning.

"Relax. It's just a joke." Bryan smirked and patted her shoulder.

When Luna didn't reply, his smile faded. "Hey, hey, hey." He leaned down to catch her eyes. "I'm sorry if I made you uncomfortable. I'll tone it down, okay?"

Luna nodded. His comment had stirred something uncomfortable in her. Once, a long time ago, it would have had her swooning at his feet. She had imagined a future with him where she would serve and he would take care of her in return. *So naïve.* Was he stirring up old feelings or was she just lonely and sad about Jacob?

"Come on. Get your stuff and let's head to the keynote. Apparently the speaker they've got lined up this year is really good."

Her body moved to obey before her mind could register his words. Still caught up in her troubling thoughts, she allowed Bryan to steer her toward the large room set up for the keynote address. They arrived just as the session started and soon Luna was able to focus on the speaker as her inner thoughts quieted.

The keynote speaker was talented! As a well-known female comedian, she had the crowd in stitches as she talked about storytelling and the challenges of finding humor in the mundane every day. Luna's earlier unease melted away as she laughed so hard tears beaded in the corners of her eyes. Beside her, Bryan's own laughter rumbled deep in his chest, and from time to time, they beamed at each other, just two colleagues enjoying an entertaining talk.

True to his word, he kept his flirting to a minimum for the rest of the day. They hung out at panels they attended together and made promises to meet up after ones they didn't. Bryan was easier to hang out with than she had expected, was a good listener and was filled with hilarious stories about his various projects. With each anecdote they told each other, each laugh they shared, each piece of industry gossip they whispered conspiratorially, her morning worries faded bit by bit. For the first time, perhaps ever, she began to grow more comfortable around him.

"So, what's your plan for dinner?" Bryan asked after the last panel for the day.

"Ah, I was going to head out with the gang at work. You?"

A shadow fell across Bryan's face, but it passed before Luna could ascertain that she wasn't imagining it. Instead he pouted, his shoulders slumping. "My work mates here are all local, so they're going home to their families. Alas, I'm alone and abandoned!" Bryan raised a hand to his forehead and rolled his eyes.

Luna giggled, shaking her head at his over-dramatization.

"Oh hey, there you are!" Luna turned as Scott approached, Jung in tow. "Come on. Joanna and Prakash are waiting in the lobby. Let's get going. I'm starving." It was only as they got closer that Scott realized who she was standing with. "Hey, Bryan, how's it going?"

"Hi, Bryan," Jung echoed.

"Good! Good to see you both again." Bryan shifted, positioning himself just behind Luna. She could feel the heat radiating from him, growing aware of how he towered over her. It was so very much like how Jacob liked to stand with her when they talked with others at the club. She stamped that comparison out of her mind.

"Nice to see you too, man," Scott looked at Bryan, then at Luna, then back up again. "Hey, we're heading out for dinner. Want to join us?"

Bryan grinned down at Luna, then nodded. "Sure, I was just bemoaning to Luna that I was being abandoned."

Luna's laugh came out a little shakier than she would have liked. As she followed Jung and Scott, she couldn't help but wonder what her co-workers had thought when they had seen her with Bryan. All sorts of awkward scenarios started playing out in her head.

"Relax." Bryan leaned down ever so slightly to whisper in her ear. She inhaled and exhaled, her mind picturing a sea of blue. She was really trying to, and she kept up with the effort as they joined the rest of the group and made their way to a restaurant.

Halfway through dinner, it no longer took any conscious effort. Bryan's charisma carried them through the meal such that the feared awkwardness never came. Time flew way faster than she expected and soon, they were back at the hotel.

Joanna and Jung both excused themselves, calling it a night. Prakash and Scott wandered off, deciding to check out the social mingle that was happening where the keynote had been held in the morning. All of a sudden, Luna found herself alone with Bryan.

"You calling it a night?"

Luna nodded. "I stayed up too late last night. I figured an early night so I don't miss breakfast would be a good idea."

"Why don't I walk you back to your room?" Bryan placed a hand on her shoulder. Over the course of the day, she had gotten used to his brief touches and gestures, so much so that she barely noticed.

"Sure." Luna gave a slight shrug and jammed her hands into her pockets to stop fidgeting. She didn't wait but started walking instead. Still, Bryan kept pace with her easily enough.

"I'm glad we got to hang out together."

She tilted her head back at his words, only to realize that he was keeping his gaze forward. Puzzled, she peered at him a little closer. Was that a shade of pink beneath that tanned complexion? She looked away, not wanting to be caught staring.

It took a few minutes before Luna realized she owed him a reply. "Me too." The words came out weak and small, but she remembered to breathe, then tried again. "I have to admit, I was really nervous, running into you again." A rueful smile graced her lips.

Their conversation paused as they joined the crowd in the elevator. The silence, heavy with words still to be spoken, hung between them until they were alone once more in the hall of her room's floor.

"I'm sorry if I made you nervous the first time. As a Dom in a new area, it's important to establish yourself right away." Luna had never heard Bryan explain himself before and maybe it was a sign that he had changed.

"I get it," she cut in, a little quicker than she intended. "Today was good. I'm glad I got to know you in a more…vanilla setting."

He chuckled at that, and as they arrived in front of her room, they turned to face each other. "Well, I can understand that. I hope after today, you are more comfortable with me and see that we can be good together."

He moved to tuck a strand of her hair behind her ear, the gesture more intimate than she expected or was ready for. "If you'd rather be friends, I'll respect that, but I won't lie and say that I won't be disappointed. I'd like it if you'd give my offer some serious consideration."

Luna, pinned down by his gaze, could only nod as he leaned forward and whispered in her ear. "Good girl." Then he shifted and placed a chaste kiss on her forehead. "Goodnight, doll."

She stared as he walked away, rooted to the spot, the warmth of his lips still lingering on her skin. Why did things have to get so complicated?

The theme song from *Deadpool 2* suddenly blared from her phone. It set her into a sudden flurry of motion as she tried to fish her phone out of her messenger bag at the same time as trying to get her room door opened. The ringtone was the latest in a long line of inside jokes with Jacob.

"Jacob?" Luna answered and cradled her phone as she tried to work the hotel keycard into its slot.

"Hi, sweetheart. How are you?"

"I'm okay!" It was good to hear his voice as it cleared away the fog of confusion in her head. She pushed the heavy door open and entered her hotel room. Only then did she realize. "Sorry I haven't texted all day. It's been pretty crazy."

"Yeah? Want to tell me about it?" There was some clanging in the background from his end. *Is he doing some late-night baking again?*

She dropped off her messenger bag and slipped off her jacket, pausing for a moment to consider her next words.

*Omission is as bad as a lie.*

"Well, actually, I spent most of the day with Bryan. It turned out we were going to a lot of the same panels."

Silence. Luna pulled her phone back to check if the line had cut out. When her phone confirmed that they were still connected, she brought it back to her ear. "Jacob?"

A heavy sigh from the other side greeted her ear. When he spoke again, his words became more measured. "How do you feel about it?"

Wasn't that the million-dollar question that she'd had at the back of her mind all day? Now it was her turn to sigh, her shoulders slumping as she fell onto the bed, lying flat on her back. "It was awkward at first," she admitted. "But it wasn't as bad as I imagined it would be."

"I see."

Another pause. Luna chewed a nail, then forced her hand down when she realized what she was doing.

"Did he try anything?"

Why would he even ask that? Was there something Jacob knew that she didn't — or was it just because of their past? Was it some green-eyed monster talking? Jacob had not been acting like himself whenever anyone mentioned Bryan, and something in her grew suspicious.

But she had to say something. Luna sat up and hunched over as she shifted to perch on the edge of the bed.

"No. But" — she chose her words with care — "he had made an offer to take me as his. He reiterated it today. When our contract ends…" *Dear God.* She'd said it. She'd said it out loud…those four words that they had both avoided. She did not want to have this conversation over the phone.

She clamped her mouth shut, lest she started babbling.

"I see." Those two words sounded so cold. Jacob suddenly felt like a stranger compared to Bryan's warmth all day. *No. No, I'm Jacob's.*

"And what are your thoughts on his offer?"

Luna burst into tears, big fat ones rolling down her cheek. She didn't trust her voice and when she tried to open her mouth, she hiccupped on the phone with a sob then covered her mouth with her free hand. Jacob shouldn't see her or, rather, hear her that way.

"Luna…" Accompanied by a sigh, his voice warmed with worry.

"I don't want it." The words tumbled from her lips, tripping over each other, her voice almost hysterical. "I hate this. I don't want to consider an offer, any offer. I…I want you… I…I love you." She cringed then. They were words she had promised herself she would never say. It sounded so desperately clingy. She tried to swallow, tried to recover her voice. He was going to disown her right here and now. "I'm sorry. No, forget I said anything. Please." She scrambled to dig herself out. "What Bryan offered is generous and no other Dominants have offered. It's something I think worth —"

"No." Jacob's single word cut her off.

"No?" It came out as a squeak.

"No." Another pause. Luna held her breath.

"I am not going to ignore what you just said. I...don't like Bryan. I don't like the idea of you with anyone else." It was as if Jacob were tasting his own words.

Luna's heart thundered.

"Jacob, what are you saying?" she whispered over the phone, not daring to hope for the intent behind those words.

"I am...not sure yet," Jacob admitted. Never had he sounded so uncertain. "I don't want to do this over the phone. Let's talk when you get back, face-to-face. For real. About the contract, the three-year term and what we want to do next."

"Okay." No, it wasn't okay! She wanted to know *now*!

"Good. We'll talk. Now go to bed, Luna."

*He expects me to be able to sleep after this?* "Okay."

"Goodnight, sweetheart."

"Goodnight, Jacob."

He hung up first. She lingered on until the dead tone came on, then hit the end call button. He didn't want to see her with another Dom. He hadn't said 'I love you' back. He'd said 'we' on next steps. Her mind went into over-analysis mode, examining each word for hints of his heart.

That night, she tossed and turned in bed. Even as she fell into a fitful sleep, a single thought remained. All she wanted was Jacob.

# Chapter Twenty-Four

"Two visits in less than a month?" Lani raised her eyebrow as she re-crossed her legs, readjusted the file folder on her lap, then tapped her pen against it. "Should I be giving Luna a call?"

Jacob growled under his breath but resisted the urge to glare at her. *Pest.* He bit into his own chocolate almond croissant to avoid having to talk. It bought him time to compose his thoughts and to exercise control of his emotions.

Since the previous night, he had oscillated between anger, confusion and an odd sense of satisfaction, coupled with some other emotion he couldn't quite put a finger on yet. He needed to sort it out before Luna came home so that he would be ready to lead them both out of such a tangled web of complications and unknowns.

With a soft sigh, Lani leaned forward, her hazel eyes warm with compassion. "Jacob, I can't help if you don't talk to me. And you know both you and Luna are dear friends."

Jacob set his food aside. By the time he spoke, he had a tight enough rein on his temper that his words came out even, neutral. "Bryan offered to be Luna's Dom after our contract ends." Across from him, Lani inhaled, but he continued on before she could comment. "He asked earlier. I think I know when, but that doesn't matter. What matters is that Luna mentioned it last night when I called her and she said Bryan had reiterated the offer yesterday."

"Wait! Isn't Luna away at a conference right now?" There was more than casual interest in Lani's tone.

"Yeah. It looks like Bryan's there too." Jacob shrugged, and it was all he could do to keep his rage back. "Not surprising, considering they're in the same field. But no, it's not a pleasant feeling."

Lani nodded. Jacob could see her tensing by her stiff shoulders.

"I told Luna as much. I told her I didn't want to see her with any other Dom."

"Oh my," Lani breathed out the words, her lips parting as she straightened. It was the closest he'd ever seen to Lani losing composure. *Great.*

"Before you ask, we didn't get much further in the conversation. I sent her to bed and said we'd talk when she gets back."

Lani's jaw dropped. Okay, now she truly had lost composure. Jacob steeled himself and resisted the urge to rub his face, despite already having raised his hand. He switched course and grabbed his coffee instead, taking a slow sip. *What the hell did I say now that made her react that way?* It had been a long time since he'd been so lost with how to proceed. Each step seemed to only propel him on to more and more shaky ground.

"You expected the girl to sleep after you dropped a bomb on her like that?" Lani's voice hit almost a full octave higher than normal, her eyes wide with shock.

He swallowed the coffee and leveled her a stare of his own, his chin tilting upward ever so slightly in challenge. "She seemed accepting of it. We said goodnight."

Lani cleared her throat and shifted in her seat, smoothing her skirt. "You know Luna would abide by any call you make and would never tell you the effect it'd have on her if she knew it would worry you."

*Damn it.* Lani was right. Usually he was sensitive enough to her needs that it didn't matter. Lately, however, everything seemed off-kilter, as if the world had tilted at a forty-five-degree angle and he no longer knew which way was up and which was down.

He shifted as well to brace his elbows on his thighs and steepled his fingers. "I need to prepare for her return. And I need a sounding board to sort myself out so I can be what she needs when she gets back."

"Of course," she answered with an incline of her head as their eyes met. The dynamics between them had always been interesting, two Dominants with the same interests and similar styles.

"I need to know two things. One, how can I figure out whether I can live with being a more permanent Dominant without being a trainer. How do I reconcile the need to grow and learn with the permanence of a longer relationship? Secondly, how can I be sure that what I feel for Luna is not just a product of jealousy or possessiveness because someone else wants her?"

To the rest of the world, he was a serial dater, three years at a time. Some thought he had commitment phobia. It appeared that there was an ounce of truth to it.

"Jacob." Lani set the folder down on the coffee table. "Let's deal with the first question by letting me ask you a question. How do you know if you would last with someone for three years and grow within that time?"

He pursed his lips. It was an easy question to answer. "I make sure we are compatible before we enter into a contract. After that, the contract binds us. For better or worse, we choose to abide by the contract."

"Precisely. The word is 'choice'." Lani leaned back, relaxing now that they had returned to her area of expertise. "A r

elationship, any relationship, is always a choice. Commitment is not some magical chemistry. It's a choice between two people to put in the work to stay together, to grow together. Three years or longer makes no difference."

Jacob slumped against the couch, blinking in surprise. He had never thought of it that way before — that three years, five years or longer wasn't as big a difference as he thought. In his mind, he had always compartmentalized. "What about the growth as a Dominant? As a submissive?"

She smiled and tilted her head to one side. "A relationship with a person is not like a relationship with a job. What makes you think that Luna won't change and continue to challenge you?" She chuckled. "Has she not in the last few weeks in ways you never would have imagined?"

Had he been looking at it all wrong? When put so simply...

"Okay, why Luna?"

"Why not?" Lani shrugged a little. "Only you can answer that for yourself. Maybe she pushes you the right way. Maybe" — Lani winked at him — "you're getting old and want to nest."

Sounds of the *pitter patter* of little feet and small giggles reverberated through his mind. What would it be like to have a baby girl with Luna? He could almost see it in his mind's eye. Hadn't he wished, all those nights ago, that Luna had gotten pregnant? It would take the decision out of his hands.

"*Shit.*"

"Oh my," Lani gasped, hand half covering her mouth, and it was only then did Jacob realized he had sworn out loud. "It seems I've hit a nerve."

"Pest," he muttered under his breath and received only a snicker in response. Jacob narrowed his eyes when he realized that Lani's shoulders were shaking as she struggled to suppress a fit of laughter. The woman was going to lord it over him for days to come.

"Okay, in all seriousness, as for your second question, let me ask you this." Lani leaned in and rested her elbow on her knee, her chin on her wrist as she grew serious again. "How would you feel if *I* took Luna?"

Jacob surged forward in one swift motion, standing to tower over Lani, his fists clenched before he realized what he had done. He blinked as Lani only tilted her head back to observe him, not one bit frightened.

"Well, we can safely say that it has nothing to do with Bryan." She sat back and waved her hand in the air, brushing the tension away "Relax, Jacob. I'm not taking Luna away from you."

With conscious effort, Jacob unclenched his jaw and bent his stiff knees to take a seat. But since he was still tense, he remained on the edge of the couch.

"And if Luna didn't come home after the conference. Say work required her to move?"

Jacob tried to imagine never seeing her eyes lit up in delight at the food he cooked, tried to imagine no more cuddling with her watching a movie, no longer waking up to the smell of the coconut shampoo from her hair, to never hear her moan his name in pleasure. He tried to replace her face with another sub's.

It felt empty and lonely.

There must have been some expression on his face that made Lani rise from her seat to circle around the table until she stood next to him. When he turned, barely needing to look up to meet her eyes, she patted his shoulder. "I think you have your answer. Now go end the torture you're putting the girl through."

Jacob was still miffed when he got back to the sea of cubicle farms that made up his office. Even as he unlocked his computer and pulled up the files he needed for the afternoon's task, his mind kept wandering. He was not torturing Luna, not on purpose. He just needed the time to sort out his emotions, many foreign to him until now. And now that they were sorted, he just had to wait until she got home. What he needed to do was prepare for the homecoming. Perhaps he should ready a dessert. Apple pie or tiramisu? Both were Luna's favorites.

"Hey, Jacob." He looked up from his desk to see Ben hanging over the cubicle wall. "A couple of guys and I are grabbing some drinks tonight. Want in?"

Well, what else was he going to do tonight?" "Yeah sure."

"Cool."

Drinks after work turned out to be five guys at the closest bar. Unfortunately, the bar also turned into a club at night and since it was Friday, others were trickling in. The lights dimmed and staff began to clear away tables to prepare for the dance floor. A DJ was setting up in the corner, getting ready to replace the sounds of the top forties — with what, Jacob didn't want to find out. Although Jacob was enjoying the beer, he wasn't enjoying the atmosphere in particular.

"Mr. Dakota, imagine running into you here!"

Jacob winced as he recognized the voice. He didn't need to see her twice in one day, especially in front of his co-workers with speculative glints in their eyes. While inwardly he braced himself, he rolled his eyes and shook his head at them before he turned to give a polite nod. "Hi, Ophelia."

Her smile was a little too bright, her eyes too calculating as she leaned down. Ophelia placed one hand on his shoulder and invaded his space to give him a peck on his cheek. He knew, even without looking, that several of his co-workers were following their interaction with too much interest, but all Ophelia was successful in doing was irritating him and he had to suppress the growl that was growing in the back of his throat for civility's sake.

The other girls who were hovering near Ophelia giggled. It was about all he could take. Then it got worse.

"Hey, you girls friends of Jacob's? Why don't you join us?" Ben called out. The girls tittered their agreement and the guys rose to pull over spare chairs.

Jacob clenched his jaws and counted to ten in his head. A sea of calm. Luna's face filled his mind instead. Nope, he was done. He rose and threw a twenty on the table. "I'm calling it a night. See you guys on Monday."

The guys were already too busy flirting to respond with anything more than vague waves in his direction.

Ophelia scrambled to rise from her chair. "Why don't I walk out with you? I need to go out for a smoke, anyway."

*Gross.* Jacob shrugged and left her to catch up. By the time they reached outside, all he could manage was a wave over his shoulder without even a backward glance before picking up speed to walk back to the office where he had left his car.

And if it seemed like he was a coward running away, he'd still prefer owning up to that over forcing himself to remain there.

# Chapter Twenty-Five

Somehow, day two was worse than day one.

With a sigh, Luna stared at the full-length mirror on the wall next to the door. Her eyes were puffy with a hint of bloodshot. Meanwhile, her fine hair, normally manageable with the use of a flatiron, refused to cooperate after her shower and had instead poofed up and stuck out every which way from the dryness of the air. She hadn't gotten much sleep overnight, tossing around in her bed as she turned Jacob's last words over and over. She knew she was overanalyzing but she couldn't help it.

When she shrugged on the khaki jacket over her plain T-shirt and jeans, it hung loose and shapeless over her frame. To salvage her appearance and make herself presentable, she adjusted her messenger bag and tugged her jacket down.

She looked like she had just been dumped, which was not what had happened the previous night? *Right? He sounded like he wanted more.*

Luna slapped her cheeks with both hands. "Wake up. Just one more day!" Stomach heavy with trepidation, she attempted a smile. It came out more like a grimace.

*Great.*

As she let herself out, the door behind her closed by itself with a soft click. For a moment, she rested her head against cool panel before she pushed off to balance on her own two feet. With a lingering, regretful last glance at her room, she found the last dregs of her energy to make her way down to the lobby where coffee and food awaited.

"You look like hell, Luna." Scott turned as she approached, coffee in hand. The guys had opted to hang by the end of the table where coffee and an assortment of tea had become permanent fixtures at the conference.

"Thanks," Luna mumbled, shuffling like a zombie as she fixed herself a cup of coffee. She'd feel better after a cup...or three.

"You okay?" That confirmed that she liked Jung better than Scott. He was nicer, more sensitive. It might have to do with the fact that he was married and a dad. His toddler was pretty damn cute too. Scott, on the other hand, had demonstrated himself to be a dude-bro.

Still, Luna held up a finger for silence as she took a long draw of coffee. She didn't even care how hot it was. If she had a choice, she'd take it as an IV, straight to her blood stream. When she pulled the mug away from her mouth, almost reluctantly, she flashed Jung a grateful smile. In her head, she pictured that grimace from earlier and prayed to powers that be that her grin

192

this time was nothing like that. "Yeah, didn't sleep well. I guess strange bed and whatnot."

"Well, one more night." Jung patted her back.

"Yeah, one more night."

"Good morning! Look who I found!" Prakash came up to them with Bryan in tow.

It was too early for Mr. Complications. Luna mumbled a good morning into her coffee mug and gestured to the food at the table. There were little yogurt cups topped with granola along with fruit, Danishes, muffins and croissants. Without waiting for a reply, she shuffled over, still dragging her heels. She set her coffee down, grabbed a plate and began heaping food on it, enough to feed three people. She didn't care. She needed it.

"Hey, you okay?" Bryan came to stand beside her, also working on putting together his own plate, albeit a lot more measured in his portions. Luna felt a stab of resentment for how perfectly put together he always seemed.

"Yeah, I didn't sleep well. Foreign bed." Best to use a consistent excuse. It worked for the guys.

"Don't lie to me." The words were soft, almost inaudible, but the steely command behind them made Luna tremble, ice shooting down her back. It was a Dominant's voice.

*Wait! Who was he to use that voice on me?* "Excuse me?"

Bryan sighed as he turned to face her in full. As Luna mustered her courage, she did the same.

"If we are to be friends, or more, I don't want to start with lies."

Luna tried to ignore his words, but perhaps he was right. "Fine," she grumbled. "There was a bit of a complicated discussion with Jacob before bed last night and it kept me up a bit after, okay? Happy?"

"Complicated?"

"I prefer to not delve into the details." Luna answered, her tone clipped. She was well aware of the implications of him asking, the ulterior motive he would have. She wasn't born yesterday and it certainly didn't feel right to share. What was between her and Jacob was between her and Jacob.

"Okay, I can respect that. But I'm sure Jacob wouldn't like the idea of you losing sleep over it." Kindness dripped from his voice. She didn't want kindness right now.

"Let's head back and join the guys before they wonder where we went," Luna said, instead of commenting more on the topic. Without waiting for a reply, Luna made her way back, already proceeding to jam the coveted food into her mouth. She barely tasted any of it, though.

If she were to be honest with herself, she spent the rest of her day trying to avoid Bryan. Every time she saw him, her mind would replay his offer, the kiss on her forehead, then switch to recalling the most confusing phone call she'd ever had with Jacob.

Luna wrenched her thoughts away from the tragedy that was her love life with an iron will. She was better than that. She was more than that. As she refocused on each panel and its speakers, she took meticulous notes and put her hand up to ask questions, sometimes challenging the very ideas being presented. If there was a speaker she admired, she made a point of talking to them afterward.

"Hi, you're Luna Weir, right?"

She was grabbing another cup of coffee when she heard her name. It was not a voice she recognized, and she turned around only to see a frazzled woman with a bundle of bouncing curls approaching.

"That's me!" Luna grinned. *The coffee must be kicking in for me to sound this preppy.*

"Oh good." The woman extended her hand and they both did that bit of awkward shuffle of getting the right hand free to shake. Luna relaxed, more at ease than she had been all day. Here was someone that understood what it was like to be too busy to keep up with appearances.

"Meredith, but most call me Merry for short. I'm one of the event organizers."

*Meredith! With a head of curls! Lani would like her.*

"I wanted to say that I loved your work on the anti-bullying campaign for the Queer Support Network."

Luna flushed but couldn't help but beam from ear to ear. That project could be considered the crowning jewel of her career so far, but she hadn't realized that her name was attached to the initiative outside of that organization and her agency. "Ah, it was a wonderful collaborative effort. We had some strong visionaries on the project."

Merry waved her words off. "*Pshaw*, take credit where it's due! We women don't step up and get recognized for our work enough as it is. Anyhow," Merry paused as someone greeted her. She waved back, then turned her attention back to Luna. "I came over to say that I'd love for you to come be on one of our panels at the next conference."

Stunned, Luna stared as if Merry had grown two heads, but the other woman paid her reaction no heed.

"Anyhow, here's my card. Would you have one of yours on you, by chance?"

Still stunned, she took the offered card in hand. When Merry continued to stare at her expectantly, Luna shook off her daze. "Oh yes!" She dug into her bag, pulled her own business card out and handed it over.

"Awesome! I have to run. There are always a thousand details to manage at these things." She rolled her eyes with a laugh. "I'll get in touch with you soon!" Then she was off, leaving Luna to stare at the woman's back as she disappeared into the crowd.

*Did that seriously just happen?* Luna shook her head, but the sense of wonder stayed with her through the afternoon.

The next panel was a bit of a blur and at last, she gave up. Luna dragged herself back to the hotel room, hoping to get some rest so that she would look somewhat more presentable for the gala that night. Without bothering to change, she set an alarm on her phone, tossed it on the nightstand then crawled under the covers.

The light from her phone faded as the screen timed out. She lay on her side, hands tucked under her head as she stared at the device and listened to the sounds of the occasional footstep or doors closing. Would Jacob call again? Text? Luna wanted to text him and let him know what had happened, to celebrate. An invitation to be a panelist at the conference was a badge of prestige for her profession. But she didn't want to draw the focus away from the more important conversation they had to have — and Jacob had decided they were not having it until they could meet face-to-face again.

Eventually, sleep found her. She didn't remember when or how, only that her eyes were closed when the alarm rang from her phone. It was as though she was swimming in molasses as she struggled to emerge from the darkness that was slumber. But at last, she triumphed, victorious in opening her eyes. She groped for her phone, brought it to her face and squinted as she shut off the alarm. Her phone informed her that she had one new message.

Luna bolted up from the bed and, with two hands cradling the phone, she swiped to open the text. Her shoulders slumped as she realized it was from Lani.

*Hey sweetie, how's the conference going?*

Better to respond now.

*Fine. Can't wait to get home.*

Luna paused with her fingers hovering over the keyboard before she resumed typing again.

*I met one of the organizers. You'd like her. She asked me to be on a panel at the next one!*

There. Sent. The news was worth sharing with someone. Convincing herself to be satisfied with that, Luna nodded and slipped off the bed. It was time to get ready.

After a shower, Luna began with dressing herself in a matching set of black lace panties and bra. She shimmied into her dress. put on a light layer of makeup and twisted her hair into an updo, all uncharacteristic of her. But she was going to have fun and she was going to do it for herself.

A quick check of her phone showed that Lani had messaged back.

*That's brilliant, lovely. We'll celebrate when you get back. High tea? There's this place that serves their scones with real clotted cream.*

Luna smiled, warmed by her friend's suggestion.

*Sounds great. I have to go now. Party time.*

*Okay, have fun!*

By the time she made it downstairs to the open ballroom, the party was in full swing. Many stood around in little groups, wine in hand as wait staff circulated with platters of hors d'oeuvres. It was all very posh and Luna felt out of place, but she kept repeating the mantra to herself. *Fake it till you make it.*

As soon as she spotted Joanna, Luna made her way over, and for the rest of the night, she stuck to her boss like a shadow. It wasn't until after dinner, when she'd had perhaps one too many glasses of wine, that she was alone at last. As she fanned the heat from her face, she leaned on the decorative railing of the terrace and closed her eyes to enjoy the kiss of the cool air on her bare shoulders.

"Ah, there you are. I've been looking all over for you."

So much for peace. *Why did I leave Joanna's side?* Perhaps if she pretended hard enough that she didn't hear, he would go away. *That would be wishful thinking.*

Bryan came to stand beside her, one elbow resting on the terrace, a glass of wine in the other hand.

Luna opened her eyes. "Hello, Bryan." From some hidden depths within, she found a smile for him.

He chuckled and chucked her under her chin. "Hello, doll. If I didn't know better, I'd say you've been avoiding me."

The smell of alcohol on his breath as he leaned in to whisper in her ear caused alarm bells to go off in her head. His use of her old pet name invoked every flight instinct she had. As he moved one arm to wrap around her waist, she took a step back, lowered her center of gravity and gave him a small push.

"Bryan, you're drunk. Please stop."

His face reddened. But she didn't give him another chance. In that split second, she understood what her hesitation with him all along had been telling her. That perfectly groomed façade hid something much darker that she had always refused to see. It took alcohol to rip the mask away.

"I'm flattered by the offer." Luna began to shuffle away, one foot at a time, to increase the distance between the two of them. "But I don't think it's a good idea. Jacob and I are still working things out and I'm not ready to enter another relationship, no matter what happens."

She could have handled rage. Bryan's eyes, however, turned cold, maliciously so. There was a promise of something akin to violence and his posture shifted as he drew himself up. She saw the subtle change through the ripple of his tailored suit as his muscles tensed, ready to spring. "Luna Weir, are you turning down my offer?"

*Show no fear. Leave no room for doubt.* "Yes, Bryan. I am." There was nothing left to say. He needed time to cool down, to sober up. "Goodnight, Bryan."

It was then she made a tactical error. Eager to leave, she turned. Without warning, he grabbed her wrist, his grip painful in how tight it was. "Don't you dare walk away from me, doll."

She winced but whipped around. *How dare he try to manhandle me!* "We're done here. Don't call me that ever again." Luna might be a submissive, but she was done being his victim. Muscle memory from her training kicked in and she curved her hand inward, pulling against his thumb. The move was enough to break his grip, regardless of his strength. Before he had another chance to recover, she stalked off, leveraging the crowd to throw him off her trail.

Luna half ran back to her room. It wasn't until she was safely alone behind the locked door that she collapsed, trembling as she sank to the ground. With shaky hands, she took out the phone from her small purse, pulling up Jacob's number.

Once, twice, three times. She counted with each ring, trying to calm the panic that was bubbling up. Then the ringing stopped and it went straight to voicemail. She hung up.

A new message arrived, from Ted this time. She hauled in gulps of air to calm herself. An unreasonable trepidation filled her as she opened the message.

*Hey, I wasn't sure if I should send you this, but I wanted you to know. Saw your boy with a blonde at the bar tonight with a bunch of other people. Looked like they might have left together too. Call me.*

A photo followed the message. It was blurry, taken in low lighting. The woman faced away from the camera, but it was obvious she was leaning over to kiss the male in the photo — the male who was unmistakably Jacob.

Her phone dropped with a soft thud to the carpeted ground. Luna pulled her legs to her chest and buried her face in her knees. The tears would come later. Right now, she just felt empty.

She spent the rest of the night that way, huddled against the door. If she made herself small enough, maybe the fears and loneliness would fade away.

# Chapter Twenty-Six

Something was very, very wrong.

Jacob knew it the moment she stepped out of the gates at arrival as he studied her, from the lifeless eyes to the jerky movements of her limbs, as if she was a marionette held together by nothing but the clothing she wore. She had never looked so fragile, such that when he pulled her into his arms, he feared he may break her. Some basic primal need, however, drove him to fold his arms around her, desperate to reassure himself that she was actually there.

But instead of relaxing against him as he expected, Luna stiffened in his arms. Horrified, he let go as if she had burned him and watched as she shuffled her way to the baggage claim. The only sign of any presence came when he tried to take her bags. She growled at him like a wild thing and clung to them like a lifeline.

His heart was breaking.

They sat in the car in silence. He had managed to coax her to leave her luggage in the trunk but she continued to clutch the backpack to her chest, staring out of the window in what he knew was an attempt to avoid eye contact, to avoid acknowledging his existence.

By the time they entered her apartment, him trailing behind her, Jacob had had enough. At some point during the drive, the agony that he ached with turned into frustration at the lack of communication. He closed the door with a soft click and noted the slight flinch she tried to hide. It scraped at his temper more, a temper, he realized with a start, which was fueled by fear. He had only ever been that scared of losing her one other time, when he had heard that she was in a car accident.

"What the fuck is going on?" Jacob struggled to keep his tone even.

"Why do you care?" There was a hint of sarcasm somewhere in that defeated voice. That was something. He would take defiance over emptiness.

"Rest position," he snapped, not even bothering with a pillow. He watched dispassionately as she struggled with herself and felt an ounce of satisfaction when her training won out as she sank to her knees.

"Explain yourself."

She stared up at him. "I turned down Bryan's offer, but maybe I should have taken him up on it instead." She had designed every word to hurt him, something he'd never dreamed he would experience from her. In a tiny part of his brain that still remained rational, he tried to remind himself that she was lashing out like a wounded animal. He just needed to find out where she was hurting.

Except most of him was no longer that rational. "Well, with the way you're acting, maybe you should have." He regretted the words as soon as he uttered them, despite his own pain propelling him forward.

"Well, maybe I'll call him back. At least he won't jerk me around the way you do." Her body shook until she was losing her hold on her position. Luna surged up to her knees. "You tell me you don't want to see me with another Dom then spend the next night with some blonde." She spat the words out in disgust, her eyes wide and her face red with fury.

*What the hell is she talking about?* His body tensed, every muscle cording as his own voice grew quieter and colder in response. "I don't know what you're accusing me of, but jealousy does not become you, Luna."

"Jealousy? *Jealousy*?" Luna exploded and in one swift movement, she rose to her feet and closed the distance between them. She held up her wrist, ringed with a faint bruise that was beginning to blossom. "He hurt me. And where were you when I needed you?" She jammed her hand into her pocket, pulled out her phone and shoved it close to his face. "There! You were there, busy with some woman you never even bothered telling me about."

Bryan had hurt her. Jacob was going to kill him. Red coated his vision, but there was nowhere to vent his rage as he barely heard anything else she had said. Jacob stared at the bruise instead of the phone and made one last attempt at being the Dom she needed at the moment. "Let me take care of that first. Then we'll talk."

"No," Luna waved the phone in front of him one last time before she jammed the phone back in her pocket. "I know we never said we were exclusive, but I thought you'd respect me — respect *us* — enough to at least tell me."

Jacob recognized the woman in the photo. That cursed bar trip he should have never agreed to go on. *God damn it. Ophelia.* He knew then that until he addressed that misunderstanding, Luna wouldn't let him near her. But part of him was even more hurt to see her assume so much based on a single photo. Had they not had more trust in their relationship than that? Whatever restraint he held onto snapped.

"Well, if you're so certain I fucked some dumb blonde, why did you bother even jumping into my car? I'm not some on-call chauffeur." Now he was yelling too.

"Because I can't stop loving you." She screamed loud enough for the words to ring in the air. Tears rolled down her cheeks, big, fat drops that fell unhindered.

"Well I can't stop loving you either, sweetheart." He snarled, his tone turning nasty as he took another step closer, their faces now almost touching. She was beautiful in her fierceness and in that moment, despite the rage and pain, he knew he was lost to her forever.

"Well, fine!" Luna huffed.

"Well, good!" he muttered in return.

They stared at each other. The weight of their words settled on Jacob's shoulders and wormed their way through all the layers of hurt and confusion into the core of his heart. Something in Luna's wide eyes told him that she was having a similar experience. In the background, the ticking of a clock counted the seconds and minutes they stood there, the anger he felt draining as he wrestled with the implications and consequences.

It was a far cry from how Jacob had envisioned their talk would go. He had dessert and roses waiting back at his place, for fuck's sake. Instead here they were, the words blurted out in the worst screaming match they had ever had in the three years they'd been together. He resisted the urge to take her over his lap, spank her until she came then fuck her hard until she screamed his name instead of those accusations before admitting she would always be his. He knew it was still the angry part of him talking.

Bit by bit, sanity seemed to resume as Luna covered her mouth with both hands, her eyes widening like in horror. It was almost amusing to watch the myriad of emotions passing through her features as she likely just realized she had raised her voice against him and had accused him of those ugly things. Then there was also probably what she'd admitted to herself in the heat of the moment. And what he offered in return. "You...I..."

With infinite care, as if afraid she would still pull away, he reached out for that hand and lifted it to press his lips on her knuckles. "There has only ever been you, Luna, and I want there to only be you going forward too. I would like to propose a new contract. Think of it as an extension."

She stared at him as if he had grown another head. "Another three-year term?" Accompanied by her squeak, her incredulous expression drained the tension from him.

He chuckled and shook his head. "We play it by ear but no, no end date."

"Oh."

Now she looked like she was in shock. When her knees buckled, he caught her just in time and helped her to the couch.

"Oh." Luna stared at him with wide unfocused eyes, still in shock.

*Dear God.* He'd broken her. His heart began hammering in his chest and he moved to brush her hair out of her eyes. "Luna, sweetheart."

She stared at him. It was the same dazed look she had whenever she entered subspace. He waved a hand in front of her face and she blinked. "Luna, I need a reply. Do you accept?" He gentled the words.

"Yes." A slow smile spread across her lips, lighting up the weary features until she was once more the submissive he knew, the submissive that was his—for as long as they would have each other.

He pulled her into his arms and savored the way she melted into him at last. She was soft, pliant and the most precious thing in the world to him. He ran his fingers through her hair and closed his eyes, resting his chin on the top of her head.

"Mine," he whispered, tasting the rightness of the word on his tongue.

She nodded into his chest and nuzzled before pressing a kiss on his chest. "I'm sorry," she murmured.

"Me too." Although he was content to stay that way, her earlier state still concerned him as he recalled the exhaustion he'd witnessed before. He trailed his hands up to her shoulders and pulled her back, noting the dark circles around her eyes, the paleness of her complexion.

"How much sleep did you get?"

The cringe and downcast eyes were enough of an answer.

"Food? Breakfast today?"

She shook her head and muttered beneath her breath. "Didn't have an appetite."

Jacob let out a heavy sigh, more exaggerated than intended. "Bandage, food, then bed."

"My wrist is okay. Really," she protested. "They're bruises. There's not much that can be done about them."

Jacob grumbled, hating the fact that she was right. "Fine. Food, then bed."

When Luna opened her mouth again, he gave her a sterner look. Her mouth snapped shut.

He marched her to the kitchen area. Unlike his place, hers was an open concept, the rest of the living room separated from the appliances by a large kitchen counter. Without another word, he pulled her to him and hoisted her up to sit on the counter.

"Jacob."

"Hush." He turned, following his most basic directive to take care of what was his, and rummaged through the fridge. Relieved that it had some basics, he scooped some vanilla yogurt out of its container, sprinkled fresh blueberries, brought the bowl over and held it up to her. "Eat."

He tracked her every move, and as she took the first spoonful into her mouth, the remaining tension in him drained. When she closed her eyes to enjoy the flavor, he picked a blueberry out from the top and held it up to her, nudging it to her lips. Luna parted them and accepted the offering with a small moan of appreciation. His jeans tightened uncomfortably.

Luna opened her eyes and, under his watchful gaze, finished the rest of the yogurt. As she held up the spoon, she lapped up the remaining yogurt with delicate little licks.

*The minx.* Now it was on purpose.

An animalistic growl emerged from the back of his throat. He slipped his hands under her ass and gave her yoga pants and panties one hard yank, pulling them down to her ankles. He returned to cup her crotch with one hand, marveling at the wet heat already gathering there while she rocked her hips on the counter, grinding against his palm. Jacob pushed her shirt over her breasts and pulled one free from the bra cup. There was no teasing, no slow build-up. Instead, he sated his hunger as he captured a nipple between his lips, sucking hard then scraping his teeth against it. He smirked as she squealed in surprise.

Jacob knew how to make her body sing and he intended to prove to her that staying with him would only mean heaven.

Even as he licked his way across, he pulled the other bra cup down, delighting in the way her breast spilled out. The taste of her skin was ever so sweet. Her nipples hardened, one glistening from his attention, the other begging for the same ministration. He obliged, sucking hard and tugging at it until it left his lips with a soft pop.

"Jacob." The breathy sigh of his name only urged him to work his way down, trailing kisses and nibbles down her stomach, watching it flex as she giggled against his day-old stubble.

He didn't wait for her to beg, but placed his hands on her thighs and parted her legs.

Her body quivered in anticipation under his touch as he observed the way her arousal caused her sex to open for him, slick with her wetness. He inhaled the musky scent. Who could resist an invitation like that?

Jacob held her hips, pinning her to the counter to ready her for his onslaught. He flattened his tongue against her and dragged it upward until he found her hardened nub. There, he began teasing, circling the tip of his tongue around it until she became a squirming puddle of mess in his hands.

She fluttered her hands before clutching his shoulders, straining against his grip as she rocked against his mouth. "Jacob, I need to come, please." Her desperate plea snapped away the last of his control.

"No," he growled as he whipped his head back. In one swift motion, he lifted and threw her over his shoulder, then wrapped an arm around her waist.

She yelped in surprise, trying to push herself up until he swatted her rear. When he was sure of her submission, he took long strides to cross the apartment until they reached the bedroom. Once they crossed the threshold, he tossed her onto the bed before he stood once more to undo his shirt, one button at a time.

"You will only come when I am thrusting deep inside you. Only then…" He snapped his jeans open, freeing his hard cock. As her eyes drew toward his crotch, he took hold of his length and pumped and down. A part of him wondered if she was aware how her legs had spread wider or that she was trailing her hand down to play with herself.

He crawled onto the bed and held himself over her, conscious of how his larger body covered hers. As he braced himself on either side of her, he lined himself up against her opening and bent down to whisper, his breath brushing by her ear. "Only then, with every moan, every thrust, will I know you are truly mine."

And at his last word, he surged forward and entered her in one swift stroke.

A scream of pure ecstasy tore from her throat as she bucked against him. He ground his hips against her, heat and pleasure driving everything from his mind until his focus narrowed to only the feeling of her pussy wrapped around his cock. He drew most of the way before slamming back into her with an almost animalistic savagery.

Luna clawed at his back and it only encouraged his pace. Beneath him, her pussy began clenching more around him and her hips began bucking against him wildly, the telltale signs of the start of an orgasm. He increased his pace, hammering hard into her. Jacob lowered his head and clamped his teeth on the spot where her neck joined her shoulder. The act of marking sent her over the edge until she was spasming against him.

He let her ride him through her climax, reveling in her pleasure before he refocused on chasing his own. Long thrusts shortened as his own body tightened. "Fuck," he swore beneath his breath as he pushed one last time and came hard, pouring his seed into her.

They stayed that way, joined, as they both struggled to recover. Only when their ragged breathing evened out did he withdraw and roll to the side, groaning as he already missed the warmth of her pussy.

Jacob turned to check on her and felt an absurd shot of pride at the sight of a dreamy smile on Luna's lips, her eyes half closed. Chuckling again, he shifted to gather her in his arms and kiss her on the forehead. "Sleep, love."

He held her that way for the rest of the morning and into the early afternoon, filled with a sense of completeness he had never quite felt before.

In his mind, he began to formulate plans for the day they would sign the contract that would seal their promise of a future together.

# Chapter Twenty-Seven

Sunlight streamed through the venetian blinds, its warmth kissing the skin of one bare shoulder peeking out from under the covers. A familiar scent enveloped Luna as her consciousness ascended and she snuggled in closer, reluctant to wake up lest the vague sense of rightness faded when her eyes opened.

"Rise and shine, sleepyhead." Jacob's breath tickled her ear and she squirmed, burying her face against his chest. "Come on, love, or you won't sleep tonight."

Luna let out a groan. "I don't see a problem with that," she muttered, the sound half muffled. She moved her hand up to lay it on his chest, her palm against his heart. Memories began resurfacing and her lips curved upward until she was grinning like an idiot, her eyes still closed.

*Love.* He never called her that before.

A sudden ache of pain disrupted her contentment as his hand brushed by her wrist.

"We should ice this. It's getting worse, not better."

Tenderness and concern mixed with seriousness gave her reason to crack her eyes open. Only the sight of his expression betrayed the undercurrent of reined-in fury as he explored the ring of bruises with gentle fingers.

"Jacob, I'm okay. It's just a little sore." Luna pushed herself up and kissed him on the corner of his lips.

"Did you report it to security at the conference?" His tone still held little humor or mirth.

Luna resettled against him and rested her head on his shoulder. She had hoped she would be able to distract him, but she should have known better. "No. It was late, toward the end of the conference, and Bryan was drunk." Jacob's chest rose as if readying to speak and she shook her head. "I know that's no excuse, and I'll talk to Joanna on Monday. It's probably best if I step away from the project."

She felt more than heard the sigh he exhaled. "Whatever you choose, I'll support you." Something told her that the words had not come easily to Jacob. He was someone who believed in an eye for an eye. "I still want to take a better look at that wrist, to make sure it's nothing more serious."

"Okay." If she didn't let him fuss over her a little, she would never hear the end of it. Lani had once mentioned that Jacob hated helplessness the most, like there was nothing he could do and that sometimes, it was more of a kindness to let him do something, anything.

Well, there was something...

"That woman in the photo..."

His chest rumbled. "That's Lani's assistant, who has always been way over-flirty. She attempted what I can only think of as a pick-up but frankly, she's not my cup of tea." Explanation out of the way, he shifted so that they looked each other in the eye. He cupped her cheek, tracing her cheekbone with the callused pad of his thumb. "Luna, do you really think I would do such a thing?"

Without missing a beat, she shook her head. "Well, I know you're not a fan of playing with someone you just met, so the idea of you picking up a blonde at a bar is kinda hilarious, now that I think about it." She grinned and poked at him with the index finger of her uninjured hand.

Jacob captured her hand in his and held it close. "No, Luna, I'm serious." His grip tightened with an urgency, though he was still careful to be gentle. "I need to know that you'll not doubt me every time you see me with another woman, that we have that level of trust." He brushed her hair back. "You know the rule. If you wanted to play with someone else, you would have to ask first. And I would never demand of you what I wouldn't do myself. You're mine. And in return, I am yours and yours only."

He took her breath away with his declaration. She saw herself reflected in the warm dark chocolate of his eyes as she nodded and her insides melted into a puddle of goo. Luna swallowed in an attempt to prepare to speak, her mind grasping for the right words. There were only three that seemed appropriate.

"I love you."

He chuckled and placed a lingering kiss on her forehead before crushing her lips with a searing one that branded her heart. It left her wanting more even as he withdrew. "I love you too, sweetheart."

All was right in the world.

* * * *

Monday found her early at the office. Post-conference catch-up was always hell and she wanted to make sure she had time to prepare for the talk with Joanna. The office was quiet, bereft of a single soul. Mornings were not very popular with agency life, especially on the first day of the work week.

Which was why she almost jumped out of her skin when a knock on the glass outside cut through the silence. That was definitely not one of her co-workers coming in. Luna poked her head out of her office. A delivery boy was peering through the glass partition that separated the reception and kitchen from the rest of the office area. The door between the two was usually open if someone was in, but she had kept it locked today so that she wouldn't be interrupted. *So much for that idea.*

She sighed and got up, resigning herself to playing receptionist. As she got closer, the boy, no more than nineteen years old, held up a bouquet of deep roses, already set in a glass vase. *Wow, whoever it is for...lucky girl, or guy.*

"Hi, I've got a delivery for Luna Weir."

*Wait...what?*

They were gorgeous, adorned with little baby breaths, but rather than excitement, Luna felt only a sense of trepidation as she accepted them. It was not Jacob's style. Roses, yes. But to the office? Not so much. They preferred to keep things on the down low.

Grateful that no one else was around, she carried them back to her office, quickening her pace until she shut her door behind her. Already, the fragrance of the roses began to permeate the air. It wasn't until she set the bouquet down did she notice the card in the middle. With shaky hands, she freed it from its plastic stand, surprised to find an USB stick taped to the back. Her vision blurred as she read the simple message.

*You will be mine.*
*Bryan*

The trepidation threatened to turn into a full-blown panic attack. Her mouth felt dryer than a desert as she attempted to extract the flash memory stick from the card. It took three tries before she plugged it into her computer.

There was a single mp3 sound clip. She grabbed her headphones and, taking a steadying breath, she opened the file.

A woman's voice. Moaning and whimpering. She broke out in a cold sweat as she heard her own voice begging for release, for permission to come. Then another scream, the sound of a woman in climax.

There was a moment of silence as if clips were being sliced then two male voices spoke.

"Well, that was quite the show."

"Please, leave. I am busy taking care of mine at the moment."

She knew both of them oh so well. In that instant, she no longer had the ability to breathe. One hand clawed at her throat, the other clutching at her chest as if it would stop the hot, torching pain in her heart. Luna doubled over and gagged until her entire head pounded.

The phone rang, its obnoxious tone cutting through her panic. She counted each ring, focusing on pushing air in and out, in and out until at last, the burning in her chest subsided. The phone stopped ringing. A minute later, it started again.

Her hands kept trembling and she had to steady one with the other as she picked up the phone.

"Hello, doll. Oh, I can call you that, right?"

*Bastard.*

"Anyhow, I hope you got my gift this morning." The pleasantness of his voice belied the nightmare quality of the situation.

"I wanted to give you a little memento of one of your most beautiful performances as of late. Of course, I have the full recording for my personal enjoyment." He chuckled over the phone. The sound chilled Luna to the bone.

"It's amazing the quality of video these little spy cameras can capture these days. Incredible."

Everything in her wanted to whimper, to curl up in a corner like a wounded animal. He had a video clip of her in the throes of a scene. When did it happen? Bits of Jacob and his dialogue came drifting back, flashbacks replaying in her mind.

That night at The Playgrounds' public dungeon. But The Playgrounds had a strict policy. Could spy cams get through? Oh God, if that was the video he had...

Somehow, she choked out her question in a hoarse whisper. "What do you want?"

"Luna, my little doll, naughty girl. You know what I want."

Her stomach dropped and the nausea returned. She tasted bile in the back of her throat.

"Of course, I wouldn't want you to break your current contract and ruin your reputation. I'm a patient and generous man. So, tell you what... As a little proof that you would make the right choice when the time comes, I want you to tell Jacob that your next contract will be with me and we can all have a nice little meeting about it."

"No…" Luna whispered in horror, her eyes round as saucers. No, not when Jacob had promised an indefinite contract with her, not when he had just handed her his heart. Now Bryan was asking her to stab it with the knife of rejection until it bled out.

"No? Luna, so brave. Would you be as brave when everyone gets to see the video at the office? I mean, who would have guessed the ambitious go-getter would be such a good little submissive, all tied up and begging to come. I mean, I didn't even know you were such a screamer. And we've played."

Images of Scott and Prakash hovering over a computer — worse, Ted, Joanna and Jung. In her mind's eye, she saw the sea of leers and disgust. It was one thing to play in public at a fetish club where everyone was in the scene and accepted each other's kinks, but quite another to be exposed to people who weren't in the lifestyle, who wouldn't understand. She remembered trying to tell someone about her submissive tendencies before. It hadn't gone well. It would be a thousand times worse. Her gut twisted.

"Now, your agency is one thing. I understand your company has quite a variety of clients — a teachers' association, a few government agencies, right? I wonder what your clients would think about such footage. I do have quite a few of their phone numbers and email addresses since I had to check for references."

Her blood turned to ice. It wasn't just her job and career on the line. It could destroy her agency if they lost those long-term contracts.

"Why don't you give my offer some thought before giving me an answer? Oh, and I shouldn't need to tell you that I wouldn't tell anyone if I were you. You're a clever girl. I trust you'll make the right choice. Text me."

As soon as Bryan hung up, Luna scrambled to the washroom. She just made it to a stall before she vomited up the entire contents of her earlier breakfast. When there was nothing left in her system, she remained there, kneeling by the toilet bowl. Her shoulders shook as the realities of her predicament came crashing down. There was no choice, was there? He had her trapped. Bryan had won.

Defeated, she cleaned herself up and staggered to the sink, all the time railing in her mind against the unfairness of it all, against whatever powers that be were up there. Her reflection, with reddened eyes and chalk-white face, stared back like a ghost out of a horror film. She envisioned the collar and leash around her neck, shackles on her wrists. Rather than being turned on, it made her gut twist in disgust.

She was so close to her happiness and now, he was blackmailing her into being his slave. Literally. The universe had some sick, perverse sense of humor.

But adaptability and resilience had been instilled in her long ago. Somehow, as impossible as it seemed, Luna adjusted to the purgatory that was going to be her life from now on, just enough to be functional once more. She dragged her sorry ass back to her office where she unplugged the USB and pocketed it with care. As if it was all happening to someone else, she picked up her phone, hands steadier than she expected, and texted Bryan back. Numbness seeped into her mind. Two simple words that traded for another two.

*I agree.*

His reply came only seconds later.

*Good girl.*

There was no turning back.

# Chapter Twenty-Eight

Luna was a wreck. All morning, she hid in her office and pretended to be busy playing catch up. But every time she achieved a flow, Bryan's name would come up and she would falter. The sheer effort of trying to stay focused was wearing on her until she kept lapsing in concentration, staring off into space. Her mind emptied of coherent thought until a numbness descended, punctuated by shots of anxiety that left her gasping for breath while her heart drummed in her ears. Time passed, seconds to minutes, minutes to hours as her life took on a surreal quality, as if she was a disembodied spirit observing the shell of a woman going through the motions.

Luna was still staring into space when her mobile buzzed. It lay faced down and skittered its way across her desk but gave no hint as to who was calling. She flinched and it took another two rings before she braved picking it up.

"Hey, Luna, you okay? Where are you?"

*Crap. Lunch with Lani.* They had booked it a while ago. Her breathing grew shallower as she entertained the idea of begging off sick. Then she would tell Jacob, then…

"Sorry. Work. Lost track of time. I'm on my way. Eat first. Don't wait for me." Her voice sound clipped, even to her own ears.

"All right, sweetie. Don't rush. I got us a table."

Luna hung up after making sufficient platitudes but paused as her hand reached for the door handle. Was she ready? Could she act normal? *Do I have a choice?* It seemed like all her choices were being stripped away from her, one at a time. *No, I can do this. I can't let Bryan take this away too.*

There was no joy in the walk to the cafe or savoring of the rich scents of the bakery as she entered. Luna couldn't even remember what she ordered as she took her food to the table to join Lani, who was just finishing up.

*Act normal. Just act normal.*

"So! Tell me!" Lani squealed.

"Tell…you…?" Luna's heart skipped a beat and her brain tripped. For a split second, she thought her friend was referring to the incident from the morning, before logic kicked in. There was no way Lani would know about that.

"Jacob! He offered you another contract, right? Details!"

Jacob must have been talking to Lani. In any other circumstances, she would have blushed then started gushing to her friend. *How good is my acting?* Luna ventured a smile, trying to recapture and emulate the feelings from yesterday, but they seemed so foreign to her. "Yeah, he did. He said there won't be an end date, that we'll play it by ear."

And she was going to turn the contract down. Inside, she wept.

"Luna, what's wrong?"

She looked down in surprise when Lani covered her hand with her own. Only then did she realize that her fingers had curled into fists.

"Nothing!" Luna offered a smile that was all too bright.

They both knew that Lani wasn't buying the act one bit, not by the way her lips tugged ever so slightly downward or how her face cooled into the professional mask of a counselor. There was still warmth in her eyes, but Luna could feel her withdrawing. "Luna, I'm not sure what's going on but, I can see you're not ready to talk about it. When you are, I'll be here."

*Stabbity-stab my heart.*

There was one thing she could ask of her friend. Realization hit her like a freight train. Before Lani could withdraw, she captured her friend's hand. "Lani, I need a favor. Please."

Lani stared at her but nodded. Worry creased her forehead.

"What...whatever happens..." Tears pooled in Luna's eyes, but she denied their escape. Her voice hitched, but what she had to do was too important to let her emotions get in the way. "Whatever happens, please take care of Jacob. Make sure he'll be okay. Do whatever it takes, just make sure he'll be okay."

"Luna, what are you —?"

She clutched at Lani's hand, tightening her grip as a frantic desperation pitched her voice higher than normal. "Please, just promise me."

Lani studied her for a moment. Luna knew there was no helping it. It was her job to be observant, after all. But she had broken none of Bryan's rules. It should be okay. The wait for Lani's answer wounded Luna's body up tighter than a jack-in-the-box.

"Okay, of course, sweetie."

Relief flooded her system for the first time that day. Luna slumped back in her seat and relinquished her hold on Lani's hand. Jacob would be okay. Hurt, but Lani wouldn't let him wallow. He would hate her, but that was okay if it meant he wouldn't grieve alone.

"You're turning down Jacob's contract," Lani whispered, her own eyes widening. The horror on her friend's face shattered her.

It was the first time the words had been said out loud. She hadn't dared, hadn't been brave enough to say them herself, to give the idea any shape or form. But now, forced to face what she had to do, a dam broke inside Luna and the tears she held away fell in silent rivets down her face.

"I need to go." Leaving her food untouched, she scrambled out of her seat and ran out of the cafe. From behind, she could hear Lani call out her name, but she paid it no heed. She just ran, the act feeling like the first natural thing to do since the disaster. Each step took her farther away from everything and she pounded her feet on the pavement with satisfying thuds, the very act giving her a sense of control and a temporary feeling of freedom.

Her run took her to less trodden territory until, somehow, she ended up at the harbor. Vendors, hawkers and performers lined along one side, vying for attention from the tourists strolling the area. Parents pushing strollers alongside dog walkers and joggers filled out the crowd. A rollerblader zipped by and, for a moment, Luna lost herself in the busyness of people going about their lives, taking comfort in the anonymity. She gazed into the distance and entertained the idea of running away from everything on a more permanent basis.

Her phone buzzed again. She had been contemplating tossing that in the water too.

With reluctance, she stepped to one side and dug into her pocket to take out the phone. Three missed calls from Lani. Another five more from Jacob. Bracing herself with a small inhale, she opened her text messages, compelled by her tendency to at least address the unread message indicator. A wall of text from Jacob greeted her and she turned the screen off with haste.

Rather than resuming her walk, she turned and leaned against the token gesture railing that was supposed to ward people away from the short rock cliffs that led directly down to the inlet. Luna closed her eyes and focused on her breathing until the din faded. Instead, the sound of water lapping at the rocks drew her attention and she breathed in the saltiness. The fresh air gave her a clarity that she had lacked all morning.

Until this point, she had been functioning on autopilot, but could she just let Bryan leak the videos? It was something she had to consider. But the idea of being so exposed made her ill. It would be the end of her job, her career or worse, if Bryan shared even more widely.

*"Come on, Luna. I thought you were smarter than that. Guys like that are basically abusive."*

The memory of Dylan's judgmental face surfaced in her mind. It was the first and only time she had ever told someone outside of the lifestyle that she was a sub and it had not gone well. Ever since, Luna had always been private about her kinks. How would Ted look at her? Brandon? Her family, as far away as they were?

A wave of nausea threatened to make her retch all over again. *No, I'm not brave enough to risk it.*

Tonight. She couldn't drag it out. She would have to tell Jacob tonight, let him know that she was going to leave him. It meant missing practice, but dealing with her Dom was important. She had to rip the Band-Aid off and let him get on with his life without her. Luna pulled up the 'compose' box and typed a quick message to let Brandon know that something urgent had come up and she wouldn't be able to go tonight. With every step taken, she was more and more committed to the course of action. She had to leave herself no room to chicken out.

It was about survival now. Luna took in one deep breath and let it out. The next one she took steeled her for what was to come. With cold detachment, she began crafting a believable story.

*Now I'm ready.*

By the time she returned to the office, she was functional again through sheer willpower. But for the rest of her afternoon, her mind focused more on what she must do that night. To avoid any doubts, she had turned off her phone. At five p.m., she took herself out of the office and transited to Jacob's place.

Luna raised her hand to knock on the door, but before her knuckles even touched the wood panel, the door flew open. Jacob stared at her in relief and, without another word, gathered her in his arms. "Oh, thank God."

She stood stiffly in his arms and began the task in her head of convincing herself to be angry. He was not the Jacob she loved once. He was the Dominant who'd jerked her around for years. He was the commitment-phobic ass. He was the idiot who'd decided they should play in public and got her into the mess in the first place, the one who stood between her and her career.

Yeah, she didn't believe any of that either. The ugly thoughts only made her want to cry.

Luna tried another tack. *I am winter and ice. I am unfeeling and merciless. I am cruelty itself.* The mantra played in her head repeatedly. That she could believe. She could be that bitch.

"Jacob, we need to talk."

He grew visibly rigid at the coldness in her voice. She watched dispassionately as he stepped back to let her in, his obvious concern giving way to confusion before he resumed a more neutral expression. Jacob never liked not being in control, but he excelled at exerting control over his own reactions.

"This won't take long." Luna jammed her hands into her pockets but remained standing in the small foyer. *Now or never.*

"I won't be able to accept your contract. I will be taking Bryan up on his offer after our term ends in a few weeks. He has asked that the three of us meet to discuss any details as required."

Jacob remained rooted to his spot, but seemingly shock and disbelief made his body rock back to the heels of his feet. Luna knew that it was a one-eighty and that she had blindsided him with the news. His reaction was no surprise. She had already played it out in her head a million times.

"Well, then… I shall take my leave now. I'll text you the arrangements." She turned her back to him. It was easier that way.

"Luna, are you under duress?"

*Damn. How observant is the man?*

"No, Jacob." Her voice was soft as she lied through her teeth and she channeled her self-pity to pitch her voice. "I'm just tired of you jerking me around. Hot one minute, cold another. Bryan's offering stability and a partnership, not just in the bedroom but also in my career." Not a complete lie. Just a very sick, twisted truth.

"Bullshit, Luna. He ghosted you," Jacob yelled out from behind. His control was snapping. She needed to end it now.

Luna had prepared for it, but she hadn't wanted to go there…still didn't want to go there. But she knew Jacob wouldn't let her go that easily. When she turned around, a sneer she had cultivated with care twisted her lips. How long had she practiced the expression in front of the mirror earlier in the afternoon, hoping she wouldn't have to use it?

"Nah, I was the one who did the ghosting, so think of this as me making it up to him. I can't believe you actually bought my sob story. I mean, what else was I supposed to tell you? Better for you to believe I was the victim." Luna laughed, the absurdity of her words lending a crazed quality to the sound. "Yeesh, I never took you for one so gullible, Jacob."

By then, her ex-Dominant was as stiff as a lightning rod, his face a mask of rage and grief. "Fine, Luna. If that's what you want, then go for it. But know that I'm not supportive of this pairing and I'll not be meeting with you and Bryan." He swallowed, and she noticed how a vein was popping on his forehead. She didn't think she had ever seen him that angry. "Remember, however, that until the end of our contractual term, you're still mine, and if Bryan wants to play, he must ask me for permission first."

The last bit was odd. She had hoped her brutal words would spur him to end their contract early. No matter... It was the best she could do.

"You can see yourself out now." Jacob turned and trudged away to his bedroom, leaving her still standing there.

Luna watched as the bedroom door closed behind his back. She would not cry. There were no tears left. Instead, she allowed her gaze to roam his apartment as she said a silent goodbye to the place that had given her so much happiness over the last three years.

On her trip home, she held on to that numbness that kept her from thinking about what she had done, how deeply she had wounded Jacob. It was for the best. She took out her phone and texted Bryan.

*It's done. He won't meet, but he understands.*

Luna turned off the phone, not wanting to see the reply. By the time she dragged her sorry ass back to her apartment building, exhaustion from pretending to be the ice queen had seeped into her. But it wasn't until she closed the door to her unit that she allowed herself any respite.

With a soft cry, she crumpled to the floor. Still no tears came, but a sharp pain stabbed at her chest. Yet there was also something else. Within the bitter ashes she tasted in the back of her throat, a new determination emerged with a startling ferocity. She was going to survive it—and Bryan was going to pay. *One way or another.*

# Chapter Twenty-Nine

None of it added up.

Jacob sat on the edge of his bed and ran a hand over his face. Over the years, he had developed a fine bullshit detector and prided himself on being able to read people. Either Luna was a grade-A manipulator or something else was going on, something she couldn't talk about. In which case, she needed help.

Which was why he would not let her leave their existing contract so easily. Reminding her of it was instinctual, but once he got over his initial anger, he knew it was the right move. He had a little less than three weeks to figure it all out—three weeks to protect the woman he loved or find out she'd never existed at all.

He glanced over at his phone. It was getting late, but he didn't hesitate to pick it up and text. Lani would want to know.

*Still awake?*

*Sort of. I am. Nathan isn't.*

Nathan? Who the hell was Nathan? He would have to ask later. For now, he needed to focus on the problem at hand.

*All right, I'll stick to text. Luna came by.*

*You okay?*

*Yes. Something's not right.*

*What do you mean?*

Jacob stared at the phone, unsure how to word the rest. He didn't want to type that Luna was going to submit to Bryan. The idea of her submitting to another sickened him, but the thought of what Bryan would do to her terrified him even more. Still, he had to text something back.

*Luna said Bryan offered her stability.*

*WHAT!*

Jacob winced. He could hear the screech all the way across town.

*We need to figure out what's going on. Luna fed me some bullshit line about me jerking her around and that's why she turned me down. If that was it, she wouldn't have looked so damn happy when I first offered it. And this thing with Bryan is too coincidental. I'm not buying it.*

No reply. He doubted that she had fallen asleep, but something may have interrupted her. Too restless to sit, he stood and paced around the room. He needed a plan, but to be honest, he had no idea where to start.

Functioning on autopilot, he pocketed the phone and made his way barefoot to his office. He considered the room in the darkness, gaze following the lines of the familiar shadows before he flicked on the light switch and picked up a marker from his desk.

He stopped when he noticed a happy winking face drawn in the corner of his whiteboard with the word 'Gotchya' written neatly underneath in block letters. A pang shot through his heart. Luna must have left it there the last time she had used his office for him to find later. She always had little ways of cheering him up in surprising and sometimes cheeky or silly ways.

*No, I can't think of her in past tense.*

He drew a careful box around the smiley face so he wouldn't draw over or erase one of the last traces of her by accident. Then he started. In the top middle, he wrote Bryan's name and began to profile the wannabe Dom.

His phone buzzed at some point, but he ignored it as he continued. At six a.m., he stepped back to survey his handwork. On the left were the knowns.

*He worked with Luna.*
*Her ex-Dominant.*
*May go to Luna's dojo.*
*Was Ted's cousin.*
*Showed poor impulse control.*
*Definitely a manipulator.*

On the right, he wrote the unknowns posed as questions.

*What was his motivation?*
*What was he using as leverage?*
*Was it some emotional guilt or something more physical and obvious?*

Ted was an information source for Bryan on Luna, maybe even Brandon. But Bryan had done his research on him, not just Luna. Who had he been talking to?

Jacob groaned and raked his fingers through his hair before he glanced at the clock. It was getting him nowhere. He needed a shower and coffee before work. Then he would go to The Playgrounds tonight and every night if he had to, to keep his ears open for any clue.

The sound of keys jingling followed by his door opening had him on high alert. It took almost a minute of him standing there before his exhausted mind reminded him that a thief would not be using keys.

"Hello?"

*Ah shit.* Lani.

He debated on hiding in the office until she left. A long time ago, when he had first moved into the city, his younger self had thought it an excellent idea to give someone a set of his keys for an emergency. At the moment, however, he had a litany of words for his younger self, mostly curses and swears.

"Jacob?" The door to the office swung open with a slow creak, like something straight out of a scene from a horror movie. Then Lani poked her head in. "Have you slept at all?"

He groaned in response. *Trapped.*

Lani stepped into the office and the whiteboard drew her attention immediately. "Oh my," she exclaimed with a breathless sigh.

"What are you doing here, Lani?" he muttered the question, half in embarrassment, not sure what was worse—caught fixating on the issue like a jilted lover who couldn't let go, which he admitted was not an untruth, or that he looked like hell with only a pair of sweatpants on.

Lani didn't spare him a single glance, but instead took a step toward the whiteboard to study it more. "I think you're right."

The impact of her words hit Jacob in the gut, knocking the wind out of him with mixed emotions. Relief that it wasn't some twisted logic his imagination had come up with gave way to an almost uncontrollable panic at the fact that Luna was in trouble.

Lani grabbed a marker as she began adding her own notes. She spoke with care as she worked, as if she were picking and choosing which words to use. "Before Luna ran out on me at lunch yesterday, she was distraught. She asked me that no matter what happened, I would take care of you, no matter what it took. She was desperate for me to agree. That's the behavior of someone who cares—and from what you've told me, that is inconsistent with the reasons she gave you for leaving."

With the last bit of info added on the whiteboard, Lani capped the marker and surveyed her handiwork, then turned toward Jacob. "So if our wayward sub is truly in trouble, what do we do?"

A ghost of a smile graced Jacob's lips. "For now, we dig. And I suggest we start at the club."

* * * *

It took four nights of wandering in The Playgrounds before he caught a break at last.

By then, Jacob had also filled Darryl in. Being a bartender meant he often overheard things that people don't mean for him to hear. It also meant he had a general sense of who was at the club when. So when Jacob approached the bar that night, Darryl wasted no time in motioning him over.

"Remember that girl Bryan was playing with when we had to intervene?" At Jacob's nod, he continued. "I talked to her earlier." There was a tightness in Darryl's voice that made Jacob take a seat and lean closer to his friend. "She was grateful for what we did. When I asked her how she'd met Bryan, she said Cassie had introduced her to him."

*Cassie. Of course. The synonym for trouble.* The girl was a switch, leaning toward a bottom who, at the same time, reveled in being a brat. She had also developed a taste for the more extreme side of masochism, even for Darryl's tastes. Those were some of the many reasons why his friend had ended things, no matter how deep his feelings ran for her.

"You okay?"

There was a tic in Darryl's jaw, but he nodded and cleared his throat. "It sounds like Bryan's been playing mostly with Cass. It would make sense why he knew so much about you and Luna. She always liked to gossip a little too much."

That was another reason, too. Their lifestyle depended so much on secrecy and discretion.

"Jacob, if Cassie's involved…" Darryl gripped the edge of the bar with both hands. "I'm sorry."

"You have nothing to be sorry for." Jacob understood his pain all too well. Darryl didn't need more guilt. "You're not responsible for her. Not anymore. Her actions are her own."

Darryl still grimaced in obvious distaste. "I should have never told her so damn much."

Jacob shrugged a little. "You trusted her. We all did. It's hard to not share when you care for someone so much." He recalled all the thousand little details Luna would tell him over meals, over texts, in excitement during their cuddles. And he remembered looking forward to unloading his own thoughts. She had always been a good listener and understood the comfort he needed.

He missed her.

"Is Cassie around?"

"Yeah." Darryl nodded toward the lounge. Jacob's gaze followed to spot the woman who lay on one of the couches. Despite making herself available for play as a bottom, she certainly posed herself more like a queen.

Everything in Jacob wanted to stay away. But it was the first chance to fill in some blanks. Each night when he returned home, the whiteboard mocked him for the lack of progress, and he was sick of it.

"Thanks." He knocked on the bar once for luck.

"Hey, Jacob."

He paused to half-turn and regarded his friend.

"I like Luna. She's been good for you. If there's anything else I can do, let me know."

"Thanks." Jacob managed a whisper of a smile for Darryl, then braced himself for the lounge. As he entered, he saw quite a few people perk up with interest, and maybe when he was younger, it would have stroked his ego more. But now it just scraped at his nerves, so much that he had to force himself to slow his pace. It would not do to rush.

"Cassie." His greeting was perfunctory as he glanced down at her.

"Why, Jacob, what a surprise!" Cassie purred as she eased up with languid grace. She looked up through her lashes, a demure smile on her lips. "To what do I owe the pleasure of this visit? I didn't think you would be interested in playing with the likes of me."

"Cut the act, Cassie." A hint of a growl underscored his impatience. He crouched down until he was at eye level with her and lowered his voice. "I need to know why Bryan's so damn interested in Luna and if he's said anything to you."

Cassie's features twisted into something uglier and she gave a jeering laugh. "Why is the infamous Jacob jealous of another Dom?"

He leaned forward until he could whisper in her ear. To any onlookers, it would be as if he was whispering intimate secrets to her. Instead, his voice dove deeper. "I'm serious, Cassie. Bryan's offered her a long-term contract." He allowed the statement to sink in, hoping it would bring her to his side. If Bryan had offered Cassie one, she would not be presenting herself in the lounge. She stiffened beside him.

Jacob shifted so that he could meet her the eye, reached for her hand and gave it a gentle squeeze, offering some comfort. He had no desire to be cruel. "You're a lot of things, Cassie, but you've never been malicious. I think Luna's in trouble and I need to make sure she's okay. Please." It was as close to begging as he had ever come.

Cassie's eyes softened. Darryl had mentioned once that Cassie had gotten into some unspecified trouble and he had bailed her out. Though the story lacked details, he understood that it had been how they'd met and hooked up in the beginning. Then there was the fact that Cassie and Luna used to be friends.

"Okay, fine." She rolled her eyes and gave a theatrical sigh. "Buy me a drink and I'll tell you what I can. It's pretty dead in here, anyway."

Jacob rose to his feet, and when Cassie held out a hand to him, he took it with reluctance to help her up. They made their way to the bar where he mouthed a silent apology to Darryl.

"You'll need a stiff one," she warned and ordered a shot of tequila with a gin and tonic chaser. Jacob took the advice and ordered his usual cognac, then paid with a few crumpled bills, leaving a large tip. After Darryl served the drinks in stony silence, the bartender made himself scarce. Jacob could understand. He wasn't sure he wanted to hear what Cassie wanted to say either, but it was something he needed to do.

Cassie downed her shot in one go and grimaced at the burn. "Bryan's obsessed with your girl," she began. The expression never left her face, long after the burn would have faded. "It got to a point where a few times when we were fucking, he would call out her name. From what I can infer, he never got to screw her, so it's like unfinished business for him."

She was right. Jacob needed strong alcohol to stomach the telling. Now he wished he'd gotten a shot too.

"Anyhow, a few days ago, we angry-fucked. He came back from his conference livid and kept yelling about something she had done and how dare she. When we played, he was super hard and muttered about how he had a plan and he was going to make her his." She shook her head a little and winced at the memory. "Not sure where it all came from, but I just recovered enough today to sit without swearing my head off. After that session, though, he just turned back to his charming self, as if he had vented enough. I haven't seen or heard from him since."

By then, Cassie had wrapped her arms around herself, her drink forgotten. Even as she lapsed into silence, she continued to stare into space. Jacob reached out and placed a hand on her shoulder. "Cassie, you don't have to put up with this. No one deserves that kind of treatment."

His touch must have snapped her out of it. She gave him a rueful smile, reached for her glass and downed her drink. "I know. I should have more self-respect, right? Who the fuck keeps going back to a guy yelling some other girl's name?" Another chuckle spilled from her lips. "Worry about yourself and Luna. She deserves better than Bryan. Thanks for the drink. And… Good luck." With that, she slid off the chair and waved without a glance backward.

It confirmed one thing. Luna was very much in trouble.

# Chapter Thirty

*Misery loves company. Yeah right.*

All Luna wanted was for everyone to leave her alone. She ignored messages from Lani. She avoided Ted's invites to lunch. She begged off with one pathetic excuse or another to skip practice. Even at work, she hid in her office and only emerged for meetings, sticking to online chat or emails for communication. Jacob, she heard nothing from. One part of her was relieved, but another part mourned.

The only one she had still been in steady communication with was Bryan, and that was, of course, not by choice. He was talkative as hell on the phone — flirty, charming, even courteous. He started the week out as they had been before the confrontation at the conference, but nothing could overcome the fact that he was blackmailing her. Over the course of the week, however, his texts grew dirtier and darker.

*I fixed up a dungeon in my basement just for you.*

That was Wednesday. By Thursday and Friday, the messages coming in were more and more explicit. She was grateful she didn't have any meetings with him through the week. It would have been too much.

*You'll truly be my doll. I'll dress you up in the sexiest things, we'll go to dinner then we'll head back and I'll tie you up. I have so many toys waiting for you. You'll love it. You'll be so filled up with every hole plugged all night long, just begging to come.*

Luna stared at her phone on Friday morning, seeing the latest in the line of pornographic messages, but before she could reply, another one came in.

*Ever felt clamps on your nipples and clit all at once then have a flogger directly land on them? You'll scream so hard you won't be able to stop.*

Perhaps for some other sub, that was a turn on, but it had never been Luna's kink. Sometimes, in the last two days, the messages would sicken her so much that they would send her dry retching in the washroom or sitting on the toilet, waiting for the nausea to subside. All she could manage were one- or two-word texts back. Sometimes, like with the ones she'd just gotten, she didn't even know how to reply at all.

In truth, there was only one person she wanted to talk to.

By the time Friday afternoon rolled around, she'd lost all ability to focus at work and had to take the rest of the day off. It wasn't hard, considering how sickly she'd probably looked most of the week. But rather than going straight home to bed, she pulled herself together enough to leave, stopping only once to pick up a bouquet. Once she stepped off the bus, she walked past the gates and up the hill until she stood in front of a very specific grave, white roses in hand.

"Hi, August. I guess it's been a while."

She sat on the damp grass, placing the flowers she bought on the stone. "I've missed you. I really wish you were here right now."

Tears spilled down her cheeks and she rubbed them away with the heel of her palm. When she spoke again, her voice remained broken. "I got myself into a mess. You know what I mean, right?" August always knew what she meant. He had been one of her closest friends, a well-respected sub in the community who had taken her under his wing when she'd first started exploring the local scene. Their style of serving was so similar that they had become fast friends, lifelong friends — until a drunk driver had taken it all away.

"I could use your advice right now. I don't know what to do. I want to say 'fuck it' and walk away, let whatever may come, come. But how would that play out? What would happen to my job? My life? That would break me, and I'd just be a burden to Jacob. I can't be that. How would he look at me after? I can't let that happen. That's what it means to serve, right? We protect our Dominants. We can't become their burdens. What if he thinks this is his fault? I can't let this hurt him too."

Her face crumpled even as she spoke those last words out loud. "Ah, but I guess I already hurt him. And I'm going to keep hurting him — his heart or his pride as a Dom. What do I choose?"

Luna pulled her knees closer to her chest. "August, what do I choose?"

There was no answer from the silent grave.

\* \* \* \*

Saturday morning, she woke to a message that chilled her bones.

*Your lack of enthusiasm for our soon-to-be relationship has really disappointed me. If you want to convince me that you'll stick to our agreement, you'll have to do something this weekend to prove it.*

Luna's hands shook as she sat up on her bed, trying to quell the panic rising within. It took some effort before she persuaded her lungs to work properly again. As she drew in another deep breath, she steeled herself and typed back.

*What can I do to convince you, Master Bryan?*

She hoped she sounded remotely sultry over the text. Maybe she should have added an emoji. Would a hand on a cucumber work? The absurdity of her situation had her giggling. Hysteria. There was a lot of that lately.

*Come to The Playgrounds tonight. Dress like the slut you are. I know you can scene with others as long as you have permission. Go ask Jacob for it. I'm sure he'll have no problem saying yes, knowing your cunt is practically mine soon.*

*He wants me to scene. With him. In The Playgrounds.* The last thing she wanted was to talk to Jacob. She wanted him as far away from it all as possible. And now Bryan wanted to play in front of Jacob, to rub his nose about the entire thing. Inside she quailed at the impossible task.

*Luna, you better give me an answer in the next thirty seconds. Don't disappoint me.*

She jumped out of her bed, panic once more threatening to overwhelm her.

*Yes, Master Bryan.*

A good five minutes ticked by before a message came back.

*Luna, Luna, Luna, what am I going to do with you? I don't know how that poor excuse of a Dom can call himself a trainer. You're still lacking as a sub in so many ways. No worries, my doll, we have all the time in the world for me to mold you to my taste.*

Luna swallowed several times to wet her lips. Her mouth was as dry as a desert.

*Yes, Master Bryan. Thank you.*

What else was she supposed to type? She tried to recall in the past if there had been any hints as to just how sadistic he was, even when she'd only known him online. But she drew a blank.

Luna threw herself back on the bed. Maybe if she went back to sleep, she'd wake up and find it would be just one long nightmare.

The darkness was a comfort, a blanket of nothingness, a void she floated in. When Luna woke, the sun was already setting. With a vicious curse on her lips, she kicked off the covers and scrambled for the shower. Briefly, she contemplated dinner but realized quick enough that with the night she had ahead of her, anything she tried to choke down would probably come right back up.

Instead, she dried her hair and opened her closet to figure out what she could wear. While Jacob always said she had a closet full of fun, they were still tasteful outfits that Bryan would likely consider as being too conservative. She chewed her lower lip, brushing her hand over the different fabrics until she settled on a short leather skirt and a grungy top that was mostly fishnet with just a band of black across the chest. She had bought both items for a biker-themed party that she and Jacob had meant to attend. They had never quite made it out of the apartment, though, and had ended up missing the entire thing.

She hated wearing it for Bryan.

Luna paired the outfit with stockings and a garter belt before she went off to find the tallest pair of heels she could, wincing as she forced herself into them. Even if Bryan's idea of fun didn't end in a world of hurt for her, standing in these heels would definitely finish the job.

She tousled her hair with hairspray. Too uncomfortable to take public transit in such an outfit, she called for a Lyft and was off, not daring to be late.

She kept her body hidden in her jacket even as she arrived at The Playgrounds. It was probably the first time in a long while that she had been so nervous there. She scanned the room, and when she spotted Darryl, she moseyed over.

"Hey, Luna," Darryl greeted. Without another word, he pushed a bottle of water in her direction. With a nod of thanks, she opened it and took small, careful sips, worried that she might not even be able to keep that down. Luna waited for questions about Jacob to start, but they never came. As if sensing how uncomfortable Luna was, Darryl moved away with only a brief nod.

Bryan came with a grin. However, his expression turned into a frown as he sighted the large jacket still covering most of Luna. She tore it off her in haste, trembling as he neared.

"Ah, better. Looks like there may be some hope for you yet." Bryan wolf whistled as he trailed a finger from her lips, down along her neck and over her breast and one nipple, all the way to her belly button. She flinched and her stomach clenched.

Bryan leaned forward and whispered, "Ah, my little cunt, already so sensitive and eager to play. Me too, slut. Me too."

He patted her knee and grinned as he shifted to slide into the seat next to her. "You just wait, my dear. We're going back to the cross tonight and I'll make you scream louder and come harder than you ever did with Jacob."

Rather than being turned on—which Luna was sure was Bryan's intention—a sense of dread settled in the pit of her stomach. Her appetite for both food and sex had taken a dive to nil in the last week. The constant stroking of her knee up to her garter belt made her skin crawl.

Fortunately, or unfortunately, Jacob arrived. He looked exhausted and unhappy but alert, scanning the room as if looking for someone. Their eyes met and Luna flushed in shame.

"Go on, Luna. Go ask for permission to be the little whore you are."

The humiliation Bryan seemed to enjoy so much tired Luna, but she didn't dare say a word. When she slid off the chair, she paused for a moment to find her balance in those impossible heels. When she didn't move right away, Bryan gave her a smack on her rear that almost sent her sprawling forward on her face.

Recovering in time, she walked over to Jacob, shaking like a leaf, like Bambi on stilts. There was no smile in his greeting, and he only gave her a wary nod of acknowledgment.

More *stabbity-stab. How much more is Bryan going to make me hurt him?*

"Jacob." She breathed out his name, wishing she sounded more like the cruel bitch she was pretending to be. "I would like to ask for permission to scene with Bryan tonight." The words stuck like tar to her throat and came out with all the formality she could muster. It was easier to pretend she was reading out words from a paper she had memorized.

Rage thundered across his face and Luna noticed his fists clenching and unclenching repeatedly. But within seconds, something replaced it, something akin to concern, pity and sadness. *No, why would he feel that way?* Better for him to be angry.

"No." The reply came quiet but firm. "You don't have permission to play with Bryan. You don't have to stay by my side tonight, but you will *not* play." There was a finality to his tone.

"Is there a problem?" Bryan sidled up behind her. There was no touching, but he towered over her, too close for comfort while Jacob stood before them both, paces away. The irony was not lost on Luna as they were in reversed positions from just weeks ago. What she wouldn't give to feel Jacob's arms around her one last time.

"Yes. You would do well to remember and respect the contract I still have with Luna."

Bryan raised an eyebrow, a sneer twisting his features. Now that he did not need to pretend, his features betrayed the cruelty that lay beneath the charm. "Well, I suppose if I was in your shoes, I'd feel the same way." Bryan inclined his head. "Of course, I'll respect your decision." He leaned in. Their height made it so that the two could converse directly over Luna's head. "I'll make her scream louder than you ever did on that Saint Andrew's Cross the other day." Then he leaned back, chuckled and clapped Jacob on his shoulder. "I should be thanking you. You're right. The anticipation of breaking in my new toy later is so much more fun. Isn't that right, Luna?"

She flinched at his words, knowing he had designed them for a specific purpose. But trapped as she was, she had no choice. "Yes, Master Bryan."

"And you're so looking forward to me breaking you in, aren't you?"

Any minute now, Jacob was going to snap and jump on Bryan. She could tell his body was readying for a fight. It would damage his reputation irreparably, despite her best efforts.

"Of course, Master Bryan. I do know how much you enjoy me on that cross, and I'm so looking forward to pleasing you on it, just like I did with Master Jacob." Luna attempted her most sickly sweet smile and looked up at her tormentor. Adoring. *What does adoring look like?* In her mind, she chanted as if she would cast it a spell. *Hate me, Jacob, hate me, hate me.*

When Jacob only stared at her, struggling to keep the disgust from his face, Luna whimpered on the inside.

It was time to leave. "Please, wouldn't you like a drink? I would absolutely love one." Luna pitched her voice higher and wondered if she should have batted her lashes.

"A most excellent idea, anything my future pet wants."

Relieved that Bryan had bought the line, she led him away. Yet, she could not help but glance back over her shoulder to see the raw pain that hunched over the man who always stood tall and proud.

# Chapter Thirty-One

Despite the red haze of fury that clouded his mind, there was something that bothered Jacob on a more logical level. As he watched them retreat to the bar, he remained rooted to the floor, torn between the need to do more investigating and the need to stay close. As long as Luna's friends and acquaintances were around, there would be a limit to what Bryan would try. The remaining days of his and Luna's contract were her last thin layer of protection.

"Jacob," Lani called out to him from behind as she came to his side and touched his arm with a gentle hand.

It was enough for him to relax a smidgen. Lani had that kind of effect on people. He rubbed his face with one hand. "How much of that did you hear?"

"Enough." Her gaze traveled toward Luna and Bryan at the bar and he turned back to study them. Bryan was chatting and laughing while Luna sat, shrinking into herself as she made weak attempts at smiling. That temporary moment of flirtation from her had evaporated, replaced by a general sullen discomfort and wariness. She was a shitty actress with an innate inability to stay in character, and Jacob was glad for it. If nothing else had convinced him that she was under duress, that just had.

"Something was odd about that conversation." Jacob needed a quick sounding board, and if Lani had heard, she was the perfect solution, as she was one of the most observant people he knew.

"How so?" Lani asked. Neither of them looked away from the bar.

"Both Bryan and Luna mentioned the Saint Andrew's Cross. I think Bryan is obsessed with proving himself the bigger Dom."

"Not unlikely. He has a classic psychopathic and narcissistic profile, from what we've been able to gather so far."

"Yeah, but why that cross?" There was a hint there, but it remained stubbornly elusive.

Lani shrugged in response. "Didn't you two play upstairs on the cross a few weeks ago? You and Luna don't play in public often and it's probably the only time Bryan witnessed you two in action, right?"

The only time… *Shit.* He had been looking at it all wrong. He had been combing through Luna's writings for days, trying to find hints of whether Bryan ever had her compromised back then. Perhaps he was looking too far in the past.

Lani regarded him in silence before she straightened, tilting her chin up as she assumed her Dominant role with haughtiness. "Darryl and I have got this. We'll keep them in public and make sure Luna goes home alone. You go do what you need to do."

Gratitude for his friend welled up in Jacob. "Thanks." It was all he could manage currently, but he promised himself he would pay her back somehow.

Lani threw a look back over her shoulders, quirking the corner of her lips upward. "Don't. Wait till you see my bill."

"Pest."

Her laughter trailed after her. Jacob stayed to observe as Lani made her way to the bar and asserted her presence with ease. He was close enough to see the mix of relief and shame that made a mess of awkwardness out of the hug Luna and Lani shared. A moment later, Darryl joined in. Bryan was all smiles and charm, but now that Jacob had learned what to look for, he saw that the man was not pleased.

*Good.*

He turned toward the stairs and sighed, not relishing the task before him. But he would walk through the fires of hell right now if it meant keeping Luna safe. It was his job as her Dominant—and his privilege.

His steps were firm with resolve as he made his way upstairs. The offices were at the end of the hall on the third floor, past all the private rooms, and he didn't pause until he stood in front of Erica's office. Politely, he knocked on the door. It would not do to barge right in, as much as he wanted to.

"Come in."

Jacob tensed as he opened the door. Rather than the easy camaraderie he had with Lani and Darryl, he admitted that he struggled much more with Erica. The woman was relentless, with her every gesture designed to be a power move. But to hold on to her domain amid all the other dominant personalities that were at The

Playgrounds, it was understandable. They were all here at her sufferance and she would let none of them forget about it.

"Jacob, how are you this evening?" The woman did not rise from her desk but, instead, rested her chin against one crooked wrist, her elbow braced against the arm of her chair.

"I...could be better." It was always a terrible idea to lie to Erica.

She gestured to the chair in front of her desk. Jacob allowed himself to sink into the seat, although he remained on the edge, his back straight.

"Luna."

Of course she knew. His shoulders stiffened.

His surprise must have shown. Erica chuckled and leaned forward. "I make it my business to keep tabs on my regulars and know if there may be any potential trouble brewing in the horizon." She shifted until she was hovering over her desk, folding her arms over each other on top of the table. "Will there be trouble, Jacob?"

It was his turn to shrug as he leaned back, feigning a casualness he did not feel. "It depends."

"On?"

"On what I find." He was growing tired of dancing around the issue. "Erica, I think Luna's in trouble and Bryan is holding something over her. I'd like to review the security footage, to see if Bryan may have done anything."

"No." The word was sharp, curt.

"Erica, wouldn't you want to know if someone managed to sneak a camera in here? If there was a security breach—"

"Precisely." Erica cut him off, tilting her head upward in challenge. "I will not suffer any damage to this club's reputation based on some hunch you have. Besides, you are still suspended from employment and I cannot just let any patron of the club review security footage simply because they think something happened." She dropped her voice. "I don't have anyone on staff who can comb through hours and hours of video right now. We barely have enough people manning the place as is."

Jacob groaned in frustration, wishing there were a way around it.

"I'll do it." Both of them looked up in surprise as Darryl walked into the room. He gave Jacob a slight shrug. "Not like I have anything better to do tomorrow, anyway." He carefully set a shot of something murky and a taller glass of a multi-colored concoction on the desk.

Erica opened her mouth as if to protest, then stared at both of them. "Fine." She glowered. "But I'm not paying you overtime. You can come in and start at nine tomorrow morning." She grabbed the shot and downed it in one smooth movement.

*That was almost too easy.* Jacob recalled their phone conversation a while back and realized that deep inside, Erica cared. He was a lucky man to have so many people helping him.

"Yes, Ma'am." Darryl nodded with a straight face.

"Get out of here, both of you."

It wasn't until they were both out of the office with the door closed behind that they turned to each other, shit-eating grins on their faces. Getting their way after Erica had already said no was a feat all on its own.

"I owe you one," Jacob started, but Darryl shook his head.

"No, you don't. I told you that I'd help however I can, and I meant it."

"Well, thanks anyway."

"Bryan left, by the way. I think by the time Lani and Luna were into the fifth dance on the floor, he gave up on waiting."

The remaining tension in Jacob drained and he slumped against the wall. Bryan had just experienced first-hand how hard it was to say no to Lani. Perhaps things were finally looking up. Jacob managed a tired smile.

"You look like hell, Jacob. Go home and get some rest. I'll call tomorrow as soon as I find anything."

With weariness seeping into his bones, Jacob yawned. It was time to go home. He clapped Darryl on the shoulder, hoping it was enough to convey his gratitude, and walked off.

\* \* \* \*

The morning found Jacob staring once more at the whiteboard, as if it would spill forth new answers to the many questions he still had. Of course, no matter how hard he studied the connections, nothing new came up, but it was better than waiting idly for Darryl's call.

"Hey, I brought coffee and croissants."

Jacob jumped at the voice and spun around to see a perky Lani holding up a tray of steaming hot beverages and food.

"You know, you can buzz up like everyone else."

Lani set the food and tray down before waving one hand in the air. "*Pfft*. Why bother? I'll do that when I have to worry about walking in on you and Luna again." A Cheshire Cat grin graced her lips. "Then again, that might be fun too."

"All right, that's it. Hand back the keys." Jacob held out a hand as he stalked toward her.

"Hey, I was kidding!" Lani pouted and grabbed his coffee and a croissant from the tray and a croissant, holding them up as a peace offering.

With a grumble, Jacob snatched both from her hands and settled into his office chair.

"We need to get Luna back for you. You're turning into a humorless old grouch."

Jacob snarled at her in response. It barely fazed Lani, but he expected that. They had been friends for too long.

Lani grabbed her own share and they ate in amicable silence before they both turned back to the board, sipping their drinks side by side. Too restless to sit much longer, Jacob stood once more and grabbed a marker, only to realize he had no actual new concrete information to add.

"How's Luna?" Jacob asked, struggling to keep the fear from his voice while his gaze bored holes in his own writing.

"She's hanging on by a thread," Lani replied, setting her tea down. "She puts up a brave front, but we all know she wears her emotions on her sleeve. The stress of it all is making her physically ill and I had moments where I was worried she was going to faint on the dance floor last night."

Something in him withered at her description.

"I took her out after. It took a drink or two to loosen her enough to relax."

Jacob turned toward Lani in alarm.

"Relax. I didn't get her drunk, only a little buzzed, enough to let me get some food into her. Once she started eating, she couldn't stop. She may have been starving herself." Lani's face was pale as she spoke. "She still refused to say much, only that Bryan's intense, but she sounded scared out of her mind, Jacob. I'm not sure how much more time we have before whatever is happening pushes her over the edge."

"Is this your professional opinion?" Jacob asked, wariness slowing his words.

"I... I don't know," Lani admitted, her own voice laced with frustration. "I'm too close to this too." She looked up and it surprised Jacob to see her eyes filmed over. "She's my friend too. Both of you are. I don't want to see either of you in pain."

Without another word, he reached out and drew her into a hug. It was the kind of comfort they both needed.

His phone ringing startled both of them. Jacob glanced at the clock, realizing it was only ten. It couldn't be Darryl already.

Jacob dug into his pocket and pulled out his phone, taken aback when it was his friend. With more trepidation than he cared to admit, he pressed the call button and held it up to his ear, half expecting Darryl to say that Erica had locked him out of the building.

"So, I started from that time you guys played in public like Lani told me to." Darryl didn't even bother with a greeting. Jacob raised an eyebrow at Lani, who was back to sipping her tea.

"Hold on. She's standing right next to me. Let me put you on speaker." He pulled his phone away from his ear and held it out.

"Oh, hey, Lani."

"Good morning, Darryl."

*Oh, sure. Lani deserves a greeting.* Jacob almost made a comment but bit it back in time. Lani was right, damn her. He was turning into an old bear.

"As I was saying, I started with the footage from the dungeon. I'm not entirely sure, but at some point, Bryan pulled out his phone and hit a single button before putting it back in his pocket. I can't tell what he was doing but it couldn't have been the phone camera, since he never pointed his phone up and he didn't have it out for long. Maybe he was even hanging up on an incoming call, for all I can tell."

"Could he have triggered a remote device?" Lani asked.

"Not sure. I'll keep scanning the later videos to see if he's ever gone back to retrieve anything." Darryl dropped his voice and both Lani and Jacob had to lean in to hear. "Erica had a team sweep through the entire place looking for bugs first thing this morning, though. I think you rattled her more than we suspected last night."

Jacob paled. "Did they find anything?"

"Nope. Nada."

Jacob wasn't sure if he was relieved or frustrated. Was it another dead lead?

"Thanks, Darryl. I appreciate it."

"No worries, man."

They hung up. With a sigh, Jacob walked over and slumped into his chair.

"Don't give up." Lani patted his shoulder. "Come on. Let's go over what we know one more time."

With a heavy sigh, Jacob nodded. At least it helped to fight the bleakness that threatened to consume him.

"All right. Let's start from the beginning again."

# Chapter Thirty-Two

Luna was sure she hadn't drunk that much the previous night, not enough to cause the relentless pounding in her head and the constant dryness in her throat. *Am I coming down with something? Hey, maybe that'll keep Bryan away for a while.* Luna almost perked up at that thought.

*Is it the last week of my contract with Jacob?* The days were blurring together. It was the last scenario she had ever expected. Never had she imagined that they would be spending their last week together like this — or rather, not together at all.

For the rest of the day, however, she barely slept, as much as she tried. When she closed her eyes, all she saw was Jacob's pain, the way he'd stood hunched over like a broken man out of a Shakespearean tragedy. When she was awake, all her mind did was replay their last conversation, the hurt that made his voice raspy and low. She was putting the man through hell.

Fresh tears filled from her eyes to her own shock and she rubbed them away. She had thought that she was done crying, but it seemed she wasn't.

Her phone rang with a short beep, showing someone was downstairs, wanting in. Fear shot through her system as she picked up the phone. Did Bryan know where she lived?

"Luna, let me in. It's Ted."

Relief mingled with apprehension as she pressed the key to allow him access. Ted had been trying to corner her all week, but she hadn't thought he would resort to a home visit. Another illogical thought wormed its way through her brain. *Did he bring Bryan? Did Bryan set his cousin up somehow?*

She opened the door a crack then let out a breath of relief when she saw it was just Ted exiting the elevator. He held up a plastic bag with a hesitant smile. "I have chocolate fudge and cookie dough. Pick your poison."

*Ice cream bribery. Not fair.*

*How can I not let him in?* Since Lani had tricked her into eating, she had regained her appetite. Luna opened the door wider and took a step back.

"Go sit down on the couch. I'll scoop us both a bit of each." Ted herded Luna toward her living room, then took charge like a mother hen. He'd look funny in a chicken costume. She giggled at the thought, aware that with her appearance, she may appear as though she had more than a few screws loose.

Once they both settled on Luna's couch, they dug into the ice cream. But her mind was spinning. She had to take control of the situation.

"So what brings you here?" Luna kept her tone casual as she tried to convince both of them she was okay. "Not that I don't appreciate the ice cream, but I know there's an ulterior motive. Let me guess. You need help to plan a surprise party for Brandon!"

"Luna." Ted set the spoon and bowl down. "Stop trying to put up a brave front. You know we're all worried about you. You're a ghost of yourself, barely coming out from your office. I've had both Prakash and Jung ask if you're okay. Joanna keeps hauling me into the office to grill me like an interrogator. She's half freaking out, thinking that you've got some terminal illness you're not telling us." He stopped himself and stared at her in horror. "Wait. You don't have cancer or something like that, do you?"

Luna wanted to laugh, but the sound died in her throat when she realized he was not kidding. She shook her head. "I'm okay, Ted. Really. I'm not sick." *Not terminally, anyway.*

With a sigh, he slumped back in relief then spooned a few more bits of ice cream into his mouth. She watched her friend, wincing at the discovery of a whole fresh source of guilt.

"Can you tell me what's going on?" Ted set his spoon down and turned toward her.

She wished she couldn't see the plea in his eyes. It made what she had to say next harder. "I can't."

Ted leaned back and looked down at his bowl of melting ice cream once more. "Luna, we've known each other for a long time. You were the first one I came out to. Remember how it was Pride and we were watching TV on this couch? I don't know what I would have done if you hadn't accepted me for who I was back then."

Luna recalled the day. Ted had expected her to reject him. It had been in his voice, in his very curled-up posture. Instead, she had facepalmed, chastised herself for not realizing earlier, then insisted they celebrate his courage for coming out. They had dropped by the parade after to check out guys and make guesses which guy played for which team. A ghost of a smile tugged at the corner of Luna's lips. It had been a wonderful day and an even better memory, knowing she had made a positive impact on her friend's life.

"So, whatever you're going through, whatever it is, you know I'd never judge. I'd never stop being your friend."

His words broke a dam within her. She still couldn't tell him everything, but...

"I'm a sub." She blurted the three words without a thought. They hung in the air and without waiting, Luna grabbed a pillow and buried her face in it. *What the hell did I do?* Her and her big mouth.

"Like... *Fifty Shades of Grey* stuff?" Hesitation slowed Ted's words.

She peeked out at Ted then groaned. "Um...not exactly. Kind of." She was not that kind of sub, and Jacob was most definitely not that kind of Dom.

Ted blinked once, then twice before a slow grin spread across his face. "I'll take that as a yes."

No, she would not dignify that with an answer. Her cheeks heated and she wondered if she could keep her face stuck to the pillow on a more permanent basis.

"So, explain it to me. I'm serious. I want to understand."

She peeked out from behind. There was no disgust or terror on his face, just an earnest willingness to listen. With a soft sigh, Luna put the pillow away and composed herself.

With a newfound bravery, bolstered by her friend's lack of judgement, she picked up her bowl of ice cream, ate a spoonful and savored the taste of sweetness for the first time in the week.

And crossing her legs on the couch, she began to explain what the lifestyle meant for her.

\* \* \* \*

By the time Monday morning rolled around, she was beginning to rethink her arrangement with Bryan. She and Ted had talked late into the night and the more she spoke, the more she realized how stupid she had been to have never told Ted all these years. The juxtaposition of Ted's acceptance mixed with Jacob's pain created an unexpected dichotomy in her head, one she was unable to shake. At some point, she realized that she had a choice. She always did.

Would she rather be broke with no career prospects but freed from this living hell or to have the shambles of a career but be caged in an abusive relationship? After the weekend she'd just had, the answer was irrevocably the former. She would deal with the fallout.

And perhaps she wouldn't lose it all? Lots of celebrities had sex tapes released online and their careers were still thriving. *Right?*

Her laugh came out more like a bark.

Underscoring it all, however, was something else she suddenly realized. Nothing was worth putting Jacob through the pain he was in. Perhaps she and Jacob could work through it after Bryan released the video. Even if that wasn't possible, it was still better to be alone than wear a collar and leash held by Bryan. And it would still be better for Jacob than to have Bryan using her to egg him on.

Or perhaps they'd run away and go where no one knew them.

Luna shook her head, twisting her lips into a bitter smile. Impossible fantasies like that only hurt more.

Things had gone too far for her to even consult him in her choices. She would have to take the risk and live with the consequences. But at least she could look at herself in the mirror again with self-respect, even if Jacob ended up hating her for her choice. At least he would hate her because of something real and not because of the façade of lies. And she would live with that, knowing she had done her best to serve him. It was a gamble, but it was one she would make, for both their hearts' sake.

Luna stared at her phone then, steady with determination, grabbed it.

*Would you be free to meet me for lunch, Master Bryan?*

He loved it when she called him that. She stared at her phone, waiting for a reply. She needed to do it before she chickened out.

*Oh? Why, I rather like this new initiative you're taking Luna. Sure. Let's meet at that soup and sandwich place we went to last time.*

*Of course, Master Bryan. I'm looking forward to it.*

And despite feeling like she was going to hurl at any minute, hope hammered in her chest.

Luna got into the office early once again, but thankfully, there were no more interruptions. Instead, she focused on dealing with the one part of the potential fallout she had any control over. Luna pulled up a new document and wrote her resignation letter. She would not drag the company and, more importantly, her friends' livelihoods down with her. If she quit, the clients, even the sensitive ones, would have no reason to cut the contracts.

That done, she switched to working on a transition document until Joanna came to work. Luna sucked in a breath and marched into her boss' office.

"Luna, are you okay?"

Luna closed the office door behind her and steeled herself for the conversation.

"Yes. No." Luna glanced down at one of the chairs, and when Joanna nodded, she took a seat before she pushed an envelope across her desk. "Joanna" — she took a deep breath — "I'm submitting my resignation."

Joanna folded her arms over the desk. "For what reason?"

Luna had a lot of difficulty meeting Joanna's eyes. "I wrote — "

"No, Luna. I want to hear it from you. I need to know why, all of a sudden."

Shame filled her and made it hard to speak, but she forced the words out. "There's a personal matter that has come up which may impact the company negatively."

"Did you do something illegal?"

Her head snapped back in surprise and she stared at Joanna wide-eyed. "What? No, of course not!"

Joanna sighed. "Then what could be so serious that you would walk away from everything you've built here?"

When Luna didn't answer and only hung her head, Joanna frowned. "I'm not accepting it." She pushed the envelope back, but before Luna protested, she cut in. "Whatever it is, I'm sure we can handle it. Tell me what you think the impact is."

There was no escaping the force of will sitting before her. "It would give reason for our more conservative clients to cut us loose."

Joanna studied her in a moment of silence and Luna shifted under the scrutiny.

"Who?"

"The government ones." Luna's voice remained small. "In particular, the ones you guys may have given out to Telcorus as reference." Even the company name was hard to spit out.

Her boss pulled herself up taller in her chair. "Luna, did something happen at the conference? Did Bryan harass you?"

*Am I that transparent?* Luna tried to take a subtle deep breath. "Please, Joanna. I know I owe you an explanation, but it's something really personal that I can't talk about."

The older woman studied her before nodding. "All right, I won't pry. But whatever is going on, know that you have my full support. You're talented and hardworking and damn if I will let some guy ruin your career—not under my watch. We'll start by getting ready to pull you off those contracts and off the project with Telcorus, then we'll see, okay?"

Luna wanted to cry, but she choked out a 'thank you' instead. She made a quick escape out of the office lest she end up telling Joanna everything, and she hid in her own office. There, she tried her best to calm the anxiety that threatened to overwhelm her. But she had done it, driven the first nail into her coffin, for better or worse.

Lunch found Luna early with a table ready. The crowd that filled the place gave her some relief. The more people there were, the less likely he would cause a scene. At a certain point, she was no longer sure what Bryan was capable of.

When he came in all smiles, the enormity of what she was about to do almost made her want to run screaming for the nearest exit. *This is it.* She was about to nuke her life. Her heart thumped so loudly in her chest that she thought the whole cafe could hear it.

"How is my little doll?" Bryan slid into his seat. Was he expecting her to go get his food? *Oh right, he probably is. The ass.*

"I'm done." *Nuclear missile launched.*

"Excuse me?" Bryan leaned forward, menacing shadows darkening his features.

"I'm done playing this sick little game of yours. I'm out. I will not be signing a contract with you. I will not be serving you. And you can stop calling me your doll, your slut or whatever derogatory term you have in your repertoire." Once she started, she lost the ability to stop. The suffering she'd gone through the past week boiled into anger that spurred her on.

"Luna Weir, I will give you thirty seconds to withdraw your statement. I don't think you quite realize the consequences of your proposed actions." Bryan steepled his fingers, tapping them to his lips. A slight tremor of his body betrayed the temper he was attempting to leash.

She leaned forward, her voice dropping into an angry growl. "No. I know what I'm doing. I won't let you control me any longer. Do whatever you want with the video you have. I don't care anymore."

That was everything she needed to say. With a stiff back, she rose from the table, drawing herself to full height as she looked down on him. Spite, however, pushed her further and provoked her to speak the next words. "I pity you, Bryan, that you have to resort to blackmail to force someone to submit to you. You're no Dom…just an abuser using BDSM as an excuse."

"You will regret this, Luna." A storm was brewing on Bryan's face and a crazed light danced in his eyes. It was time to go.

She gave a soft, bitter laugh. "I regret the day I let you convince me to hurt Jacob. This is just righting a wrong."

Before he could utter another word, she walked away. Luna tucked her hands into her pockets, dodging his attempt to grab her wrist. She kept walking as he rose from his chair, shaking with promised wrath. She kept walking as she left the cafe and took in the first full breath of freedom.

But Luna was not done yet. There was one last wrong to right.

# Chapter Thirty-Three

Luna didn't dare to buzz up to Jacob's, unsure if he would even tolerate seeing her. So she waited outside his building around the corner like a stalker until she saw someone going in. With a quick smile, she ducked in before the door closed completely, acting as if she lived in the place. It was fortunate that she had been here enough times that she was a familiar face to his neighbors.

As she rode the elevator up, Luna chewed her lips. Talking to Joanna or even confronting Bryan hadn't made her as nervous as she was now. When the elevator arrived at Jacob's floor, she sprinted out and almost fell flat on her face as she tripped over the uneven spacing between the elevator and the floor.

She caught herself in time, then tried to pace herself, walking up to Jacob's door with as much dignity as she could muster. It wasn't a lot.

On her way over, Luna had tried to compose the right words to say in her head. An apology should be there somewhere, but somehow 'I'm sorry' seemed too insignificant. She knew she wasn't there to beg him to take her back, but he deserved to know the truth. But how could she put it so it didn't sound like the pathetic excuse it was?

For the third time that day, she pushed herself forward before she lost her nerve and she rapped her knuckles on the door. No answer. She tried again. *Oh God, what if he isn't home?* Or worse, what if he was with someone and she was interrupting? *What if he's in the middle of playing with someone?* Luna's face reddened, fear of what she would see making her hesitate to knock one more time.

No, she would still owe him an apology. She would come back another time. Tears began spilling down her cheeks as her mind spiraled downward, out of control. She couldn't do it. She wasn't brave enough. She—

The door opened and an exhausted Jacob opened the door. His half-closed eyes widened when he realized who it was. "Luna?" Incredulity dropped his voice into a whisper.

She rubbed at her cheek with both her palms. "Can... Can I come in?" Luna braced herself for a no as Jacob stiffened before he sighed and stepped aside for her.

Luna struggled to get her crying under control as she stepped into the dimly lit apartment, almost surprised to find herself there once more. She had expected to never be back, and yet here she was.

"What do you want, Luna?"

*Ouch.* She deserved that. She'd done nothing but hurt him. But it still stung. Luna had thought that she had given up on earning Jacob's love back, but his chilly attitude made her heart ache all over again. She stopped in the foyer, afraid to intrude any more than she already had, afraid the very place itself would reject her in some unexpected way.

"I wanted to let you know I'm no longer going to serve Bryan." She faltered as her voice cracked and it took several tries before she found it again. "I'm not asking you to take me back. I hurt you in so many unforgivable ways." Her shoulders trembled and she tried to lean against the wall to steady herself without him noticing.

Jacob stared at her with a distinct lack of warmth in those deep eyes. Luna swallowed, then cleared her throat. "I need you to know that I didn't do it willingly... Well...not entirely. Bryan said he had a video of me that he would share if I didn't do what he said." It was the first time she had admitted that out loud to anyone, and she shuddered with revulsion.

"You're saying he blackmailed you."

Why was it so hard? The tears just wouldn't stop coming now and she struggled to keep talking. His bluntness made her flinch, but she kept going. Just a little more. "It's no excuse for what I did to you. I should have been braver, should have told you. Should have said no. But I was... I was so scared. I'm sorry. I'm so sorry for being such a coward."

Her body was going to give out any minute now, but somehow, she found the strength to turn, to lay a hand on the door handle. "I'll...go now. I just wanted you to know. It wasn't because I didn't love you."

Luna pushed the door handle down, but before she could pull the door back, he enveloped her in his strong arms and pulled her tight against him.

"Don't you dare leave." Jacob's whisper tickled her ear and he buried his face against her hair.

His words sent her trembling as Luna let go of the door handle and slumped against him. In that single moment, she understood at last just how much he was her shelter and strength.

"I've got you, love. I've got you." He tightened his arm around her, but his words made little sense as her emotions threatened to overwhelm her. The tears that wouldn't stop falling clouded her vision. Then, against the seriousness of the moment, she hiccupped.

Luna busted out laughing at the ill timing of the childish sound while Jacob chuckled behind her. She found comfort in the rumble of his chest against her back.

With a light touch on her shoulders, he guided her to turn around and cupped her cheeks to lift her face to his with infinite gentleness. The love she saw on his face took her breath away.

"I knew early on something wasn't right. If I were pissed, it'd be because you didn't trust me enough to come to me with it." When she opened her mouth to explain, he shook his head. "I'm glad you are here now, though."

*Me too.* It was worth it, worth the world of pain that would descend on her head. She would always have this moment to see her through. "I rejected Bryan this afternoon and tried to quit my job, but Joanna just took me off the contracts with more conservative clients."

When Jacob drew in a sharp breath and stared at her with widening eyes, Luna wondered what she'd said. Did he think she would come to him without tying up the loose ends first?

"You— But what about the blackmail?"

Luna shrugged, trying to appear as nonchalant as possible. "Come what may."

"That would mean you gave up everything…" It was the first time she'd ever seen Jacob, the eloquent charmer, at a loss for words. There was an awe in his expression that she didn't feel she deserved.

"I couldn't see you in pain anymore. I didn't want him to use me to hurt you anymore," she admitted, her voice growing smaller.

The next thing she knew, Jacob descended on her with a passion that left her weak-kneed. He kissed with all the desperation and thirst of a man parched for eons. At first, caught by surprise, Luna only trembled as the tidal wave of his passion washed over her.

Then her body awakened.

As if finding familiar ground, she melted into his embrace. When she reached up with one hand to thread her fingers through his hair, he pulled her in closer and nipped her lips before he trailed lower to nibble along her jaw down to her neck, scraping his teeth against the skin there. "Mine."

The single word sent a shot of heat straight to her core and soaked her panties.

"All yours," Luna whispered as she clung to him tighter. She swore to herself with a renewed fierceness. She was never letting go, never again.

Without another minute wasted, Jacob picked her up in a bridal carry and took them to the bedroom.

When he laid her out on his bed, she stared up into his eyes. Jacob broke the gaze first, only to retrieve jute rope from one drawer of the bedside table. That crooked grin she'd missed so much graced his lips once more.

"Got to make sure you're never escaping again."

It was odd how, if that same statement had come from Bryan, Luna would have freaked out. Perhaps it had to do with the fact that behind Jacob's words, she knew there was respect and love. In Jacob's hands, she knew she was safe and cared for. It was the trust they had built together since the beginning.

"Strip." The command was soft, but it sent shivers down her spine. She lifted herself from the bed, pulled off her T-shirt and tugged down her jeans without ceremony, revealing a matching set of red lace halter bra and thong. All week long, she had put on the ugliest granny panties and bras she could find, but this day, it was as if her subconscious had dared to hope that he would take her back.

A hum of appreciation from Jacob spurred Luna to lie down, sliding her thighs together in a tempestuous effort but also to provide some relief to the burning need brewing at her core. She trailed her hand from her stomach up along the center of her body until she reached her breast and could scrape a fingernail across one of her nipples. She parted her lips in a moan and arched her back up at him. He hadn't even touched her yet and he'd already stoked the embers of her arousal into an inevitable storm that threatened to break at any second.

Jacob grinned as he watched the show until her back arched. With a hiss, he surged forward, prying her legs apart to kneel between them, refusing to let her give herself the much-needed relief. When she reached down with both hands, whimpering a protest, he captured and moved them to either side of her head. "Hold still."

Without missing a beat, he tied each of her wrists to D-rings anchored to both sides of the bed so that he had her stretched out in a V. She had almost forgotten about those things that he had so thoughtfully built into his bed.

Luna tugged at the rope to test her restraints only to discover that there was little give. *Jacob always does tie a good knot.* She looked up at him and gave a brief lick of her lower lip before she rolled her hips up on purpose to grind against him.

His eyes darkened, but humor lit his face up. "Hmm, someone missed me, didn't she?"

Despite the heat that rushed to her face, she pouted. Luna held still once more, as much as she could. "You're laughing at me."

He chuckled and shifted to rise on his knees as he undid his own jeans until his cock sprang forth. "Not at all, sweetheart. See? I missed you too."

Mesmerized by the sight of his hardened cock, she licked her lips, begging for a taste with that gesture.

As if he read her mind, he shook his head and inched closer. "Not tonight, little one. Tonight is for me and I want to feast on you."

He had designed every touch, every word to encourage her arousal until he had reduced her thong to a useless piece of soaked fabric. When he dipped one finger below, he left it wedged between her folds. Her body quivered with delight.

"You're not going to last very long, are you?" He teased as he scraped his nails across her inner thigh then reached back up. When he slid his arms underneath, she arched her back again to let him unsnap her halter bra and pull it off over her neck. Her nipples were pebbles begging for kisses.

"Soon, love," he whispered and obliged with pressing a light kiss on each one. Luna let out a long groan of frustration. A little more, even a few licks of her nipples, and it might have been enough to push her over the edge. But he gave her no such satisfaction.

Instead, he shimmied his way down. As the opportunity rose, she tried to take advantage of it and press her legs together, but one stern look from him made her part her legs once more, albeit with great reluctance.

His gaze never seemed to stray far from her sex, outlined by the red lace, even as he reached down for something underneath the bed. Her eyes widened into saucers as he pulled out the spreader bar and laid it on top of the sheets. With loving touches, he took one foot and kneaded her arch before moving to strap her ankle to one cuff. Then he gave the same treatment to the other leg.

Now he had her spread out for him and she was at his mercy. Luna trembled, held over the edge of the cliff, ready to be lost in the desire only he could bring.

"Jacob, please, I need you."

"Almost, sweetheart." Jacob trailed kisses up one leg, reaching her inner thigh. "First, I need to make sure there's never any doubt again about who you belong to." Without warning, he bit down on her thigh.

The light pain soon gave way to pure pleasure as he sucked and licked the spot. He traced lazy circles across her flesh with his tongue, teasing her with its proximity without touching her where she needed him to the most. She tensed and strained to watch him between her legs as she waited anxiously for the next bite that never came.

Instead, he rolled to one side, careful to not crush her limbs. Propping his head up with one arm, he drew slow circles around one nipple but avoided touching the hardened nub. When she tried to shift to meet his touch, he stopped and withdrew until she held still again.

"Jacob," she whimpered, wanton longing dripping from her voice.

"Shh, we have all night." He pressed a kiss to her forehead and trailed his hand down, leaving her nipples aching with need. When she remained unmoving for him, he skimmed across her stomach and tugged her thong up. In response, she gave a long moan full of desperation. *So close. Oh God. Please, don't stop.*

"No coming," he commanded, but did not cease his ministrations. Just as her body tightened, about to peak, he withdrew and slackened his hold.

"No," she whimpered with frustration. Her chest rose and fell, panting while she wrestled with the need for a release. Everything that was her consciousness narrowed to focus on that singular goal.

He chuckled once more, this time pulling the thong away with a deft hand. She groaned as her wetness trickled down onto the sheets. Soon he replaced the fabric with his palm while he slid his fingers past her folds. She ground against them, wishing she could press her legs together so that she could keep his fingers there. Almost.

Again he withdrew them. At his mercy, she trembled, her body driven and held over the heights of desire. "Please, Jacob. Please." Watching his eyes darken with wanting, she wondered if she was on the right track. At this point, she would do whatever she needed. "Please, I need to come. I need you inside me. I need to feel your cock in me. Please, Jacob." She was babbling out of her mind.

"All night," he whispered in her ear instead. "I will prove to you tonight that you're mine, that you'll always be mine. Every moan, every bit of arousal, every orgasm you have is mine and mine alone."

He plunged two fingers into her and thrust back and forth. The sudden intensity caused her to buckle, her eyes squeezing shut.

"Open your eyes, Luna. I want you to look at me when you come."

She snapped her eyes open. The naked hunger on his face drew a long, low moan from her as he pushed her higher and higher.

"Come for me. Give me everything," he whispered and curved his finger upward, pressing his fingers against her g-spot. At the same time, he moved his head and bit down on one nipple.

She flew apart by his hand, her body spasming as the mix of pain and pleasure pushed her headlong over the cliff into the abyss. He never stopped, moving his fingers back and forth as she rode them through her orgasm while he swept across her nipple with his tongue. Stars and spots filled her eyes as he drew out the climax, such that every time she started calming, a new sensation, a different angle, a scrape of teeth, a light tugging, would cut through the haze and make her come harder still.

At last, he had wrung every imaginable sensation from her. Jacob slowed his fingers until he held them still within her. Her nipples pulsed and her entire body thrummed with energy. Through it all, she had somehow kept her eyes open, and when he shifted to hover over her, ripping away her thong with one powerful tug, a more primal part of her growled out his name. "Jacob."

"That's it, sweetheart. My name on your lips. No one else's."

Then he entered her, filling her with one hard thrust...and it was the most wonderful feeling in the world.

# Chapter Thirty-Four

She lost count of how many orgasms he brought her to that night. Fingers, tongue, cock and later adding toys to the mix. Jacob kept her tied to his bed, sometimes waking her up to experience the build-up, other times starting in on the next round without her even being conscious, until she wasn't sure what was a dream and what was reality. She lost herself to the pleasure he wrought in her and it kept her in a constant state of bliss.

When sunlight filtered through the windows at last, she woke to the ability to move her limbs for the first time.

"Good morning, sweetheart," he murmured, pressing a kiss on her forehead. The air was pleasantly cool against her skin. Everything else, however, felt...sticky still, her thighs coated as if her last orgasm had been recent. And she wasn't sure if all of what remained between her legs was hers.

She groaned and curled up closer against him, refusing to open her eyes. Her throat was raw from screaming all night. Luna took her time to work it until she was sure she could speak. "How much sleep did we get?"

"One or two hours, by my estimation." There was an unabashed glee in his voice, and when she ventured to open her eyes to look up at him, she found him grinning like the cat that had just swallowed a canary. *Yeah, me.*

"Come on, love. We still have work."

With that, reality came crashing back down. She whimpered, drawing the covers closer to her naked body, not that it mattered. Soon everyone in the office would know what her naked body looked like.

"Luna, talk to me."

She choked back tears as Jacob's warmth steadied her. "He'll send the footage to everyone in the office…somehow."

No need to mention who. Jacob tensed next to her.

"Luna, what did he say he had, in his exact words?"

It was an awfully specific question and Luna tilted her head up to study Jacob's expression. There was something she was missing here.

"He said he has footage of me tied up on the cross that night we played in the dungeon." She spat out the words, surprised at the bitterness still within her.

"And did you see proof?" Jacob's line of questioning was scaring her.

"He sent me some audio clips. I could hear the session. I even heard your voice after." Realization dawned on her and she bolted up. "You think it was a bluff?" The last word came out a near octave higher.

"I'm...not sure." Jacob's forehead furrowed. "Darryl reviewed the security footage. We knew he may have recorded some audio on his cell but not video, at least not with his phone. He never went back to retrieve anything either. Erica also swept the place for bugs and found nothing, which limits the possibility of an external camera..."

"That son of a bitch," she whispered beneath her breath as she trembled, the enormity of the possibility shaking her to the core. Had she put them through hell for nothing but a bluff? *How could I have been so stupid?*

"Hey, Luna, hey," Jacob called out, but he seemed distant.

A hand under her chin forced her attention back as she met Jacob's gaze. With an effort to still her trembling, she pulled herself out of her head where darker and darker thoughts began to surface.

"Listen... We can't be certain that it's a bluff, but no matter what happens, I will be right here for you, okay? We'll make it work. You can move in here if we need to cut our bills down and eat more at home. If we look at combining our budgets..."

She blinked at him once, then twice. "Did you just...suggest I move in here?" The rest of his words hadn't even caught up to her mind yet. He wasn't just proposing a long-term Dominant-submissive relationship. This was a plan for a life together.

Jacob stared at her, as startled as she was, but he recovered more quickly with a chuckle before he smoothed a hand over her hair. "Luna, when the time comes for you to move in with me, it won't be a suggestion."

There was the Dominant she knew and loved. She wasn't sure if she was disappointed with his answer, but she also knew there was no need to rush their relationship.

"Now come on. Go shower. I'll drive you to work and walk you in. I won't let you face this alone." He smiled at her and she grinned like an idiot until her cheeks hurt despite the situation, her heart full of love.

When they arrived, everything was eerily normal. Ted waved good morning. Luna introduced Jacob to Jung, Prakash and Scott. No one made a single lewd or off comment. When Luna got to her office and turned on her computer for the day, there were already emails from Joanna about a new project queued up for her.

Wednesday rolled by. Same thing.

"Hey, kinkster, you sound way better this week." Ted had taken to calling her that when alone, just to tease. More than anything, he said she deserved it for feeling like she had to keep that secret for so long.

"Yeah, yeah." She took a sip of her coffee as they walked back toward the office. "Hey, Ted?"

"Yes, Luna?"

"Thanks for not judging." She smiled into her cup. Although she couldn't tell him that he was the one who had given her the courage to break away from the nasty situation, Luna resolved to express her gratitude, nonetheless.

"You're welcome." Ted paused mid-walk suddenly, looking as if lightning had just struck him. "Oh my God, is that why you never wanted to double date? Because Jacob is your…" He paused and tilted his head. Luna had explained several terms that night and the subtle differences between them. She was pretty sure by the end that she had just confused the hell out of Ted.

"Dom, yeah." Somehow, Luna was hoping Ted wouldn't put two and two together. It was a dumb hope.

"So does that mean we can double date now?" Eagerness lit up his features and she couldn't help but giggle.

"Yeah. I'll ask Jacob."

Even with the looming threat, she felt lighter than she had in years, and for the rest of the work week, she was finally able to refocus on her duties.

By Friday, Luna began to allow herself to believe in the possibility that it was all a bluff. No footage came. All her co-workers acted normal and she didn't hear so much as a peep from Bryan. Part of her kept kicking herself for being played like a fool, but a general sense of relief overshadowed any regret or shame.

"Do you want to try The Playgrounds tonight?" Jacob asked after dinner Friday evening. Out of a need for solace or perhaps savoring their new reunion, she had stayed over every night. It meant less sleep, but had been definitely worth it.

Luna hesitated, chewing her lips. At Jacob's frown, she let go but remained quiet.

"I'd like us to go — live our life, see our friends. Darryl and Lani have both been asking for you." He smiled, rubbing the back of his neck. "It's like they don't believe me when I tell them we're okay."

Over the course of the week, Jacob had revealed Lani's and Darryl's roles in trying to figure out what had been going on. The whiteboard, in particular, had a rather chilling effect. When she saw all the facts about Bryan laid out, she realized just how much worse things could have gotten had she stayed.

But that wasn't important anymore. What was, was living her life, and that meant seeing her friends — the ones who had jumped in to help, despite her attempts at pushing them away. And she would not let Bryan have any hold on her anymore. Only one man did, and he stood in front of her waiting for an answer.

"Let's go party!"

* * * *

The place was packed, the music already in full swing as dancers filled the floor. A wall of people in various states of dress and undress separated them from the bar but Jacob, using his height, parted the crowd with ease while he hovered over her to keep others from pressing in. The move was completely dominant and she had to admit that she may have swooned a little. Just a little. *Okay, a lot.*

As they made their way through, they found Lani already there, her latest submissive in tow.

"Lovelies!" Lani's eyes shone as she pulled Luna into a tight hug. Luna lost no time in returning the hug, relieved to be back among friends for real. "I'm sorry," she started, but Lani waved her off.

"Lunch is on you next week and I'm ordering the most expensive tea latte and an extra piece of cake."

Luna laughed. "Done. Lunch next week sounds wonderful." She was getting her life back, come hell or high water.

"Welcome back, Luna," Darryl pushed a fruity drink over, complete with its own little paper umbrella. "To celebrate." He winked before moving away, the number of patrons keeping him swamped.

Out of the corner of her eye, she glimpsed Bryan and stiffened before she felt Jacob's arm around her waist. His breath tickled her ear as he whispered. "Don't be afraid. You're safe here. I'll be right back."

Before Luna could reply, Jacob left. Already she missed his warmth against her, but as if on cue, Lani tugged at Luna's hand, likely to distract her. "Sweetie, I'd like you to meet Nathan." The man behind her wasn't very tall compared to Jacob and Darryl, but he had the build of someone who worked out in the gym—toned and muscular, but not so much that he came off lumpy.

"Hello, Nathan," Luna greeted with a smile and the other sub inclined his head. Luna eyed Lani and raised an eyebrow in question.

"I'll tell you over lunch next week," her friend replied with a giggle, her cheeks pinking.

*Oh, dear God.* Lani was blushing and giggling like a schoolgirl. *What did I miss last week?*

Something however tugged at her, an unease that made her scan the floor despite Lani's best attempts at distracting her. Her eyes widened when she saw Jacob walking out with Bryan and, in that moment, a sense of fear and trepidation filled her.

"Luna?"

"I'll be right back, Lani!" She had to shout a little over the din as she pushed her way through the crowd. It was much harder without Jacob around, but as determined as she was, she made it through to the doors after a while.

Jacob and Bryan stood together, a way away from the door, but as she neared them, careful to still keep out of sight, she had no trouble hearing the words as they echoed in the parking lot. Neither of the men had bothered to keep their voices down.

"There was no video, was there?" Jacob's voice appeared calm, but Luna recognized the seething rage in the undertone.

Bryan laughed, the sound mocking even to her ear. An ugly sneer twisted his features. "It was pretty good, wasn't it? She was so damn gullible. Is she still dreading that all her co-workers will see her all naked and strapped down in some first-class porno? Who knows, perhaps that's one of her secret fantasies. Has she been hotter lately? Do you two fuck to the thought of that?"

*God, he's a sick man.* Jacob clenched his hands into fists, the threat of violence hanging in the air.

"Recording of any kind in the club is still breaking the rules and will get you banned," he stated instead. There was an odd flatness to his tone.

In an instant, Bryan's humor evaporated. "You are treading on thin ice, Jacob. I will not tolerate you taking so much from me."

It all happened at once. Jacob half turned away with a shrug. Luna spotted a glint of something reflecting the streetlights that illuminated the parking lot. Bryan lunged forward.

Her mind screamed. She leaped out, her body acting on autopilot. She couldn't reach Bryan, but she managed to throw enough of her weight to knock Jacob off balance. Her hands reached out of their own accord as the muscle memory of her training kicked in. She tried to redirect the path of the blade with her extended hands, but she was too off balance herself. The next thing she knew, hot, searing pain like none she had ever known blossomed across her midsection.

Everything happened in slow motion as her body hit the pavement.

"Luna!" Jacob's voice was already fading into the din of the background noises. Strong arms repositioned her and she noted with a detached mind that she was being moved to recovery position. Why? There were other voices and she sensed other presences around her, but her vision was fading fast.

"Stay with me, Luna. Don't you dare black out on me, you hear me? Stay with me."

She tried, she really did, but she was so tired. "I'm sorry," she whispered. Her eyes drooped, the sight of Jacob's frantic, desperate face the last thing she saw before the darkness took her away.

# Chapter Thirty-Five

Jacob hardly heard the beeping from the machines as he sat next to the hospital bed, Luna's hand in his. He hadn't let go since they'd moved her into the current room and let him back in. Whenever a nurse came in to try to tell him visitor hours were over, he just glowered until they went away.

He brushed Luna's hair back and regarded the woman who held his heart in the palm of her hand. "You silly girl. I'm your Dominant. I'm supposed to be the one protecting you, not the other way around."

Bending over, he pressed his lips on her forehead. The little touches kept him balanced and anchored, kept his hope up as he waited. "Luna." His voice was hoarse with raw grief. "Luna, you've got to wake, sweetheart. We have so much to do still." His voice cracked. "I want to travel with you, to take you all over the world. I want to go on that double date you have planned with Ted. I want to see you give that talk at that conference."

The memories of the last week they'd spent together flitted through his mind — all the little moments as Luna caught him up on everything else that had happened in her life while they'd eaten, while they'd cuddled, while they'd simply just enjoyed being them. Jacob couldn't remember ever having been happier. He raised her hand to press his forehead against it. "I want to spend the rest of my life with you. Don't leave me now, not when I've just realized this. You need to wake up and give me a chance to show you."

When there was no sign of consciousness, he slumped back, looking up only as Lani entered the room. How much she heard? Not that he cared. He would bare his soul to the world if it meant Luna would open her eyes.

"You need to eat something, Jacob." Lani handed a coffee to him as she approached, her gaze never straying far from the frail, still form on the bed.

"I'll eat later." It was the automatic response he gave every time she or anyone else suggested it.

With a sigh, Lani pulled up another chair and slid into it with only a little more grace than Jacob. They were all exhausted from the last forty-eight hours. "What did the doctors say?"

Jacob lowered Luna's hand to his lips and pressed a kiss on her knuckles. "They said she's stable. Moving to recovery position and applying pressure helped. But it'll be up to her when she'll wake up." He refused to entertain any other possibility.

"You saved her life, Jacob." Lani patted him on the shoulder.

A broken laugh was his first reaction. He shook his head, refusing himself the easy comfort. "It should have been me. Bryan was aiming for me."

"Bullshit. It shouldn't have been anyone." Lani squeezed his shoulder. "You had no idea, none of us did. Not all psychopaths are violent. We had no way of knowing he was that unhinged."

Before he could reply, the door opened and Darryl let himself in. Both of them looked up with a nod of greeting.

"How is she?" Darryl came around to stand by them, his large hands holding a pot with a beautiful blooming purple orchid. Lani rose to take the plant from him, setting it down in one corner close to the window.

"Stable," Jacob replied but left it at that.

Silence filled the room as the three watched Luna, her chest rising and falling steadily.

"How's The Playgrounds?" Jacob lifted his head once more to regard Darryl, although he never moved from his chair.

"It'll be fine. Since it technically happened in the parking lot, there'll be minimal fallout." Darryl cleared his throat and shifted his weight from one foot to another. "Erica and Dominique send their thoughts and well wishes for a speedy recovery. Erica said if there's anything you or Luna need…"

"Tell them thanks." If it weren't for Erica giving them access to the security footage, Luna might still be stuck with a violent psychopath as her master. Despite where they'd ended up, Jacob wasn't so consumed by sorrow yet that he didn't recognize the help. It led to the other loose end.

"And Bryan?" He spat out the name. They all remembered the number of times the cops had questioned them.

Darryl swiveled his head in surprise when it was Lani who answered instead of Jacob.

"Nathan asked his friends on the force this morning. He said that given the USB stick you provided and all the testimonies from us and the other witnesses, he's going to be locked away for a long time."

Jacob waited for a sense of relief or satisfaction to sink in at Lani's news, but there was only a deep weariness that seeped into his bones.

The events that had unfolded after the confrontation had been hazy. After Luna had collapsed, he remembered little else. But he recalled Lani's new submissive immediately calling nine-one-one then assuming crowd control duty until Darryl and others got there to help.

"Why don't you head home and take a break. I can stay here a bit until you come back," Darryl suggested.

Jacob only shook his head. "I don't want to leave in case she wakes up."

"I'll head over to your place and get you some more clothes then," Lani suggested and when he nodded in agreement, she got up and dragged Darryl out of the room with her.

Left alone once more in the room, Jacob shifted in his seat, his eyes heavy with fatigue. He had managed only fitful bouts of dozing, startling awake every time he thought Luna was showing signs of consciousness. A part of him was terrified that if he slept too long, he would wake to find all the machines hooked up to Luna silent or her bed empty.

But a person could only physically take so much, pushed to the limits, whether his mind was ready for it or not, he put his head on the side of her bed and drifted off to slumber.

*The white dress on Luna was stunning, with a train that trailed after her as she walked down the aisle, graceful in her every step. Jacob straightened, his heart beating wildly as he glimpsed her smile. Filled to the brim with love for her, his face softened and he saw hers do the same. Here was the woman he would spend his life cherishing and protecting.*

*The aisle felt like the longest one ever. A minute passed. Two. Luna was no closer. The wedding music had long faded into a deafening silence. Sensing the wrongness of it all, Jacob started to walk before he sped into a run down the aisle. But the more he ran, the farther away she seemed, until only the shape of her remained. Then that too faded into nothingness. No, he couldn't lose her. Not again.*

"Jacob? Jacob." A voice cut through the void he found himself in. It was raspy from disuse but unmistakably Luna's. "Jacob, wake up."

His eyes snapped wide open, dark brown meeting baby blues in the darkness of the room. His hands still trembled from the desperation that had overwhelmed him in his dream and it took him a moment to realize she was truly awake and he was back in reality.

"Hey," Luna whispered.

"Hey, you," Jacob replied. A single tear of relief rolled off his cheek and on to their still-joined hands.

"Were you having a nightmare?"

He stared at her, as if trying to figure out why the hell she would be concerned about him when she was the one in a hospital gown. When he said nothing still, she spoke again.

"I heard you." There was a mix of shyness and awe in the way she looked up at him. "You called for me." Then she grinned, so much like the spunky submissive he'd known before everything had happened. "You said you'd go on that double date with Ted."

Jacob groaned but could not help as his lips stretched ear to ear with a playful grin. "Anything you want, my love, but it may cost ya." Tension ebbed out of him and he gave her a suggestive wink.

Luna laughed while clenching her stomach, then winced in pain. "Ow, you're not supposed to be riling me up when I'm still bandaged."

Guilt and a fierce sense of protection made him tug her blanket down to check the bandage and tape over Luna's stomach. No blood. She hadn't broken her stitches. *Thank God.*

"Jacob, I'm okay. I promise. I'm alive and I'm here." She turned her palm upward to give his hand a light squeeze. "Fill me in? I remembered hearing Bryan say there was no video, but then everything was a bit of a blur after that. How long was I out?"

He sucked in a breath. "A little more than two days. You lost a lot of blood." His gaze traveled down to her wound again. The knife had gone in deeper than they'd all thought, and it was likely she would carry the scar for the rest of her life.

"He had a switchblade in his pocket. I knew there was a possibility he'd get violent when I turned, but then you jumped out of nowhere and..." Jacob swallowed hard and tightened his grip on her hand. He never wanted to relive those moments ever again. "The cops came after and took him away. We did what we could until the ambulance came. They tried calling your brother, but he was away on business. Lani used her connections to get you set up in this private room and that's pretty much it. You're caught up."

Aware that he was babbling, Jacob allowed his words to drift into silence. *They say when couples have been together long enough, they start picking up each other's mannerisms. Am I starting to pick up Luna's?* He wasn't sure, but he was interested in finding out if there was any truth to that concept.

Luna blinked once, then twice, staring at him with her mouth hanging open as she obviously was struggling to absorb his recounting.

A few minutes passed before he spoke again. "Don't you ever do that again."

When she shook her head in reply, he felt a growl emerging from the back of his throat.

"I serve you, Jacob."

"Not with your life," he snapped back.

"With everything I am. You know that."

Her words rocked him and shook his very being. Here was a woman who would be as fiercely protective of her Dom as he was of her. *How the hell did I ever get so lucky? And how dumb am I that I almost let her go?* She was the gift he'd never asked for but had waited for his entire life.

With all the tenderness and adoration he had for her, Jacob rubbed his thumb gently across her lower lip. "Luna Weir, I love you. Three years or forever, my heart will always be yours." And with that, he replaced his thumb with his lips, bestowing a kiss that promised everything.

# Epilogue

Luna paced back and forth in her apartment, stopping occasionally to smooth the slinky black dress over her calves, aware of how much skin the slits on either side exposed. At the rate he had her wound up, she was going to leave a very obvious stain on it before she even left her home. It didn't help that he had instructed her to not wear any panties...or a bra.

He had teased her all day over text with tasteful yet suggestive comments about the night to come. It had riled her up so much that she'd had to resort to cold showers to calm herself down. It wasn't just a guy thing.

Despite being mostly healed and having a body that no longer ached constantly, work had insisted on Luna taking more time off. Meanwhile, everyone kept dropping by to visit. Poor Ted had had it the worst, dreading that she would turn him away at the door because of his cousin. Instead, she had embraced him, and they'd had a rather tearful session mourning all the things that had happened.

Yet, memories of that visit did not distract her enough from the fact that she was so aroused that even an accidental brush against her nipples was enough to send tremors across her body. It didn't help that she and Jacob had been forced to abstain throughout the healing process lest she reopen her stitches. It only proved that neither of them was suitable for a life of celibacy.

The creak of her door opening spurred her to action. She grabbed her purse and draped a shawl, a rather pathetic attempt at covering the hardened nubs that showed through her dress. Once she was out of the hospital, she had given Jacob a set of keys so that he could drop by anytime to help her take care of her wound. It was just practical, but it did mean he had caught her by surprise a few times.

As Jacob stepped into her apartment, Luna almost had the wind knocked out of her. Dressed in a pair of black slacks and a crisp white shirt with a dark gray suit jacket over it, he cut a handsome figure, blended with a different kind of dominance from his usual easy-going assertiveness. In his hand was a single long-stemmed rose and on his lips was that crooked smile she loved so much. Luna wasn't sure she was going to survive the night.

Jacob handed her the rose then closed the slight distance between them and pulled her to him, hip to hip. She almost failed to hold back a moan as he reached down and dipped his fingers between her legs to check her attire, or rather her lack of. "So sexy," he whispered in her ear before he leaned back.

"Ready to go?"

Weak-kneed, she took his offered arm with gratitude, letting him lead them out to her car.

Throughout the drive to the restaurant, Jacob was the perfect gentleman. When he stopped in front of the valet at La Lumiere, one of the most expensive French restaurants in town, Luna's eyes widened into saucers. And when the maître d led them to a private booth in the back, dimly lit to create the right ambience, her heart almost stopped.

"Jacob, what's this?" Nervousness returned when she took a seat in the booth. Jacob only shook his head with a grin, sliding into the booth next to her rather than sitting on the opposite side.

When the sommelier came to suggest wine pairings, Jacob listened with a singular focus and asked a few questions. It was a side of him she'd never expected and for a moment it was almost as if she were sitting next to a stranger, until his hand crept up her skirt underneath the table. With that, she lost track of their conversation.

They must have decided on a wine as the sommelier left. He leaned in toward her and, with a Cheshire grin, whispered in her ear. "Spread your legs for me, sweetheart."

They were in public! She was going to leave a puddle on the seat. There were at least a gazillion reasons it was a terrible idea. Instead, she obeyed and pried her knees apart for him. In return, he wasted no time tracing idle circles along one inner thigh.

"Jacob," she whispered then bit back a moan as he reached her mound and, unhindered by underwear, slid lower to part her folds. A gush of her arousal soaked his hand and he chuckled in her ear, the sound more delicious than any food she could think of.

With feather-light touches, he stroked from her center up to her clit and back again. Helpless against his ministrations, she gripped the edge of the table as he increased the pressure of his stroking and narrowed the length his fingers traveled until he was just circling her clit.

"And how are monsieur and mademoiselle this evening?" The waiter approached just as Luna thought she was going to explode. Her cheeks grew hot and she hoped against hope that the waiter couldn't smell her arousal. When Jacob wiped his hand on her thigh, then lifted it to open the menu, she thought she was going to die.

They struck up another conversation. By the end, Jacob had ordered a small feast, but all she could think of was how the hell she would be able to leave the restaurant with the growing wet spot on her dress.

"Relax, no one will notice, and I'll sneak you out," he whispered once more, as if reading her mind as he placed her hand on her leg again. For the next while, he toyed with her, bringing her to the edge only to back off over and over, until she was a sopping, strung-up mess.

When the food arrived, he showed some measure of mercy at last and stopped his ministrations under the table, but he refused to let her pick up a fork. Instead, he took great pleasure in feeding her, course after course. In revenge, Luna took every opportunity to sexualize the way she savored the food, flicking her tongue out to taste each dish, licking her lips with small moans of appreciation. At one point, she slipped her hand under the table and accidentally not-really brushed his crotch. A deep satisfaction settled in her when she discovered just how hard he was.

With the meal completed, Jacob waited until they cleared the plates before he pulled out a white envelope and placed it in between them on the table. Rather than playing with her more as she expected, he gestured to it with all the seriousness and gravity that contrasted the playfulness that had prevailed so far.

Luna stared at it, her heart pounding in her chest, her desire to climax forgotten for a moment. She reached out with shaky hands and opened it, pulling out neatly folded pieces of paper. Tears welled up in her eyes. *I really am becoming a cry-baby.*

It was the same contract she had signed three years ago. A promise to cherish and protect, to guide and lead for the Dominant, to serve and follow for the submissive. A commitment to respect, trust, open communication, self and mutual care for both. Luna noted the subtle differences as she read through the pages with care. There was a new clause specific to exclusivity and an additional statement about involvement and discussion from both parties around life decisions. A declaration of living arrangements rounded out the clauses and taped next to it, a key.

The pounding turned into a roar in her ears.

"Is there anything you have questions about, wish to discuss or negotiate?" Jacob asked, trying to appear nonchalant. Only the way his muscles tensed beneath his shirt betrayed any sign of nervousness.

A little dazed, Luna shook her head.

"Good." Jacob took the paper out of her hand with care and flipped to the second page then set it down on the table before offering her a pen. His signature was already there above the line denoting 'Dominant'.

There was a decided lack of an end date.

The tremor of her hands faded and an unexpected peacefulness settled over her. As she turned back toward Jacob, she gave him a most serene smile. With no hesitation, she took the pen from him and added her own signature above the line left for the submissive.

Jacob swept the document back up, detached the key to hand it to her, then folded the papers up to tuck them back into the envelope.

She laughed with a newfound delight as he rushed to summon the waiter to settle the bill.

"We're going home. *Now.*"

"Wait! How am I going to get out?" she whispered back, alarmed.

"I'll stay close behind you. Now git."

Somehow, they got back home in one piece.

As they crashed through the door to his apartment, Jacob almost ripped her dress open in haste. They unzipped and pulled it over her head before he hurried to reclaim her lips, thrusting his tongue into her eager mouth. She undid the buttons of his shirt, tearing at least one off in the process until at last he could shrug the damn thing off.

When she raked her nails across his back, a guttural sound emerged from deep within his chest. Without warning, he pivoted them and slammed her against the wall, his arms cushioning her from direct impact. Jacob slid his hands up from her shoulder blades and entangled his fingers in her hair to pull her head back and expose her throat.

"Mine." He bit down on her neck to brand her once more. As if that sated his immediate need, he leaned back to survey his work then licked the mark to soothe it.

Whimpering as pain gave way to pleasure, Luna arched her back. She moved her hands downward, tracing his stomach before lowering to undo the clasp and zipper that held up his slacks.

He hissed and grabbed her hands, pulling them to her side. "Keep them there," he warned and took another step away.

She stood there, her naked breasts rising and falling as she panted, with evidence of her need dripping down her thighs. Still pressed against the wall, she kept her hands flat on her legs as instructed, but she subtly rubbed her legs together, trying to relieve some pressure.

"Minx." In one swift movement, he hauled her over his shoulder, strode across the room and tossed her on to the couch, face-down. When she tried to turn, he pressed down on the small of her back to prevent her from doing so. "Stay."

Luna took a deep breath and held herself still, her shoulders digging into the couch. When Jacob stroked her ass, she raised it higher in the air and wiggled. He traced the curve down to her thigh, then moved over until he reached her pussy. She sighed in relief as he dipped his fingers into her opening and she pushed back with wanton eagerness.

He chuckled and withdrew, to her chagrin. As his touch became notably missing, she wrestled with all her might to not turn around to search for him.

The wait wasn't long. The next thing that assaulted her senses was the single jute rope he used to tie her hands behind her back. He then looped the two long tails around her body, knotting them in strategic places to create a sturdy harness. As if centering her for display, he draped the remaining length over her rear to frame it.

"Beautiful." The word he breathed out struck a deep chord within her. Knowing he was watching, admiring, sent another shot of molten desire through her body until it vibrated with desire.

"Do you need something?"

She could hear the smirk in his voice. He knew very well what she needed.

"Your cock," she whispered, the heat in her cheeks rising as she forced the words out. Some things, it seemed, she would never get used to.

"Hmm? What's that?" His chest pressed against her back and Luna figured that he must have bent over. A sound of zipper and cloth made her shiver in anticipation. But she didn't have to wait long as he rested the length of cock against her sopping pussy while he rubbed the head against her entrance.

Luna pushed back again, forgetting her previous lesson, only for him to chuckle in amusement. He gripped her hips to keep her from moving. "Sweetheart, you need to tell me what you want."

With a groan of frustration, she squirmed more, hoping it would give him the right incentive that would drive him crazy enough to lose control.

But she lost the contest of wills as he parted her with gentle fingers. When Jacob found her clit, he rolled it between his fingers. She shuddered, pushing back against his hand as her entire body tightened, about to come.

"Please don't stop. Please," she begged with a desperate whimper.

"Tell me what you want," he whispered in her ear, then nibbled along the ridge.

"Come. I need to come. I need you inside me." Driven mad with need, words, any words he wanted to hear, spilled from her lips in almost incoherent babbling. "Fuck me, please. Fuck me with your cock."

"Well then." Oh, he was pleased, she had no doubt. Not when he sped up playing with her while applying more pressure. *Close, so close.* She held her breath.

"You can come now." Jacob pinched her clit and she screamed out her orgasm, crashing headlong into ecstasy. She rocked her hips against his fingers until he relented and she began coming down, her body starting to relax.

Without warning, he slammed into her, his cock thrusting in with one smooth stroke. The unexpected intrusion drove her to climax all over again and she clenched hard around his cock, holding him in.

"God, sweetheart," he groaned, tensing and holding himself still behind her. She couldn't see but heard the words behind his gritted teeth.

Then he moved.

As he pulled back until just his cockhead was inside, he reached with one hand to grip the rope around her and used it as leverage to once more push into her. Again and again he drove in, his pace increasing as he sought his own pleasure. At that angle, he seemed even larger than usual, stretching her, filling her.

Luna's moans grew higher in pitch as she neared orgasm once more. "Please. Come…again… Oh God, again." She was babbling.

"Come." The command came as a grunt and her entire body spasmed, jerking against him in all her glory. Her vision became spotted with stars as her fingers and toes curled and the most intense orgasm yet kept her suspended in the heights of pleasure until she knew naught else. He bellowed as he came, pouring himself inside her.

She fell forward, taking him with her as they panted. Luna waiting in silence for the world to stop spinning. Time stood still until, at last, he pressed a kiss on the back of her neck and withdrew from her with a groan.

After untying her, Jacob helped her up, but when her legs proved too wobbly to support her weight, he smirked with pride and changed tack, settling on the couch with her and pulling a thick throw over both of them.

Luna shifted to nuzzle him then rested her head against his shoulder as he wrapped his arm around her. She blinked and yawned.

"I think it's time for bed, sweetheart."

She pouted in protest, looking up at him with puppy eyes. "But…"

Luna's breath caught as she saw the love he held for her reflected in the warmth of his chocolate-brown eyes. She ducked her head in a moment of sudden shyness. But he tilted her chin back up toward him with one finger. With a tenderness that made her tremble, he brushed his lips by hers.

"Patience, my love. We have all the time in the world."

And for the first time in three years, they truly did.

# Want to see more from this author? Here's a taster for you to enjoy!

## Some Like it Haunted: The Fae Effect
## P. Stormcrow

### *Excerpt*

The old-style English pub was the little university town's best kept secret, and tonight, it was filled with sexy witches, grotesque murderers, charming devils and not-so-innocent angels. After all, it was the Saturday night before Halloween, when most parties were taking place. No one wanted to risk a 'hangover Monday' in the middle of midterm season.

In contrast, Keenan, a grad student in the Department of Computer Science, and three of her friends, all in normal attire, sat at a round table in the back, observing the revelry with amused smiles.

"Is that one of the jock babies over there in a chugging contest?" Keenan whispered to Aisha, the raven-haired woman beside her.

It was what Keenan and her fellow grad school friends called the group of undergrad jocks they'd had to teach this year. The university had admitted most of them based more on their athletic merit than their academic abilities, and it showed in their reluctance to learn.

"Oof. Yeah. I think you're right. Aren't you TA-ing his class this semester?"

Keenan winced as the third-year frat boy by the bar slammed his pint glass onto the bartop, threw his head back and howled—never mind that it was rather appropriate, considering he was dressed like a werewolf in a flannel shirt. "I'm not looking forward to marking whatever he ends up handing in on Monday."

"Forget about that," Dale waved at the two women for attention and leaned forward, his eyes flashing with excitement. His freckles were growing more prominent with the flushing of his normally pale cheeks. "Tell us, Kee… What do you have planned for your Halloween episode?"

Keenan grinned. She wasn't too proud to admit that she loved talking about her passion project. It had turned into a full side gig. She even had fans! "Well, a couple of weeks ago, I was covering this urban legend about peeling an apple at midnight. I figured I could air that one on the channel tomorrow."

"An apple?" Aisha shivered and wrapped her arms around herself.

"Yeah, there's an urban legend that says if you peel an apple in front of a mirror at midnight, you'll see an image of the one you'll marry one day. And every time the peel breaks, a scar will appear on their face and you would have cursed your future spouse with that scar."

Aisha gasped, her eyes round with fear.

At her friend's look, Keenan laughed and patted her back. "Relax. I did not see my future husband and there were no scars. It's just a myth, obviously."

"Luckily. I still think you're crazy, doing what you do." Aisha pursed her lips and shook her head.

"But brave." Jonathan pushed his glasses up the ridge of his nose then grabbed the pitcher sitting right next to a bowl of peanuts to refill everyone's glasses. "Besides, all this stuff has no basis in science. I think what Kee's doing with her YouTube channel, debunking these myths and legends, is doing the world a service."

"Here's to scientific inquiry." Keenan lifted her beer.

"Hear, hear!" Her three friends mirrored her gesture and they all took long, satisfying gulps from their respective pints.

"That said, I think you should do something different on Halloween. I mean…it being *that* time of the year." Dale was often her source of inspiration for her episodes.

"What do you suggest?" Keenan tucked a stray red curl back behind her ear then folded her arms on the table.

"Local rumor has it that the hill behind the old Donovan property is a fairy mound. You know what they say…"

"That they're really fairy forts and, on All Hallows Eve, you can see fairies dancing there?" A familiar thrum of excitement coursed through Keenan's body. Dale was on to something.

"I dare you, Keenan O'Brien, to spend Halloween night at the fairy mound." Dale smirked.

*Ah, he planned this all along. The sneaky bastard!*

To be fair, however, Keenan had already been planning in her head what to pack before he'd even dared her. *I'll need to shoot on my phone to livestream, so that means an extra battery pack. And a sleeping bag. Oh, and I better tweet out an announcement. It'll be touch and go with such short notice.*

"Earth to Keenan." Jonathan waved a hand in front of her face.

"She's off in planning land. You can see it in her eyes." Aisha's voice drifted back to her attention.

Her friends knew her too well. "I'm here. I'm here!"

"So, you going to do it?" Dale asked, affecting his most innocent smile.

*Ha! If he's innocent, then fairies are real.*

"You knew I was going to do it as soon as you opened your mouth." Keenan mock-glared at him but failed to hold it for long.

Dale only widened his grin as Aisha stared at the two of them and sighed. "Just be careful, Kee. Sleeping alone outside is not safe, no matter which way you look at it."

"Aisha has a point. I'll be up all night anyway, the way my block parties. Why don't you check in with me?" Jonathan offered.

Before Keenan could respond, Aisha clapped her hands together and spoke again. "That's a splendid idea. She can call in every hour, and if she misses a call, it means something's gone pear-shaped and you can call for help."

Keenan almost choked, and her face heated from the alcohol. "Every three hours."

"Two," Aisha shot back while Dale tried to stifle his laugh, and Jonathan watched with an arched brow.

"Fine, *Mom*," Keenan groaned with exaggerated exasperation. With that, Dale burst into laughter.

Aisha rolled her eyes at their antics.

"Well, I for one will be watching from the comfort of my nice, warm, comfy bed." Dale winked at them.

At that, Keenan threw the peanut that she had been shelling at him.

Home of Erotic Romance

Sign up for our newsletter and find out about all our romance book releases, eBook sales and promotions, sneak peeks and FREE romance books!

# About the Author

P. Stormcrow has always been an avid reader across the fantasy and sci fi genres but early on, found herself always looking for the love story in each book. Coming to terms with her love for love later in life, she now writes steamy romances that examine social norms and challenge conventional tropes of the genre, usually on her phone. And yes, she has walked into walls and poles doing so.

When she's not reading or writing (or even when she is), she enjoys copious amounts of tea, way too much sugary treats, one too many sci fi / fantasy / paranormal TV shows (team Dean all the way) and every otome game she can possibly find.

P. Stormcrow loves to hear from readers. You can find her/his/their contact information, website details and author profile page at https://www.totallybound.com